The Border Crosser

D1571336

Other Bella Books by Cindy Rizzo

The Split Series
The Papercutter

About the Author

Cindy Rizzo is the author of four previously published novels, including her first book, *Exception to the Rule*, which won the 2014 Goldie for Best Debut Author. *The Papercutter*, the first book in The Split trilogy, was awarded a 2022 Lesfic Bard Award for Best Fiction. Cindy's short stories and essays have appeared in *Unwrap These Presents, Conference Call, Language of Love, Our Happy Hours: LGBT Voices from the Gay Bars* and on Medium. com. She is a member of the board of directors of SAGE, the national organization that serves and advocates for LGBTQ+ elders, and is a member of Congregation Beit Simchat Torah in New York City. Cindy lives in NYC with her wife and has had a long career in social justice philanthropy.

The Border Crosser

Book II of The Split Trilogy

Cindy Rizzo

BELLA
BOOKS

2022

Bella Books, Inc.
P.O. Box 10543
Tallahassee, FL 32302

Printed in the United States of America on acid-free paper.

First Edition - 2022

Editor: Katherine V. Forrest
Cover Designer: Kayla Mancuso

ISBN: 978-1-64247-410-7

PUBLISHER'S NOTE

Acknowledgments

This book, its predecessor *The Papercutter*, and the final book to come in this trilogy, would not be possible without the support and encouragement of Linda Hill, publisher at Bella Books. Linda's enthusiasm about my idea to write about a split United States of America has carried me through this entire process, because, really, who wants to disappoint Linda Hill?

Enormous thanks to Jessica Hill and the entire crew at Bella for all of their assistance with production and promotion. Your patience with me is much appreciated.

It was a privilege and an honor to once again have Katherine V. Forrest as my editor. Katherine helped me strengthen the story and cast her eagle eyes on all of the text. Katherine, I really did try to stop over-using the word *that* in this manuscript, but I'm grateful you were still able to catch my continued lapses, among others. *The Border Crosser* is a much better book thanks to you.

I never underestimate the value provided by the people who devote their precious hours to beta reading my books and providing feedback. Thanks to author Alison R. Solomon for your careful reading and your feedback on Orthodox Jewish practices. My colleague, Erica Lim, helped make sure I didn't mess up too badly in introducing Kim Ji-Joong (Will) and Kim Ji-Kyung (Ann) to the cast of characters. I value her feedback as well as any I might still get from other Korean readers. Millie Ireland provided valuable assistance so I could make sure I was writing accurately about Meyer Lipsky's life and the way he uses his wheelchair to create a distraction. My pal, author Jaycie Morrison, not only beta read the manuscript, she helped me finish it by joining me on virtual writing dates over a period of months when we both needed to meet deadlines. Her help and support were invaluable. Finally, my teenage beta reader, Nuri, provided one particularly important piece of insightful feedback that I so appreciated.

Encouragement to continue with the trilogy after the publication of *The Papercutter* was especially helpful from

Idit Klein, the executive director of Keshet; my rabbi Sharon Kleinbaum; and the amazing Urvashi Vaid, whose memory is indeed a blessing.

Finally, I am fortunate to have married well. My wife, Jenny, is an incredible supporter of my writing and provided a key plot point for this book that drew on her many years reading true crime books. When I asked her, "How does someone get broken out of jail?" she answered, "It's easier when they're sick and in the hospital." Thanks, honey. I love you.

Dedicated to:

Hannah Senesh, Sarah Braverman and their comrades in
the Jewish Special Operations Executive
Who parachuted into occupied Europe to save Jews

And to the memory of
Urvashi Vaid,
A visionary leader and tireless activist
Who fought hard for social justice

"*In America, time was supposed to be a straight line
where only the future mattered;
in Judaism, it was more like a spiral of a spiral,
a tangled old telephone cord in which the future was the present,
which was essentially the past.*"

Dara Horn
People Love Dead Jews:
Reports from a Haunted Present

*What is occurring occurred long since,
And what is to occur occurred long since:
and God seeks the pursued.*

Ecclesiastes 3:15

THE SPLIT

After decades of increasing polarization, the United States of America became ungovernable and split itself into two nations. Each state joined one of the new countries—the God Fearing States of America (GFS), a majority white Christian conservative nation; and the United Progressive Regions of America (UPR), a majority non-white, liberal nation.

All except Ohio, which was divided in two.

CHAPTER ONE

Judith

South Ohio, God Fearing States

"I thought weddings were supposed to be joyous," my friend Isaac Leventhal mumbles quietly as he walks by me at the reception.

"Not this one," I respond as I look around at the synagogue's social hall crowded with round tables of ten, each filled with most of the important people of our Orthodox Jewish community smiling and enjoying their time at the wedding of two of the most evil people in existence—Yetta Freundlich, my classmate at Kushner Academy for Girls, and Simeon Rausch, the son of our turncoat city councilman, who supports every horrible new action of our government designed to isolate and confine the Jews of Cincinnati.

Isaac doubles back and whispers in my ear. "Lots of bad souls?" He's referring to my gift of being able to see souls, or *neshamot*[1], of some but not all people.

---

1 The plural of neshamah, meaning soul in Hebrew.

What was once a secret known only to a few is now common knowledge among the network of Minyans[2] of Resistance, independent communities of prayer and action that have sprung up throughout the God Fearing States.

"More than I can usually see in one place," I tell him. "I've spent most of the time looking down or to the side."

The oozing green stuff inside those blackened souls of Yetta and Simeon standing under the *chuppah*[3] is making me feel like my stomach is leaping up into my throat and is about to be expelled through my mouth. At one point when I looked at some members of their families and saw the same thing, I stopped making eye contact with anyone.

Well, except for thirteen-year-old Naomi Blau, one of the only members of our First Minyan of Resistance to attend this wedding of the hateful couple, Yetta and Simeon. But every time I try to get a fix on Naomi's *neshamah*, I see something unusual. The first time I looked, which was during a meeting of our minyan, her soul shimmered like fading fireworks, similar to other good souls. But lately I see instead a dark gray wall, the color of a slate roof, with a faint light behind it. Today, the light seems only slightly brighter but still hidden behind the gray.

Focusing on the mystery of Naomi's soul, normally an inscrutable puzzle that would frustrate me, has instead been a welcome diversion. It would have been much easier to get through this horrible wedding if Hannah Goldwyn and Jeffrey Schwartz, my two best friends, were here to distract me with their snarky remarks. But Hannah's family declined the invitation, using their weekly commitment to volunteer at a soup kitchen as a convenient excuse, since none of them wanted to attend; and Jeffrey's family, who campaigned for Simeon's father's opponent in the city council election, wasn't invited. Had he been here, I could easily imagine Jeffrey shaking his head every time the look on my face registered disgust from seeing another evil soul.

"SJ," he'd say, using his nickname for me, Super Jew, a sarcastic reference to the fact that I use my art as a means to express my devotion to Judaism, "you need to stop looking at

2 A minyan is a group of at least ten Jews needed for prayer.
3 Wedding canopy

these people. Why not stare at Hannah or Isaac or me—though I know I'm not much to look at." I've decided the reason Jeffrey belittles himself is because he likely thinks it hurts less than when someone else does it. As his close friend, this habit of his is as frustrating to me as his teasing about the fact that I am so devoted to my faith that I use the craft of papercutting to create art that celebrates Jewish holidays, symbols, and scenes from the Torah[4].

I can see him sitting at a table, his plate piled high with food, complaining that the meat is too overcooked as he shovels another forkful into his mouth.

Hannah would grab me by the arm and lead me to the ladies' room where she would check to make sure we are alone and then spend the next few minutes on an angry tear about Yetta, Simeon, and their families, calling them Jewish traitors who've aligned themselves with an evil government, an attitude shared by only a few in our community.

"They're *kapos*[5], Judith, plain and simple," she'd say. "Can't you just see them leading us all into cattle cars and beating those of us who refuse?" Then, without missing a beat, she'd soften and get this dreamy look on her face, her eyes half-lidded, hands on her chest, fingers interlaced. "Isn't Isaac amazing? So intelligent and sensitive. I had to stop myself from running into his arms when we arrived. I'm so glad we can be physically close in our real minyan."

Both Hannah and I have broken through the no-touch boundary our community imposes on people of the opposite sex outside their immediate families. But Hannah's shows of affection with Isaac have a romantic purpose that is lacking between Jeffrey and me. Ours is more like brother and sister, though on more of an equal footing than when I hug my little brother, Morty.

Feeling alone at this wedding without my friends, I am relegated to sitting next to my mother for the ceremony, enduring her endless sighs of happiness at seeing two members of our Orthodox Jewish community joined together, and grimacing at

4 The Torah is the first five books of the Bible.
5 Concentration camp prisoners assigned to oversee other prisoners, often using violent methods.

her whispered comments that it won't be long before I'll be the one standing under a *chuppah*. It's not difficult to guess who she imagines me with since most of the adults here already assume I'll be marrying Jeffrey. Out of necessity, he and I have agreed to neither confirm nor deny these assumptions. But in reality, nothing could be further from the truth.

It's just too dangerous to let anyone outside our minyan know that Jeffrey is gay and that I am…I don't really know. Still figuring it out, is the best I can lay claim to. Though it's been months since my first and only kiss, which was with another girl, I still have no idea about anything more. I mean, how much does that kiss even count when it only happened because a mysterious force greater than both of us pushed us together? I admit that once we did kiss, I just wanted to stay close to her with our arms wrapped around each other and her soft lips pressing on mine. Plus, there was that warmth that radiated throughout every cell of my body when her soul with its many shades of blue appeared to me, a feeling that returns whenever I think about her, and once again I yearn for that closeness.

According to Dvorah Kuriel, a member of our minyan who has the gift of prophesy like her famous father, this girl, Dani Fine, is my *bashert*, my chosen one. And while I know it isn't wise to disbelieve Dvorah, I wonder how meaningful this pronouncement can be. After all, Dani lives over the border in North Ohio, a state in the United Progressive Regions, which while only one hundred miles away, may as well be one hundred thousand. We've only met that one time when we kissed and since then we've exchanged short, secret messages through codes embedded in my papercuts and in the holograms she emails that are hidden behind a set of secret keystrokes.

I wonder if all over the world there are people who live separated from their *basherts* by oceans and borders, who will never know the kind of intense connection I felt with Dani for those precious few moments when we met.

Now, once again seated next to my mother at the wedding reception, my jumpy stomach hasn't quieted since I took that first and only look at the bride and groom. I stare down at the plate a waiter has placed in front of me. It's a *fleishig* wedding with meat entree choices of chicken, brisket, or prime rib. The Freundlichs have pulled out all the stops, determined to show that their precious daughter, the dreaded Yetta, who has always used her posse of followers to exclude people like me and Hannah who are deemed inferior, is worthy enough to join the Rausch family.

I excuse myself from the table, still unable to eat and wanting to avoid my mother's inevitable questions. I'm sure if Jeffrey had been here, he would have gladly eaten my dinner in addition to his own. That boy can certainly put away whatever food is placed in front of him, though he prefers what we call *milchig* or dairy meals over courses of beef and chicken that are served at *fleishig* dinners like this one.

It's when I begin to wander around the social hall trying not to look too conspicuous and avoiding coming face-to-face with the evil souls that I run into Isaac, and he quickly shares his opinion about this dismal wedding. Like me, he doesn't want to be here, but we are still young enough at seventeen to have to go with our parents to these types of events.

After our short exchange, Isaac rushes past me and I turn to follow, figuring that tagging along after him is preferable to having to listen to my mother heap praise on the Rausch family.

I follow Isaac out of the social hall where the reception is in full swing, with a klezmer band playing some kind of mournful tune very fitting to the occasion. I'm hoping he's not on his way to the men's room, which would just be embarrassing with me on his heels. But instead, he turns a corner and heads up the stairway to the first floor of the synagogue. When I hesitate at the bottom of the stairs and look up at his receding figure, I'm surprised that he motions for me to follow, an arm waving me forward. Up until that moment, I had no idea he knew I was there.

At the top of the first landing, he turns and whispers, "I need a witness," then heads to the right to continue his ascent. I follow quickly, wondering just what it is he wants me to see.

When I get to the first floor, I spot him entering the corridor that leads to the rabbi's study. He must be going to see his father. But why in the middle of this wedding?

Sure enough, he enters the study, closing the dark wooden door with its frosted glass window, the words Rabbi Yehuda Leventhal etched in gold.

Immediately I hear raised voices and can recognize the rabbi's deep baritone and the high-pitched wail of his wife. Isaac's voice occupies the middle ground, more measured with an emotional emphasis that helps me decipher some of his words.

"My decision is final," I hear him say. "I am not attending that seminary."

The *Rebbetzin*[6] is practically screeching, "It's that girl, that Hannah Goldwyn! All this started when you took up with her."

Isaac's calm voice doesn't allow me to hear his exact words, but I know he is defending Hannah.

"So just what do you intend to do when you graduate this year? Become a bum like that Solly Herschel you admire so much?" That's the raised voice of the rabbi talking about Solly, a member of our minyan, who ran for city council against Simeon's father.

I know Isaac has been pushed beyond his limit. First they attack Hannah and now Solly, the man who's taught Isaac to defend himself so he doesn't wind up beaten to a pulp again by the red-hatted God Fearing Boys, a gang responsible for dozens of attacks against Jews and who always escape punishment by the police.

"I'd be only too proud to wind up like Solly who fights for justice," he shouts, his tone defiant. "And, if she'll have me, Hannah and I will have a wedding that will be a true celebration, not like this travesty downstairs."

The *Rebbetzin* is sobbing. I hear a loud *bam* and wonder if the Rabbi is going to start throwing books at Isaac. Instead, he bellows so that I can hear every word.

"*Get out!* Get out. You are no son of mine. From today, you get nothing more from me. Leave my house, leave my *shul*[7]. I have other sons who listen."

My body tightens and there's a lump in my throat at the finality of those words. My hands are shaking.

6 Wife of the rabbi.
7 Synagogue

There's another *bam*, and again I don't know which of them is expressing their anger. I just hope no one is getting hurt, especially since Isaac now has the ability to knock his father to the floor.

"Gladly," shouts Isaac over his mother's keening. "You are no holy man to me. I'll be gone by sundown."

With that, the door swings wide open with a force that slams it against the wall. I do my best not to be seen by the two people who remain in the study. Isaac rushes into the hallway, his body bent forward, his hands tightly fisted. When the door closes, I run down to catch up and find him in an empty Hebrew School classroom, seated at the teacher's desk, elbows on the wooden surface, head in his hands. I hear him sniffling and see his head bobbing up and down. He is crying softly.

I go to him and whisper his name, my hand lightly on his shoulder. In the next moment he is standing and folds himself into me, his head buried between my shoulder and neck. He's clutching me, sobbing.

It is the first time we've touched, but this is no occasion to worry about tradition or ancient rabbinic proscriptions. I hold him just like I've held Jeffrey when he told me he was gay and then later confessed the abuse he'd suffered at the hands of Simeon Rausch.

After a few minutes, Isaac gently pulls away.

"Thanks Judith," he says. "For…" and he gestures toward the hallway, "for all of this."

"I'm glad I could be here for you, especially since Hannah and Jeffrey couldn't."

He nods and is silent while I hand him some tissues I've pulled from a box on the teacher's desk. I wait while he puts himself together, unsure if he wants to talk about what just happened in his father's study or if he isn't ready to deal with it. I remember that right after kissing Dani, I was unable to speak about it for weeks despite Jeffrey's constant prodding.

Isaac adjusts his posture so he's standing straight and resolute, his chin tilted up, tears gone from his cheeks, which are still a light shade of pink.

"I need to go get my things and figure out where I can live."

"I can come with you and help."

"No, Judith, I've asked enough of you already. I'll be okay." He breathes in audibly and sighs. "This showdown with my parents has been a long time coming. Figures it would finally happen during this day when so much evil is present in the synagogue."

I nod. "You're sure?"

His hand is on my forearm, "Yes, you're a good friend, Judith, a valuable comrade in our resistance. Just, when you get a chance, let Hannah and Jeffrey know and tell them I'll be in touch soon when I have a plan."

A few minutes later I find myself once again seated next to my mother. Her eyes closed and her head shaking, she tells me, "They took your plate away, Judith. But they're setting up the dessert buffet, so at least you can eat a little something."

I nod silently, just to satisfy her. There's no hunger that could make me eat a crumb from this wedding of evil.

CHAPTER TWO

Jeffrey

South Ohio, God Fearing States

"SJ we really need to find a new clubhouse," I tell her. "This place gives me the creeps."

Judith insists on holding our secret get-togethers in this dilapidated shed behind the *mikvah*[8]. It's a place she and Hannah discovered a while ago when they would steal away to look at all the photos Hannah was collecting of antisemitic graffiti spray-painted around our neighborhood. Over these past few months as violence against Jews increased and groups like the God Fearing Boys felt they could attack us and leave their messages of hate without worrying that the police would come after them, Hannah's collection of photos grew quite a bit. But still, I've never understood why she even bothers. How are all these pictures of hate going to be useful to any of us? Not that my opinion matters to someone as stubborn and determined as Hannah Goldwyn. She's resolved that we must have a record, or an archive as she calls it.

8 Ritual bathhouse.

"For posterity," she said in that slightly condescending tone she regularly uses with me. My response is always to roll my eyes and make some snarky retort like "You mean, if none of us survive, right?"

Three of the four of us sit, crowded among dusty boxes and discolored PVC pipes, long forgotten *mikvah* supplies. Although Judith assures me that no one ever comes here, it is still too close to the women's ritual bath for my comfort.

But there are more important things to worry about this evening, now that Judith has told us about poor Isaac being thrown out of his parents' house.

In this tiny place, Hannah has found a few square feet of floor that barely accommodate her nervous, angry pacing. Her arms are folded over her chest and her head is bent forward. Her light brown wavy hair hangs down covering the sides of her face. Her normally penetrating hazel eyes are almost closed. Her mouth, usually a bit open as if she's about to lecture you about something, is shut tight into a straight line. She stomps and then whips around when she reaches the limits of forward motion.

"They've never appreciated him the way we do," she exclaims. "He is a million times the rabbi his father is!"

Stomp, stomp, stomp, whip around, stomp.

"Hannah please sit down, you're making me dizzy," says Judith.

To my amazement Hannah obliges and sits on the box next to Judith, still with arms folded and her body leaning forward, ready for another round of pacing at the least provocation.

"They could never love him like we do," she whispers, and I can see her blinking away tears.

"Love, huh?" I ask, wondering if she and Isaac have already made those declarations.

Hannah glares back at me. "Don't you also?"

I worry that this is more of an accusation than a question. Luckily, as always, Judith comes to my rescue, which is a good thing since Hannah's question has left me mute.

"We all love him, Han," she says and inches over so their shoulders touch.

My body sags with relief. No one except Judith can know that I also love Isaac, though unlike Hannah, my brand of love is most definitely unrequited. That isn't to say he doesn't regard me as a close friend, perhaps his closest. But that still leaves a chasm of feeling between us, and I work hard every day to become more accepting of that chasm.

Later that night I sit in my little attic room with the small black iBrain affixed to the side of my head, right above my ear. Another marvel of its engineering is that it never pulls on my hair. We can't get these tiny computers in the GFS. The only reason I have one is because when I met my UPR pen pal Dani Fine after she ran across the border for a brief visit a few months ago, she gave me her iBrain, hoping I could get it to work so we could communicate more easily than through Judith's papercuts and emails with hidden holograms. Now that we've been able to reverse engineer the device and use a 3D printer to make more of them, our minyan is able to communicate with other groups across the country who oppose the government.

I turn on my iBrain by speaking to it by name. "Fredy, please let me know when connectivity opens."

My device is named for Fredy Hirsch, one of the gay Jewish heroes that the all-knowing Dvorah Kuriel has introduced me to. The real Fredy lived during the *Shoah*[9] and did his best to care for children imprisoned under inhumane conditions in Theresienstadt and Auschwitz. And during those horrible times, much worse than now, he lived openly as a gay man, even taking a male lover in the camps and never caring who knew. If I could ever be even one percent as brave as him, I'd be forever grateful to *Hashem*[10].

My primary iBrain group is our so-called Minyan of Resistance, the first of many minyans that came together across the GFS to figure out how to stop the government's growing restrictions against the country's Jews. Not that we've done much resisting these last few months. Lots of praying for sure and lots of commiserating and a little bit of plotting. I don't know. I'm not on the governing council or whatever it's called.

9 Hebrew for the Holocaust.
10 The term religious Jews use for God outside of the synagogue.

I leave the big decisions, the life-and-death stuff, to Hannah, Solly, Binyamin Fine (the brother of Dani, my pen pal in North Ohio), and the clairvoyant Dvorah.

To be fair, the minyan has made a few strides. Judith, for example, is now not only an artist for the resistance—her posters are all over town, even beyond our enclosed area—but she has also been enlisted as a document forger. That's how we are all able to travel outside the two-mile perimeter around our neighborhood imposed on us by the government. Signed permits magically appear that have enabled Solly, Hannah, and even Dvorah to leave what we now all refer to as our God Fearing Ghetto and, under cover of darkness, affix Judith's art in places where we think our messages will be appreciated.

Binyamin's knowledge of the University campus, where he used to teach until the Jewish Studies Department was eliminated, has enabled our team to make sure that when students wake up for their morning classes, they are greeted by one of Judith's finest works of art. It's the image of a bull's-eye with our little village in the interior circle in the shape of the Star of David. The next circle out marks the two-mile boundary and then beyond that is a collection of guns, cannons, and tanks in the outer circle pointed right at us. The words *Don't Be Fooled By the Lies* are above the bull's-eye, with *We Know What's In Store* at the bottom.

My iBrain vibrates against my head notifying me that it's eight p.m., the start of the second daily hour of connectivity.

"Fredy, connect me to my group."

"I'm okay, Arc, I promise," is the first thing I hear. It's Isaac. He's using the fake names we've created for iBrain communication. Solly calls them our *noms de guerre*. A little dramatic for my taste. In addition to our real names and the names we've given our iBrains, I now have to keep track of the fact that Judith is Chagall, Hannah is Arc (for Joan of Arc, more drama), Solly is Dayan, our chief engineer Meyer Lipsky is Einstein (I gave him that one), and Binyamin is Heschel. I can't remember Dvorah's so I hope someone refers to her during our conversation.

I am Chef, named for my love of cuisine. It was Isaac's idea and I accepted it, especially after Judith thought I should be called Dish, because I always have a dish in my hand piled high with food. Or so she claims. When I rejected that, she offered up Kugel, which made Hannah break into hysterics.

"No and no," I told them, which is when Isaac gave me his magnetic smile and said, "What about Chef?"

The most curious name is thirteen-year-old Naomi's, Binyamin's niece and the daughter of the beloved departed Rivka Blau, our first casualty, victim of a planted bomb. May her memory be a blessing. Naomi insists on calling herself Nixy and refuses to tell any of us why. Whatever.

"Where are you?" I interject to Isaac, cutting off whatever Hannah was going to say in response to his assurance that he's okay.

"Oh, Chef," he says. I warm to the affection coming through in his voice, hoping I'm not imagining it. "I'm staying with Dayan. It's a bit cramped, but his couch folds out and is quite comfortable."

"That's not a permanent solution." Hannah. Not pleased.

"It's gotta be for now. He's even been nice enough to set up some empty drawers and shelves for my stuff."

"But all your books," responds Hannah, sounding like she's on the verge of tears.

"I have them." Dvorah. "I wish I could have taken you in, Reb, I really do."

Yes, Isaac is our Reb, a name he adores since it connotes both Rabbi and Rebel.

"You can't compromise your reputation for neutrality," says Solly, the resolute tone in his voice signaling the end of this part of the conversation.

Normally Dvorah would have been the natural choice for Isaac's relocation. Since the death of her father, the Great Rabbi Yakov Kuriel, Dvorah has an entire house to herself, with enough room to accommodate Isaac and all his belongings. She was the first option I thought of when I heard the news of his break from his parents, telling Judith and Hannah how fitting it would be for Isaac to inherit the mantle of one of the most respected spiritual leaders of our community.

Isaac leads our minyans and has even begun to compose a liturgy for all the other minyans like ours that are springing up around the GFS. He may not be going to his father's beloved seminary, but, ordained or not, there's no way that Isaac Leventhal will be anything other than a rabbi. Our Rebel *Rebbe.*

But of course, Solly is right. Dvorah must maintain her façade as the revered and departed rabbi's daughter, the long-suffering widow who leads a Torah study class for adult women among whom is Judith's mother.

"You must remain untouchable," I've heard Solly tell her, "uninvolved in any of this as far as they know."

So for the duration of our senior year at Kushner Academy for Boys, due to begin in a few weeks, Isaac will remain on Solly's couch.

Binyamin has just let us know that he's going to leave our meeting to connect with Queen Olivia of the Gullah Geechee nation on the islands off the coast of South Carolina. After the United States split in two, most non-white communities settled in the United Progressive Regions. The Gullah Geechee, though, refused to leave their ancestral islands and remain one of the few Black communities in the GFS. We are allied with Queen Olivia's people, who have also been confined to live in a small area, forbidden to visit the mainland. But before Binyamin signs off, we are all interrupted by a crackling sound and then a loud pop.

Fear and dread fill my chest. My heartbeat quickens and my breathing becomes labored. They've finally tracked us down and now we will all be arrested and sent who knows where. But as I continue to expound to myself on this worst-case scenario, a female voice breaks through, with a "Hooot, hoot, *buenos noches* comrades."

"Owl?" asks Binyamin. "Is that you?"

"*Si, hermano.*"

Owl is Dani's friend Julia, the tech genius, who figured out how to let us use the iBrains in the GFS. Even though we've only had two hours of connectivity a day, it's two more than we ever had before. Now she's figured out a way to talk to us using iBrains, something we haven't been able to do before. This will make communication so much easier.

Binyamin is laughing, likely in relief. "*Baruch Hashem*[11]. But how? How did you…?" He trails off. "Oh never mind, I wouldn't understand anyway."

"I would, Owl." Einstein, of course.

"Ah, *Senor* Einstein. One day I will explain, but I only have a little time and this is a trial run just to make sure this is feasible and to check in on you."

"This is Reb. All is well with us, Owl."

"Not all." Of course, Hannah.

"Just a few bumps in the road," counters Isaac. "Nothing too serious."

I hear Hannah breathe out in exasperation. Clearly she thinks Isaac's banishment is much more than a mere bump in the road. I'm of a different school of thought; that away from his father's influence, Isaac is now free to chart his own course, one much more meaningful and important than Rabbi Leventhal's.

"Chagall, are you there?"

"Yes, Owl."

"Abby Cadabra says hello. I will make sure she can be here very soon."

"Thank you." Judith's voice is soft and sweet. It's that tone she uses when she talks about Dani, who is apparently using the name of the hologram character who carries her messages to us.

Binyamin's voice is urgent. "Please, Owl," he begs, clearly anxious to connect with his sister.

"Can you tell Abby hello from me." That's Judith's lovestruck voice. I suppress a giggle that I know would annoy her. I'll wait and tease her about it when we're together.

11 Blessing to God, an exclamation used to express gratitude.

CHAPTER THREE

Dani

North Ohio, United Progressive Regions

It's no wonder everyone calls these last two terms the Year of Decision. It's not like we have to figure out the rest of our lives, just make the choice of where to spend the next two years in UPR National Service, a requirement we all have to fulfill after high school. If that's not enough, we also have to decide what to choose to focus on for our Capstone Project, a graduation requirement that's viewed as the culmination of our education. No pressure, right?

For a long time, Julia, one of my closest friends and a member of my school project group, agreed that we'd both sign up for the UPR Security Service. We're hoping that my *visi* designs and her tech skills will qualify us for the Intelligence Bureau. Our former project team member, Ibi, who graduated last year, is working at the International Bureau, which I'm sure thrills his mother since she's set her sights on Ibi becoming the future UPR ambassador to Nigeria, their family's home country. Ibi told us that so far it's been a bit dull. He's in a French class, a language he already knows, and he's learning all about the governmental structures of countries in Africa, something you can find out just using an iBrain. So for his sake, and for my own, I'm hoping things pick up for him as the year progresses.

As for my Capstone, I am totally at a loss. I've already mastered holograms, video, and still photography. There's really nothing left for me there, though I guess something multi-media could work. I don't know. Lately, because I'm thinking about national service, I wonder if I should learn more about encoding and decoding and use that as a topic for my Capstone. I could become a modern-day Alan Turing, the gay guy in England who helped win World War II by breaking the Nazi's secret code. Something to ponder.

Aisha, my ex-girlfriend who's also in my project group, is writing a web series about the Gullah Geechee, from whom she's descended. She's spent the last year on a research project, meeting with, of all people, my mother, who wrote her PhD dissertation on the island nation's climate change mitigation practices.

These meetings with Aisha have transformed my mother's opinion of her from heartbreaking, polyamorous anarchist to burgeoning literary talent who's on the brink of doing more for the cause of climate change mitigation than any single scientist or engineer. It's been a fascinating turnaround that would be easier to appreciate if my mother didn't spend every family dinnertime regaling us with Aisha's brilliance. It's not that I don't agree to a certain extent, but as my GFS pen pal Jeffrey put it in one of his more amusing emails, "What am I, chopped liver?" Of course, in his case, he'd decided that he undoubtedly was.

To round out my little project group, my trans pal Trey is also undecided about their Capstone. They could easily compose a collection of songs, since they're a great musician. But they say that idea just doesn't do it for them.

I turn back to my course and activity schedule projected in front of me by Kat, my iBrain. There's enough advanced work on the list to place me right into my second year of college if

I decide it's worth attending after national service. College is different here in the UPR than it was during my parents' era in the USA. Then, just about everyone wanted to go, though it was so expensive that not everyone could afford it.

Now, only people who know exactly what they want to get out of it go to college. Future doctors, lawyers, scientists, academics. The rest of us don't need it. We learn what we need to from courses on the 'net, which are either free or cost very little. People trade lessons. Like I could trade teaching holograms with someone who would teach me code breaking.

As my father tells it, "College in the USA just sped out of control. People ended up owing hundreds of thousands of dollars, and for what? The ability to spend their late teenage years away from home partying and playing sports with a little learning thrown in? It became more about the college experience itself than about education."

When he gets going on the subject, he always concludes with the final verdict that college "was a bubble that was bound to burst." I guess The Split that created the UPR and the GFS was kind of the last straw. The creation of a new country enabled us to rethink, well, everything.

I'm playing with my schedule—adding, deleting, and then re-adding physics—when Kat's melodious voice in my head announces a communication from Trey, my buddy and lifelong friend. With this newest version of the iBrain, I can message them by thinking the words and they'll be transmitted, but I'd rather speak aloud.

"Hey there pal, how are things?"

"Yo," they say. "I think I figured out my Capstone."

"Well that makes one of us. I'm trying to get excited about code breaking."

"Sounds interesting."

"Maybe. So you?"

"Okay, so, you're the first person I'm telling?"

"Wow, even before your girlfriend?"

"Yup."

"I'm honored and also surprised."

"Yeah, well, Julia's not gonna be thrilled because it involves spending time in the Autonomous Region of New England."

"What? Why?"

The Autonomous Region of New England, the ARNE, is the only autonomous region in the UPR that is not reserved for indigenous tribes. Before he relocated to the GFS, my brother Binyamin wrote a paper about the creation of the ARNE. The region was carved out from the rest of the country at the request of a group that my mother refers to as "principled conservatives," but who Aisha, Julia, and Ibi refer to as "right wing infiltrators." These are people who, although conservative politically, didn't see themselves fitting in with the GFS and their distinctive brand of nationalism, racism, and Christian white supremacy.

My brother's paper detailed the negotiations that preceded the establishment of the ARNE, along with the protests by those who didn't believe the UPR should give up any of our precious territory to people who didn't want to live in a country that regulated business and technology, taxed at high levels, but also guaranteed the right to health care, housing, food security, and education.

But despite the protests, the ARNE was permitted to impose fewer regulations on its businesses, tax at lower rates, and opt in or out of the UPR's guaranteed protections. Otherwise, the region was subject to the same laws that govern the rest of us—national service, climate change mitigation, non-discrimination, and even reparations compensation.

"Doesn't the ARNE fascinate you, Dani?" asks Trey. "I mean, it's a self-contained area in the UPR up in Maine and New Hampshire filled with people who believe differently than we do but aren't extremists like the GFS."

"Not according to your girlfriend and my ex-girlfriend."

"Yeah, well, that's why you're the first to know. I'm working up to telling them."

"How long will you be away for the research?"

"I have to work it out with Jackson, my new coach-advisor, but at least six weeks."

"Geesh, Trey. Why don't I just give you Binyamin's Capstone paper and you can be done with it?"

"Oh, that's great. Now my oldest friend who crawled around with me on my living room floor when we were babies is recommending I become a plagiarist."

"Yeah, I guess that won't work. They'd scan your paper before they even read it and up would pop my brother's."

"Dani, I'm not refusing to use Binyamin's paper because I'd get caught. It's because I'm going to come at the ARNE from an entirely different angle. I want to be there for a while to soak up the place, to interview regular people who live there, not just the leaders. I want to understand how kids our age live in the ARNE and if, being in conversation with me—a trans non-binary person who uses a gender-neutral pronoun—will make their heads explode or not faze them at all. Those are the questions I have."

When Trey puts it that way, I have to agree it sounds fascinating. While it's true that there's a lot we can learn about the ARNE just from using our iBrains—their regional government is on the 'net and there are various news sites, plus, even the UPR national news sites carry news about the ARNE—all of that is filtered through journalists and politicians. What Trey wants to do is go to the source.

Then a question comes to me that makes me a bit nervous. "Are you thinking of actually living there one day?"

"I have no idea," Trey says. "It's not an active question of mine, if that's what you mean."

I'm relieved, but only just a little. It's not like they've ruled it out. I decide to focus instead on more immediate concerns.

"Are you worried about what Julia'll say?"

"A bit. She's gonna think that spending so much time in the ARNE will influence my politics. But the truth is Dani, even now I'm just not as radical as her or Aisha."

"Or me?" I ask, thinking maybe he's just trying to spare my feelings.

"You're an enigma."

So much for sparing my feelings. "What's that supposed to mean?"

"Well, you're not out running around protesting with the Emma Goldman Anarchist Cell. You defend your brother living in the GFS. You're obsessed with antisemitism. And then there's Judith."

I can jump on Trey for a number of things in this rundown, but it's only the mention of Judith that catches my attention.

"What about Judith?"

"You're in love with a very religious girl, Dani."

"That's not why... That has nothing to do with... I mean, it can't be helped. And I never said that word." I pause for a beat. "Love."

They laugh at me. "That's because you don't have to. That dreamy look on your face where you stare off into the distance at the mention of her name says enough."

"Great," I say, my voice dripping with sarcasm. "Glad I'm so transparent. Anyway, we were talking about you."

Even though they're probably right, I don't see the point of openly admitting what they're saying is true. It's not like there's much of a chance that anything can ever happen between me and Judith Braverman, even if those few minutes I spent with her feel like this gigantic defining moment of my life.

But what does it matter if we can never be together? Maybe one day I can feel this way about some other girl, though I know deep down that's unlikely.

"Well," Trey says, "I guess if Julia ends our relationship because I want to spend six weeks in the ARNE, that'll tell me a lot. Don't you think?"

"Don't say that, Trey."

I'm shocked by how cavalier they seem. It's a bit depressing. I have such strong feelings for Judith, but I can't be with her. And here's Trey, who can be with Julia all the time, acting like it's no big deal if they break up. It all makes me wonder if there really is such a thing as true love in my generation.

"How 'bout we just leave this one up to G-dash-D as your friend Jeffrey would say?" Trey finally says, likely trying to lighten the mood.

I let a short laugh escape. "Don't make fun of his beliefs."

I guess Trey is right that my politics are a bit murkier than Aisha's and Julia's, both of whom think religion is a fairytale used to control the masses.

"I'm kidding and you know it," replies Trey. "Jeffrey is a total stand-up guy."

I smile in agreement, even though Trey can't see me.

"Well, *adios* and good luck with the Capstone decision," they say. "Hey, you know I looooove you."

"Yeah, same here Trey, you maniac. Enjoy your time with the right wing."

"Now who's making fun? *Ciao*."

I look up at the projected image of my schedule and have Kat turn it off. I'm no longer in the mood to worry about school since Trey had to go and mention Judith. Now I can't stop thinking about her and our nearly hopeless situation.

Julia says she's going to try to break into the Minyan of Resistance's evening connection hour. I worry she'll be unable to do it without compromising their security. But if she's successful, then I can actually talk to Judith without the use of papercut codes or holograms. I'll be able to hear her voice. Not as good as seeing her, but it's more than we have now.

CHAPTER FOUR

Judith

About a month after the horrible wedding, I begin to think there's something different about my mother. I'm observing little things that maybe aren't noticeable to other people. With my older sister Shuli married and out of the house, I'm now the eldest girl, which means I'm the one who is expected to spend more time with my mother, preparing meals, shopping, and cleaning. We do laundry, each holding the ends of a large sheet and stepping toward one another for that last fold when I give her the section that I've been holding, hoping she won't find fault that all of the edges aren't lined up perfectly.

Growing up I thought my mother never stopped running, doing work around the house or shopping in town. She was like one of those remote-controlled race cars that my brother Morty plays with, speeding forward in one direction and then suddenly going off in another. But now that I'm around her more often, I notice she does have a bit of free time to pursue her own interests. She usually relaxes in our living room, knitting or crocheting. That is, until two weeks ago, when I walked in on her with a book in her hands.

"For my Torah study group," she tells me. But that explanation doesn't seem to make sense, since instead of the heavy red *Chumash* or Torah volume on the table in front of her, it looks like she's holding a regular book the size of a novel. This surprises me since I've never known my mother to read anything other than a prayer book or the newspaper.

Another change is that she is less quiet at mealtime. At first it was little things, like worrying out loud about whether my father will be able to get a permit so Morty can get to the Cincinnati Symphony now that Jews aren't permitted to travel beyond the two-mile perimeter the government keeps us confined to "for our safety."

"Ruchel, don't scare the boy," my father admonishes. "I'll figure something out."

"Reuben, I just don't want you making promises you can't keep. That can be just as harmful."

When did my mother ever talk back to my father like that, especially in front of her children?

But the most incredible change just happened this morning when my mother finally agreed that I can attend Isaac's minyan for Shabbat morning service instead of going to synagogue.

"That poor boy," she says, shaking her head. "What parent turns their child out of the house like that? And a rabbi, no less."

I nod in agreement, but really, my mother seems not to need any encouragement from me.

Her arms are up in outrage, her voice raised. "I mean, what did he do? Did he murder someone? Did he get a girl pregnant?"

That question really gets my attention. Never, ever, has my mother talked about such a thing in my presence.

"No," she goes on. "He simply decided not to follow in his father's footsteps. And for that, he's an outcast, treated like a homeless orphan."

I think maybe she's given me an opening. So I take a risk and add my own contribution to the outrage. "You know, Mama, Isaac's parents blame Hannah for all this."

"Ridiculous," she spits out. "How long have you and Hannah been friends, Judith?"

I shrug. "Forever."

"She's been here in this house hundreds of times. Never gave us a minute's trouble. Always offers to help. She's a good friend to you, Judith, isn't she?"

I nod. "The best." As I say that I think, so why haven't you told Hannah about Dani?

"Go on to Isaac's minyan at Binyamin Fine's, Judith."

"But Papa…" I say, worried he'll overrule her.

"Let me worry about him. You're my daughter too."

That's all the permission I need to quickly leave the house wondering if this change in my mother is permanent or likely to fade away at the insistence of my father.

Wide eyes of surprise greet me when I enter the Fine's apartment. It's the first time I've been able to join them on Shabbat morning. I couldn't let them know ahead of time during our early morning iBrain meeting because we agreed not to use our devices on Shabbat except in an emergency. Jeffrey and Meyer Lipsky were the holdouts.

"Oh, because our whole lives aren't enough of an emergency already, we have to wait for something worse?" Meyer countered.

They are assembled in the living room, on the worn beige sofa and an old beige armchair. Some dark wood dining room chairs are set up as well for the more than ten of us. It's our original minyan plus Jeffrey's parents and the three Fine children, who are seated on the rug. I spot Naomi Blau on one of the wooden chairs and once again try to get a fix on her soul. Still slate gray, with light peeking through at the edges. So strange. Her blond hair is tied back in a ponytail and I'm surprised to see that she's wearing dark gray linen slacks instead of a skirt or a dress. A white button-down Oxford shirt is adorned only by the gold Star of David that hangs from a delicate chain around her neck.

"SJ, are you here undercover?" asks Jeffrey. "I mean, did you slip out of synagogue when no one was watching?"

My smile is broad. "No, it was more like a Shabbat miracle. Mama said I could be here for the morning service. I think she's mad at the Rabbi for what he did to Isaac."

"I always liked your mother," says Hannah as she pats the place next to her on the couch.

Isaac is at the front of the room, standing at the makeshift *bimah*, a table with a tall wooden box stacked on top, reaching up to his chest. The *Chumash* sits on it open to what is likely the weekly Torah portion. Isaac holds the *siddur*, or prayer book, in his hand along with some sheets of paper.

"Friends," he begins, "*Gut Shabbes*."

All of us respond in kind, using his title, Reb, including Jeffrey's parents who sit next to one another on two of the chairs. They gaze at Isaac with such reverence, likely in the same way they've regarded his father in synagogue. Warmth fills my chest as I watch them, certain they're the reasons why they have such a sweet and caring son.

Isaac has us begin the service with the usual Shabbat morning songs before we reach the central prayers. I follow along in the *siddur* though I have most of what is in there memorized.

Because I can move through this part without thinking, I let my mind wander to my latest artwork assignment for the resistance. Hannah says I can't use pictures of papercuts for my posters because everyone will know they came from me. She's right, of course, but it's still frustrating that our cause won't be able to benefit from the artform I love most, and at which I'm most accomplished.

Instead, I think about the protest art that Dvorah has shown me, remembering that one slogan, Silence = Death, white letters set against a black background beneath a pink triangle. A simple, yet compelling, warning that you either speak out or perish. It's like that reading from the Torah where *Hashem* tells the Israelites in Deuteronomy—"I have put before you life and death, blessing and curse. Choose life, that you and your descendants may live!" Choose life by refusing to remain silent.

I need something powerful like that. Something enduring that will always make people think about us and our cause.

I lean back on the couch. A small sigh escapes and I quickly continue singing *Mah Tovu* to cover it up. I wonder if maybe I'm trying too hard, thinking about this slogan too much. I decide to let it rest. Sometimes ideas come to me when I'm doing something mindless like polishing the silver before Shabbat or dusting the bookshelves in my father's study.

Isaac then leads us in the *Shema*. Each of us places a hand in front of our eyes to concentrate intensely on the command that is the key to our identity as Jews.

"Hear Oh Israel, the Lord is God. The Lord is One."

The word *Shema* is an admonition. Listen! Heed these words! Pay attention!

As the prayer concludes and I lower my hand to rest on my prayer book, it hits me.

Shema lanu! Listen to us! *Shema lanu haolam!* Hear us world!

I want to jot down these words so I won't forget them. But I can't write until after the sun goes down on Shabbat.

Later as we rise for the silent prayer, the *Amidah*, I whisper into Hannah's ear. "Remember *shema lanu*, so I won't forget."

She looks at me with one eye squinting, like I've lost my mind. "Uh, okay," she responds then shrugs, shaking her head.

We continue the silent chant of praise for our ancestors, another prayer I know by heart. But when I happen to look down at the page, I notice that the *Amidah* includes not just the names of the patriarchs—Abraham, Isaac, and Jacob—but the matriarchs—Sarah, Rebecca, Leah, and Rachel—as well. When I'm seated again, I take a closer look and realize this is not the same prayer book we use in synagogue. I nudge Hannah and point to the Hebrew letters that list the female names in the prayer. She nods and her smile is broad.

I make a mental note to ask Isaac where he's found these books, though I feel certain they've come from Dvorah.

Sometime later, as he announces we will end the service with a concluding song, Isaac hands a pile of papers to Naomi and asks her to distribute them. Similar to the prayer book, the paper has Hebrew on the left, and English on the right.

The Partisan Song is the title in English. I try reading the Hebrew, but it makes no sense. "*Zog nit keynmol*" What does that mean?

Before I have a chance to ask Hannah, Isaac speaks.

"I don't know how many of you know this song, but as I watch you take a first look at the paper, I see a few nodding and smiling, and some very puzzled faces. If you are trying to read this as Hebrew, then I'm afraid you'll quickly feel frustrated." He breaks into an open-mouthed grin and lets out a short laugh.

Although I've never been attracted to Isaac it's not difficult to understand why Hannah and Jeffrey are so entranced by him. His light brown hair flops over his forehead when it's not gelled into place. His eyes are the color of brown honey, with a lighter shade at the edges. And he truly does have a smile that makes you feel special, like you could be his best friend. I don't think I need Dvorah's gift of prophesy to predict that Isaac Leventhal will one day be revered by many as a great rabbi.

"The letters we most associate with Hebrew," he explains, "are also used for Yiddish. This song, written by Jewish partisans living in the forests of Eastern Europe and Russia and fighting the Nazis with homemade bombs and whatever else they could lay their hands on, was their battle cry. It is their song of resistance and of survival. Take a look at the English and you'll see why these words are so meaningful for us today."

Never say that there is only death for you
Though leaden clouds may be concealing skies of blue
Because the hour that we have hungered for is near
Beneath our tread the earth shall tremble: We are here!

As I read the lyrics, I feel my heart speed up. That last line that ends with the pronouncement "We are here!" *Mir zaynen do* in Yiddish, translated to *Anach'nu kan* in Hebrew, is another powerful message. Suddenly, instead of feeling like the least creative person on the planet, I am filled with possibilities for our battle cry. Now I just have to figure out the surrounding design.

As we fill our plates with food piled on platters laid out on the Fine family's dining room table, I overhear Binyamin and Dvorah discussing Isaac's *drash* or sermon.

"We may be facing the great spiritual, moral and, yes, violent battle that the Torah speaks of," he'd begun. "Fortunately, God has provided us with an abundance of guidance."

"Reb," says Binyamin, "you are a master at connecting the Torah to our struggle. I hope you are saving this *drash* along with all the others so that our network of resistance can benefit from them."

Before Isaac has a chance to respond, Dvorah speaks up. "Yes, Isaac and I are working on a Resistance *siddur* for all of the new *minyanot*[12] and it will include readings from all of his *drashot*."

I feel a tap on my shoulder and turn to see Dvorah's smile. "I'm hoping our new *siddur* can benefit from the talents of a certain young artist."

This is a big responsibility. It's one thing to design a poster, but to illustrate a prayer book, I just don't know if I have the level of skill it would require.

Dvorah has not removed her hand from my shoulder. I feel her gentle, reassuring massage communicating that she believes in me.

"I...I'll try."

"Oh Judith," says Isaac, brimming with enthusiasm. "That would be amazing."

For years, Hannah and I have taken a walk after the Shabbat *kiddish* meal. All our friends know that this is our time, so not even Jeffrey asks to come along.

"Enjoy your Sabbath walk," he says, punctuated by a little knowing smirk, and a waving of his hand in front of his face as if to fan himself.

It's a hot August day, so Hannah and I head over to the shaded area of a nearby park. The leaves on the maple trees are drooping from the summer heat. When Hannah rolls up her sleeves, I turn my head in every direction worried that someone will notice her bare arms.

"Relax Judith," she says. "At this point, I really don't care what anyone thinks about me. I'm already that girl who corrupted the Rabbi's son, so how much worse could it be."

She's standing against the thick, dark gray trunk of a tree, and is tying up her wavy light brown hair in a messy bun, likely

12 The ot ending for minyanot and drashot is the plural form of the words in Hebrew.

another reaction to the heat. "Here," she says and hands me a black scrunchy.

I take it and tie my unruly dark curls into a bushy ponytail.

"Judith, turn around," she says in that voice that makes me worry she's losing her patience with me.

Though I do as she asks, my annoyance seeps through. "What?"

I feel her untie my hair, then grip, twist it, and secure it with the scrunchy. I have to admit that even the feeling of hot air on my now bare neck feels good.

Her back against the tree, Hannah slides down the trunk and sits on the grass. I make sure the ground is free of dog doo or anything else I wouldn't want to sit in and plop myself down.

"I was really glad you came to the minyan's service today," she says in the sweet voice I most associate with my best friend.

I nod in agreement and a moment later realize we've been sitting in silence. Knowing that I've put this conversation off way too long, I take a deep breath and begin.

"Hannah, I need to tell you something."

Even as I tell her the story, there's still a feeling of unbelievability to it. I explain to Hannah how I stood there in the dark parking lot of a church in New Hope, that small town right near the border with the UPR. I was only there to support Jeffrey, who had to tell Dani he wasn't going to come with her and seek asylum in the UPR, but instead stay and fight against the growing antisemitism in the GFS. But instead, when I looked at Dani, all dressed in black to keep from being noticed, I felt this strange pull toward her. It must have been mutual, because in an instant we were drawn together, embracing. Then our lips met and we were kissing. I don't know which of us initiated that. I'm pretty sure that was also mutual. I tell Hannah that Jeffrey yelled at Dani to stop, and that when we pulled apart she apologized, but I looked at the ground and softly told her not to. Then, as Dani turned to go, her soul appeared to me in different shades of blue, unlike any others I've seen.

The words pour out of me like candies from a bag into Hannah's hand, slowly at first and then suddenly, in a torrent, spilling all over the place.

I watch her face as I speak. First her eyes are wide, then her mouth is agape and finally, she covers her open mouth in shock.

"A girl? You kissed another girl?"

I have no response since I've already admitted to that.

"But…but what about Jeffrey?"

I've told her so many times that Jeffrey and I are not a couple. But I've promised Jeffrey I won't tell her that he is gay.

"He was angry at Dani at first, thinking she instigated this, somehow taking advantage of me. But he knows now that it was a strange but mutual thing, something beyond our control. When I asked Dvorah about it, she said it was a sign that Dani is my *bashert*."

Hannah steadies herself on the tree trunk and pulls herself up. I don't want her towering over me, so I stand as well.

Her voice is shaking. "You told Dvorah?"

I nod. "I thought she'd be able to explain it."

"Who else knows?" I hear a hint of anger in her voice.

"Binyamin, Dani told him."

"And this happened months ago when we went up to New Hope and got stopped by the police?"

I nod and a small shudder goes through my chest. I feel like some kind of trap has been laid for me.

"And you're just telling me now? Me, your best friend?"

The trap snaps and I am caught.

"Hannah, this was so big and shocking and unexpected…"

"But not so much that Dvorah, Binyamin, and Jeffrey know about it."

I close my eyes. She's past the point of being reasoned with.

"Hannah—" I'm all but shouting at her at the same time that my eyes fill with tears, "Jeffrey was there when it happened and I couldn't even talk to him about it for weeks."

We are staring at one another locked in anger, so I don't hear the sound of running footsteps approaching until Jeffrey is almost next to us. He's out of breath, crouching with his hands on his knees trying to talk. His sweaty, damp hair is plastered to his forehead.

"So…so glad I found you," he says, still gasping.

It takes me a minute to switch out of my argument with Hannah. "Wait," I tell him, "catch your breath."

He shakes his head. "No time. Too important."

Hannah's face changes from tight annoyance to the serious expression she wears when she's speaking to us as a member of the governing council. "What's happened?" she asks.

Jeffrey seems to be recovered from his run. He straightens, wipes the sweat from his forehead, and breathes out audibly. "There's been a second Order of Protection, restricting Jews in the GFS from serving in the military and in all government agencies. Also, no more visas, even to Israel. They say again that they're doing it to keep us safe. But really the noose is tightening."

I'm gaping, but Hannah nods at him. The serious look she gives him reminds me of all the times Jeffrey has told me how much she intimidates him.

"Go on ahead," she tells him. "We'll be along in a minute."

He squints in confusion, shrugs, and turns to walk away. I see his head shaking as he leaves us.

Poor Jeffrey. He's run all the way over here in the heat to deliver his message and all he gets in return is dismissal. I'm about to lay into Hannah when she steps into my personal space and puts her hands on my shoulders.

"About before," she says in a quiet voice, "I'm sorry. I know you have your reasons for not telling me sooner. Plus, there are so many bigger things to worry about, and now I have all this responsibility." She breathes out and looks down at the thin blades of grass at our feet. I stand there waiting for her to finish, realizing for the first time that there is a real struggle going on inside that strong and imposing person she shows to the world. She raises her head and I am confronted by the tears she is holding back in her light brown eyes.

"The thing is," she finally says, "I know I can't do any of this without my best friend."

The tears silently roll down her cheeks. I grab onto her waist and pull her into a hug.

"I'm here," I tell her. "Always."

CHAPTER FIVE

Jeffrey

I'm like some kind of Jewish Paul Revere scurrying around alerting everyone that the antisemites are coming. But unlike ol' Paul, I have no horse. It's just me running through the sauna of an August afternoon from house to house, letting our minyan know what my father (who seems to have abandoned his Sabbath piety) heard on the radio.

It was a recording by that traitor, that Jewish Benedict Arnold—to keep the historical comparison going—our esteemed city councilman Barak Rausch. Of course, they would release it on Saturday while we are all obediently keeping our various devices off, except thank goodness my papa.

It's not like I have any desire to join their horrible GFS military or work in their Christian government where every day begins with some kind of Bible study and prayer. If I'm not a big fan of my own religion's practices, there's no way I'd go near theirs.

But just the same, we are slowly but surely being shoved aside, and it makes me wonder if we'll end up like those Gullah

Geechee people we talk to on the iBrain, confined to our islands, considered "guests" of the GFS instead of citizens.

When I reached Binyamin, Solly, and Dvorah, each of them wanted me to take a break from the heat and have a cold drink.

"No time," I told them, "have to tell the others."

That's when I set off to find Judith and Hannah who were on one of their ridiculous Sabbath walks they insist on taking, even during the worst weather, which seems to be all the time lately. What could be so important that they have to get away where I can't find them when I need them?

I ran to the shopping area, thinking maybe they'd stopped in a doorway somewhere to get out of the heat. I ran to that awful little shack behind the *mikvah* which is as hot inside as an oven today and was actually glad I didn't find them there all dehydrated and close to passing out. What is wrong with them?

Finally, I saw two figures under the trees at Ronald Reagan Park, the last place I could think of to look for them. My body was drenched in sweat. My eyes stung and I was completely out of breath.

I stopped in front of them unable to speak. Crouching forward to catch my breath, I felt the stirrings of nausea rise from my stomach and instantly regretted the huge mound of whitefish salad I'd piled onto an onion bagel after today's service. It took all of my effort to keep it down.

Neither of them looked very happy. I don't know if I'd interrupted some kind of serious conversation or they just weren't thrilled to see me. Frankly, I don't really care. Whatever made them so unhappy before I got there didn't compare at all to what I had to tell them. And then, for all my effort, I got a stare down and dismissal from Hannah…

Our Reb Isaac has decreed that, except in the case of life and death, the Minyan of Resistance can only meet during *Shabbes* for prayer. Meyer Lipsky and I, who are not quite as devout, try to convince Isaac and the others that living under the order of protection means that each day constitutes a matter of life and death. But our pious friends see it differently so there's not much we can do until the sun sets.

Solly invites the whole group back to his place for *Havdalah* [13]
followed by a meeting. Only the original First Minyan members
are included, except for my father since he was the one who
heard the announcement on the radio. I'm ready to argue that
my papa's decision to violate the Sabbath commandment and
turn on an electrical appliance should be considered a matter
of life and death, but luckily, none of the more learned minds,
who can argue rings around me when it comes to Talmud, raise
the issue.

It's an understatement that I'm not much for all the
religiosity when it comes to being Jewish. I've told Judith, to
her horror, that I'm more of a Food Jew. But of all the services
I have to sit through, *Havdalah* is my favorite. For one thing,
the service marking the end of *Shabbat* is short. So it has that
going for it. Also, I like that moment when the Rabbi takes the
flame of the blue and white braided candle and extinguishes it
into the cup of wine, even though it does ruin a good shot of
vino. Then there's the spice box; that small silver box on a stand
about the size of a candlestick that houses the sweet-smelling
combination of spices, mostly cloves and cinnamon. Now that
I'm praying with the Resistance and its Rebel Rabbi, each of us
has a few seconds to experience the spice box, instead of limiting
it to only the important men at the front. There's something
about that point when I'm handed the box, and I bend forward
to get a good strong whiff of the sweet aroma, that lights up my
brain with endorphins of happiness. Of course, it would be an
even better moment if I had a nice young man to pass the spice
box onto next. But you can't have everything. Or so they tell me.

Isaac explains that the sweetness of the spices helps cushion
the sadness that, as *Shabbat* ends, we each lose an extra soul
that has joined our regular soul for the Sabbath. This is an
interpretation we've never heard from his father, and I start
to wonder if our Rebel Reb has been dipping to the Zohar or
other mystical texts. I also wonder what Judith, the seer of souls,
makes of this. As the sun sets, is she able to look around and see
all our extra souls departing for a weeklong vacation to who
knows where? What if I bargain with God and say I'll trade

13   A short service marking the end of the Sabbath.

away my extra Sabbath soul for a boyfriend? Would *Hashem* possibly help a guy out?

See, this is why I'm just not suited to piety.

Dvorah and Solly carry in plates, cups, a coffeepot and, to my delight, a babka from the bakery. Now, this I can get behind. As we all dig in, the four members of the governing council—Binyamin, Hannah, Solly, and Dvorah—stand together and a few minutes later call us to order.

"Mr. Schwartz," begins Binyamin, beckoning my father to stand, "please tell us what you heard today."

My father stands, but his thin, wiry body still appears a bit bent over. He's dressed in his Sabbath navy blue suit, white shirt, and blue and black striped tie. He speaks slowly, still likely intimidated by the man he refers to as "Professor Fine," even though Binyamin is no longer at the university and has told my papa on numerous occasions that he does not have to be so formal.

My father recounts exactly what that rat, Barak Rausch, said on the radio. We are banned from military and government service and from travel outside the country. His voice dripping with disgust, his mouth twisting around the words like he's eating a lemon, my father repeats the lie that this is all about our safety. When he is again seated, his head is still shaking in disbelief.

So now we can have the discussion I've been waiting for all day. What are we going to do?

"I've got an iBrain meeting," Binyamin tells us, "with the other GFS minyans and the Independent Jewish Network tomorrow during our connectivity hour." This is the Network that Rivka Blau, of blessed memory, set up just before she was killed by the bomb set off in the office of the Jewish Federation of South Ohio.

"I want to work with you on that, Uncle Binyamin."

The high-pitched voice belongs to Naomi Blau, Rivka's daughter. I hadn't really noticed her tonight, but now, with everyone's attention on her, I see that she's cut her blond hair short above her shoulders and she's wearing gray slacks and a white button-down shirt. It's the first time I've seen her in pants on *Shabbat*. With that haircut and outfit, she looks kind of boyish. I file that away so I can mention it to Judith after I tease her about the extra soul thing.

I can't imagine that Binyamin will let Naomi come to this meeting of the IJN, so I'm a bit shocked when he agrees. Hannah and Solly announce they will be heading up all operations outside of our fenced-in community, leaving our area with forged permits to seek out allies and spread our message.

"Judith," asks Hannah, "any progress on the slogan we'll use?"

Judith seems flustered to be put on the spot. I wonder if that's how she reacts in school when she's called on by a teacher.

"Um, yeah, I have a few ideas," she says in that halting voice she uses when she's caught off guard.

"Tell us," says Solly. It's more like a command that he might have used in the Israeli army. He pauses and I can see his features soften in response to Judith shrinking back in her chair. At ease, soldier. "Maybe we can help you choose," he says in a more soothing voice.

Judith bends down and lifts her sketchbook out of her brown canvas shoulder bag. "I've been thinking about the *Shema*, which is a call to listen. So, something like *shema lanu*, listen to us. Or *shema otanu haolam*, hear us world."

There are nods all around and I hear a few yesses. But Judith is still staring down at her sketchbook and turning the pages.

"Then there's that song Isaac…sorry, Reb Isaac, taught us. The Partisans' Song. The last line, 'we are here,' is *mirzaynen do* in Yiddish and *anach'nu kan* in Hebrew." She looks up from her sketchbook and I see her scan the room. "So, I'm working with 'listen to us,' 'hear us world,' and 'we are here,'" she tells us and then immediately looks away.

I'm relieved that she's ended this recitation sounding much more sure of herself than how she began. This group can be intimidating, and I don't just mean the grownups. Even little Naomi has a strength of purpose that can set you back on your heels, a lot like her mother, if not quite as polished. It's depressing to realize that a thirteen-year-old has more of a sense of purpose than I do, but that's my life.

Dvorah takes a step toward Judith. "I like all of them," she says in that kind voice she reserves for my pal, SJ. "They speak to our resilience and our resistance." She turns back to her cohorts on the governing council. "Why don't we wait for Judith to finish the artwork and we can decide then. We might find a use for all three."

Solly is back to being nice. "And once that message is out there, we can figure out the next stage of messaging so we are making sure the world knows that if they can do this to us, they can do this to anyone."

"I'll th-think about that," Judith responds, returning to her meek voice.

I notice that Binyamin has taken my father aside for a few minutes and I can't imagine what they are talking about. Hopefully it has nothing to do with me. As they shake hands, I see my father eyeing the door.

"I want to thank Mr. Schwartz for coming tonight and alerting us to this new development," Binyamin announces.

As they all approach, I rush ahead and my papa gives me a quick hug. "I'm proud of you," he whispers.

I'm overcome with emotion, unable to speak through the lump in my throat. All I can do is grab hold of him again and kiss his cheek.

When the door closes, Binyamin pulls out his iBrain and affixes it to his head.

It's time.

CHAPTER SIX

Dani

Julia promised me that this would work, and I have no reason not to believe her. She was able to make contact last time. But still, my hand shakes as I place Kat, my iBrain, on my head and execute the contact parameters that Julia programmed into it. Will I actually be able to talk to my brother or will I be placing him in danger? What if the GFS government is able to listen in?

Then I think of Judith and I can hear her quiet voice in my head when I apologized that night in New Hope for whatever made me draw her close and kiss her.

"I'm sorry," I told her, only to hear her say in response, "Don't be." Those two words were just about all she actually said to me that night, but they meant so much and became lodged in my heart. Would I be able to talk to her now?

There's a shushing sound, like static on the line, and a pop, all of which Julia told me to expect. Then I hear a familiar male voice.

"Hello? Hello?"

My heart is racing. The parameters Julia created restrict the iBrain to out loud voice communication. No video and no thought messaging.

"Ben?" Oh no, I need to call him by his secret name. What is it? Hesh... "Heschel? Is that really you?" I realize I'm almost yelling.

"Abby!"

I figured it would be less confusing if I didn't create a new secret name and continued using Abby Cadabra, the hidden hologram character, a cartoon pixie, a kind of mystical, magic creature I've been sending to communicate with Jeffrey and Judith.

I blink back tears. "Yes, it's me," and I know he can hear the sob that escapes. Then a second later I am laughing with relief.

"Oh my God, oh my God. It's you."

"*Baruch Hashem*," says someone else. A woman.

"Abby, it's Chef," says Jeffrey. "All of us are here."

"Hi." There it is. Judith's quiet voice that has been echoing in my head these last few months.

I breathe out her code name. "Chagall, hi."

It's quiet for a few seconds and then it's like they are all speaking to me at once until one voice finally emerges.

"Abby, it's Arc." I look down at the list of names in front of me that Judith hid in a papercut. Hannah. Her voice is strong and commands my attention.

"Things here are getting more difficult. New bans on military and government service. No travel visas."

Suddenly the excitement I've been feeling in finally connecting with them is replaced by fear. "Oh no. What can I do? I want to help."

"I need you to do two things." That's my brother again. He's speaking quickly, likely worried that our connection could be cut off at any time.

"First tell your parents everything."

My parents? They're his parents too, but maybe that's giving too much away. But tell them? That I crossed the border and met Judith and Jeffrey? That they all have iBrains and we can talk to each other? They'll freak out and want to take all of this over, telling me it's too dangerous. I'll never get to talk to Judith and my brother again.

"Why?" I'm trying to push back at him in my response, but it comes out more like a whine.

"The world needs to know," he says with a tone of finality that makes me realize I have little choice. It also makes me worry that this might be my only chance to talk to Judith.

"I want to talk to Chagall in private right now." Great, now I sound like a teenager arguing with her parents. I might as well be stomping up the stairs on the way to my room.

"Abby, it's Heschel's wife here."

That's Miriam, my sister-in-law who I've never met.

"It's so good to hear your voice."

I wonder if she doesn't have a secret name yet. "Ohmygod, are your kids there?"

"Not right here," she says. "I'll try to see if I can have them around when your parents contact us."

I sigh out loud. My parents. He really wants me to tell them. I decide to switch back to something more pleasant.

"Chagall? Can we talk?"

"Wait," says Binyamin, "there's a second thing."

Oh, right. I just hope it's easier than the first.

"Contact Rabbi Weissberg at Congregation Beit Tzedek and help her get in touch with me."

"What?" The name Weissberg rings a bell, and then I remember the book Binyamin called "the Weissberg Torah" that I had to use to decode Judith's hidden message in her papercuts. "Did she write that Torah book?"

"Her father did. Listen Abby, we'll sign off now except for Chagall. Just please know how much I miss you."

I'm crying again and my voice shakes as I say, "Me too Heschel."

I wipe the tears with my sleeve and do my best to stop crying. "Wait don't go yet," I tell them. As much as I want to talk to Judith, there's a part of me that doesn't want the rest of them to leave. "I wish I could meet all of you."

"You will, Abby. One day." It's that same woman who spoke earlier.

"Chef? Please stay safe," I tell Jeffrey.

There's a short chuckle. "Don't worry about me, Abby. I'm very risk averse, which is a nice way of saying I'm a coward." I hear more laughter and can make out Hannah's voice again.

There's a few seconds of silence and then she speaks. "I'm here," says Judith. "Just me."

I breathe in and then out at the realization that her voice has the same effect on me as a full meditation session. I'm calm and my muscles are relaxed. I sit back against the pillows on my bed.

"Your voice is so soothing." The words are out before I realize I've said what I'd been thinking, relieved that this connection doesn't support the iBrain thought function. I look down and feel my cheeks warm.

"Really? No one's ever said that to me. Usually they tell me to stop mumbling."

I smile. "That's not how I hear you."

"I'm glad."

We are both quiet. There's so much to say but I have no idea how to begin. I just know we can't let this opportunity go to waste because it's unclear whether someone in the GFS government could realize what's going on and block the connection. I lean forward and lay my hands flat against the forest green comforter on my bed.

"This is kind of awkward, right?" I say at last.

"Oh," she pauses. "I'm sorry."

She thinks it's her fault. I wish I could launch myself off this bed and run to her. I speak quickly to reassure her. "No, no, it's both of us. I think because we've gotten things backward, you know?"

"Backward?"

I'm starting to read the emotions behind the cadence of her voice. So, I know from the halting soft tone, she sounds worried. I wish she didn't think I was blaming her for something.

"Yeah, see, people usually meet and get to know one another and then, well, what happened...I mean, what we did when we met, that usually happens after. But for us it was the reverse. Do you know what I mean?"

"Yes." Her voice is quiet again. "That night, we didn't, you know, have a lot of control over our actions."

Now I'm the one who's worried. I flop back down on the bed. "Do you regret it?"

Her voice is forceful. "No, I don't. I just want to figure out how we get to that first part that we skipped."

I'm relieved that she hasn't been scared away, thinking that kissing within seconds of meeting one another was a crazy mistake. I sit back up so I'm comfortable against the pillows and take a stab at a corny getting-to-know-you question.

"What's your favorite color?"

"Huh? My favorite…"

"Yeah, it's silly I know, but I thought we could start with something easy."

"Oh, ah." She pauses. "It's just that…for me, colors aren't really simple."

Right, of course, she's an artist. I think I've screwed this up until I hear her reply.

"I guess I'd have to say that it's all the shades of blue I saw when your soul appeared to me. It's a vision that is with me all the time."

Now I'm right back in that post-meditation contentment. I wish for the millionth time that Julia could get the video utility for the iBrain to work when we contact the GFS. I want Judith to see the big grin that she's put on my face.

She says, "Chef told you I can see some peoples' souls, didn't he?"

This is where things get a little confusing for me. "He did, but I'm not sure I understand."

"Yeah, well, that makes two of us," she says and I hear a short chuckle. "Golda says there's a reason that *Hashem* has given me this gift, but the reason may not have been revealed yet."

Wow, I am so out of my depth here. I bend my knees and hug them to my chest. This is like one of those dreams where you're sitting taking an exam for a class you never attended. Judith's explanation about her soul thing might as well have been in a foreign language. It's opened up a chasm between us into which all the gooey romantic stuff I've been floating on has dropped out from under me and I've fallen to the ground with a thump that reminds me how our worlds are so very different. I take a deep breath and let it out slowly. Then I do it again. The calm that begins to spread into my chest helps remind me of my determination to one day again feel what I felt the night we met. It propels me up from the bottom of the chasm and I am once again rising because I can't imagine living without that pull toward her, that warm embrace and the electricity of our kisses. So what if I need to learn some new things.

"Who are Golda and Hashem?"

"Oh." She pauses. "I have to remember you don't live here, even though right now you feel so close."

And with that, I'm right back on the gooey cloud.

She explains that Golda is the daughter of a famous mystic rabbi who inherited her father's gift of prophesy and has become like a second mother to her. Now I'm in familiar territory since I know so many kids my age with two mothers, though I'm not sure Judith is talking about the same thing.

"Golda was on the group call earlier," she tells me.

"Yes!" I say with some excitement. "I remember hearing her. And it was also great to hear Arc."

Judith giggles. "That name. So dramatic. She's my best friend. You know she and the Reb are together. I'm pretty sure they'll get married one day."

I relax back against the pillows, relieved to hear there are no romantic feelings between Judith and her best friend, Hannah. This whole distance thing is hard enough without the element of jealousy entering into it. And after my disaster of a relationship with Aisha, I'm convinced I cannot be with somebody who is also interested in other people.

"Tell me about Hashem," I ask, still filled with glee and this desire to know everything about her life.

"You don't…" Another pause. "Chef said you are Jewish but not religious. Can you explain that? I don't really understand."

Once again, I'm on the ground at the bottom of the chasm. But it's okay this time because just like me, Judith wants to learn.

"I didn't grow up with religion, like going to synagogue or stuff like that. But my parents have always been clear that our family is Jewish. That's why I understand when Chef writes about all the food. We do some things, like have a seder on Passover, and I've read just about everything written about the Holocaust. Does that make any sense to you?"

She doesn't answer directly. "*Hashem* is how we refer to God outside of the synagogue. *Baruch Hashem* is what we say to express gratitude to Him."

Ugh, Him. She really thinks God is male? I have a feeling the ups and downs of this relationship, if I can even call it that, will continue for a while. Yet, I still feel it's worth the ride.

"You didn't answer my question about whether my explanation about how my family is Jewish made sense," I tell her.

"I know," she says. "I need to think about what you said so I can decide if I really do understand."

This worries me because I don't know how I could explain it any better. Will this difference in how we are Jewish be a deal breaker for her? Then I realize there's someone who might be able to help.

"Heschel can help you understand. Will you ask him?"

"Yes, I'll do that, very soon." The excitement in her voice makes me know that she is also not ready to walk away.

We're quiet again until her sweetest, softest voice returns. "Abby, this talking is so good but not as good as it would be to see you."

I'm sure she can hear me breathe out "Yeah" in agreement. "I have to believe that can still happen."

There's a pop sound and I know we're about to be cut off.

"Can we do this again?" she asks in a rushed voice.

"Yes. I promise." And I seriously hope it's a promise I'll be able to keep.

"Take care Abby."

"Please stay safe, okay? You're important to me."

"I'm glad. I'll be thinking of you," she says, and I can picture her looking down to hide her shyness.

The static is louder, and I shout over it, hoping she'll hear. "I think about you all the time!"

I can tell that we have been cut off because the energy I felt from her has disappeared. I remove my iBrain and lie flat on my bed staring at the plain white ceiling.

This is crazy. We live in different countries that might as well be on different planets. I should just try to find a girlfriend here in the UPR. But like the pull I felt on that night Judith and I met, I'm still unable to back away, and I know deep down I don't ever want to.

CHAPTER SEVEN

Judith

"Where are the lovebirds?" Jeffrey asks as we walk down the dark streets of our neighborhood on the way to his father's shop. Hannah and Isaac have agreed to meet us there in a little while.

"Don't ever let Hannah hear you call them that," I warn him. He shakes his head in response. "She's still in the Governing Council meeting and Isaac is waiting for her."

The night is warm, but now that the sun is down, there's some relief from the intense heat. It's after ten so there aren't a lot of people out and we pass only a few stores and restaurants that re-opened after *Shabbes*.

Jeffrey stops under a streetlamp and turns to me. I recognize that funny smirk on his face and the twinkle in his hazel eyes that means he is about to tease me.

"So, did you see them all fly up at the end of *Shabbes*?" His eyes are wide open and he's using his hands to mimic a bird in flight, his thumbs hooked together and fingers flapping.

I place my hands on my hips. "What are you talking about?"

He lets a giggle escape that quickly turns into a laugh. "The second souls, SJ. You know, the ones we lose at the end of the Sabbath."

I roll my eyes.

"Do I have one? I'm willing to give my extra to someone else in exchange for something I really want. I mean, what use is a second soul one day a week anyway?"

I motion for him to keep walking. "What would you exchange it for, a kugel?"

Even in the dark I can see his grin.

"I was thinking of something taller and more handsome."

Now I'm laughing. "A one-day-a-week boyfriend?"

"Hey, I figure if things start out slow we can build from there, which by the way, leads me to ask how things went with one Miss Abby Cadabra."

I have no idea how to talk about a conversation that left me with so many questions. "Mostly good," I tell him.

"What does 'mostly' mean? Did you have your first fight?"

"Jeffrey, no!" I can't even imagine fighting with Dani. Just the fact that he would ask that annoys me.

"Well then?"

"It's just… She asked me who *Hashem* is, like she expected Him to be a member of our minyan."

Jeffrey unlocks the door to his father's shop and uses a flashlight to guide us to the back room. "Sorry for the cloak and dagger," he says, "if I turn on the overhead light, some wandering Jew will wander in with a broken blender or something, and I don't exactly want to deal with that now."

Once we're in the back, he turns on the light. The clutter of wires and metal parts on every surface always unsettles my innate sense of order whenever I step into what is Jeffrey's father's workshop. How does he find anything in here? I sit on a stool and look around.

"SJ, you'll never make sense of this place, so stop trying. My papa and I know where everything is."

"I don't see how," I tell him as I wonder why they don't see the value of putting all the screws in one bin and the metal rings in another. How do they know which random parts go with a mixer and which with a computer? It would drive me crazy to try to work here.

"You're avoiding the subject by mentally organizing the workshop."

"How did you...?"

He rolls his eyes. "You're not as mysterious as you think you are. Now, back to the crisis of the hour." He raises both hands and moves them back and forth. "Dani Fine doesn't know who *Hashem* is, a calamity of epic proportions."

His attitude toward religion is even more annoying than Dani's lack of knowledge. He clearly doesn't know me well if he doesn't realize how difficult this is for me. I don't appreciate the fact that he thinks this is all a big joke. A girl who doesn't know *Hashem*! Where would I even begin?

I sit there seething in silence thinking about hopping off the stool and making a dramatic exit.

He's across from me in a desk chair, his back to the large computer where we first saw Dani's hologram of the cartoon pixie, Abby Cadabra, leap off the screen like some kind of mystical, magic creature. Jeffrey's arms are folded over his chest and I can tell he's just as annoyed with me as I am with him.

"You know," he says at last, his voice sounding like a parent chastising a child, "you should be grateful that you even have somebody. Not everyone's that lucky." He's actually pointing his finger at me.

Now I'm really thinking of leaving. No one my age gets to talk to me that way. I'm sure he can see the tension in my body and the angry glare I'm sending his way.

We sit there like fuming bookends for what seems like forever but is more likely a few minutes. Does he really think I asked for this? That I wanted to meet another girl and be drawn to her this way when it would have been much easier for it to have been him? Dani should have been his *bashert*, not mine. Then he could have left with her and be happily settled in the UPR.

But that would have been impossible because neither of them could fall in love with a person of the opposite sex. It's just not who they are. It's not the way *Hashem* made them.

So where does that leave Jeffrey? He's right to feel jealous. He yearns for something that I didn't even know I wanted, though now that I have it, I can't imagine going back to my life before that night in New Hope, even with all of our differences.

So maybe he's right to remind me how lucky I am.

I unfold my arms and drop them to my sides. I tilt my head a bit and whisper, "I'm sorry."

His body relaxes and I hear him sigh. "Me too, SJ. I know I can be a jerk."

"Our first fight," I say and smile.

He chortles. "Hopefully that satisfies our quota for a long time." He gets up and walks to stand next to me. "Do you want to say more about your talk with Dani? I promise not to act like an idiot."

I grab onto his arm. "It was actually nice. She said I have a soothing voice." I let out a giggle. "No one's ever told me that."

"I've heard that love can mess with your hearing."

I look up at him, eyes wide, silently asking if he's starting up again.

"I'm kidding," he says. "Will she be able to talk to you again soon?"

"She said she'd try to."

The dinging of Jeffrey's device echoes in the small room. "That'll be Isaac and Hannah," he says. "I have to let them in."

I listen as the front door is unlocked and opened followed by voices I know well coming from the front.

Hannah walks right over to me. "Hi, how'd it go with Dani?"

"Mostly good," I say for the second time.

"Judith was all freaked out because Dani doesn't know who *Hashem* is, but I think we've worked that out," Jeffrey interjects as he and Isaac move a collection of metal and plastic off a counter so they can sit down.

"That's what you talked about?" asks Hannah, her head shaking. "I was hoping for something more, I don't know, romantic?"

Jeffrey laughs and I do my best to ignore him.

"There was some of that," I tell her. "There's just a lot we don't know about each other. And it's so much harder because we come from such different worlds."

"Binyamin told me that many Jews in the UPR aren't observant of *Halacha*[14]," Isaac says. He seems more and more to be inhabiting his new rabbinic role. "And others who do observe," he continues, "well it's really different from the way we do. I'm actually eager to learn more."

I nod. "I really like some of the changes you've made, Reb."

Hannah is smiling with pride. "The fact that I can be counted in the minyan means so much."

"And I finally get to smell the spice box at *Havdalah*," adds Jeffrey. "I know it's a silly thing, but maybe because it's related to food and cooking, it means a lot to me."

I smile at him. It's the first positive thing I've ever heard him say about a Jewish ritual. Maybe Isaac's new ways of conducting the service will change Jeffrey's mind.

14 Jewish law.

CHAPTER EIGHT

Jeffrey

Judith and I are quiet as I walk her home, but it's a good quiet, not like before when we were silently seething across the small back room of my father's store. I'm incredibly relieved since Judith is the only person who knows all my secrets. Who else can I tell that I'd trade my *Shabbat* second soul for a cute boyfriend? When I joke around with her like that, I feel more like my true self than at any other time.

As we turn to walk up the flagstone path to her front porch, I realize I meant to ask her something. "Hey, what's up with Naomi Blau?"

She looks at me with her head turned at an angle. "What do you mean?"

"You know, the haircut, the different clothes."

Judith pauses for a few seconds before responding, nodding. "I'm not sure. It could be nothing or it could be some delayed reaction to her mother's death."

"You mean murder."

"Yes. But then again, it could be related to what's going on with her soul."

"Which is?"

Judith grabs hold of the brown strap of her shoulder bag as if it's a tether keeping her firmly standing on the ground. "It's hidden behind this thing that looks like a dark gray wall, and all I can see are little shimmers of color around the edges."

Judith's soul thing still confuses me. It seems impossible that she can actually tell whether some people are inherently good or bad. I mean, how could science even explain such a thing? And yet, it's hard to deny that she sees something, I just don't know what. Maybe she's a psychic or an empath? At this point, I've decided to stop trying to figure it out and just take a leap of faith with her.

"Is it a bad soul?"

Judith shakes her head. "No, the little I can see is good, and the first time I met her, the good soul came through with a silver shimmer and no wall in front. Something's changed."

We are interrupted by the opening of the Braverman's front door and Judith's father standing before us still in his Sabbath coat and tie. He looks right at me. "So late you bring her home?"

The man gives me the willies, just as much as Isaac's father the rabbi. "S-s-so sorry, Mr. Braverman," I murmur, staring at my shoes.

"Goodnight Jeffrey. Thank you for walking me home," Judith says in a clear, strong voice that signals to her father that there's no need for further conversation.

After a quick goodnight in response, I'm more than relieved to turn around and walk home.

It's about eleven thirty when I open the front door of my house, surprised to see both my parents sitting in the living room. My father is in a white T-shirt and blue striped pajama bottoms and my mother has her yellow and white-trimmed robe tied tightly around her waist. Usually there'd be a screen on with the news or something, but tonight it's dark and the only light in the room is a lamp on the end table next to the couch.

"You're still up?" I ask. They both wake early on Sundays. My father opens the shop at nine and my mother is usually up at six making his food for the day.

"We were watching the news," says my father. "I just turned it off. I don't have a good feeling about this upcoming election."

He's always glued to whatever device or publication can fill him in on the news, even in the front of the shop when the customers are there. Politics, weather, the economy, and always the plight of Jews. My father might as well be the town crier, he is so up on the latest happenings. His newest obsession is the upcoming GFS presidential election. Ever since The Split, the New Republic Era Party, or NRE, has won every national and local election. But now, their opponents, the Christian Patriots, are gaining in popularity and it's looking like their candidate might even win. The CPats stand for the worst aspects of our country, including and especially antisemitism.

"I know you're a big boy, *tattele*," my father says, using that Yiddish term for "little father" he always calls me. "But these are dangerous times and we stayed up to make sure you got home safe. Remember what happened to your friend, Isaac?"

Isaac's beating by the God Fearing Boys last year is still fresh in my parents' minds like it happened yesterday. "But now we all know Krav Maga so we can defend ourselves," I tell him, recalling with great satisfaction how I was able to use my newfound martial arts skill to send Simeon Rausch crashing to the floor that last and final time he tried to abuse me.

"Israeli judo, or whatever Krav Maga is, can't help you when someone comes at you with a knife or worse."

I can try to reassure them by explaining that our training involved learning how to take weapons away from attackers, but he'll only come back with some other paranoid argument and we'll go on for another round.

"Jeffrey, if you're not too tired in the morning, I'm planning on baking," my mother says.

This gets my attention and I respond with a big smile. "What are we making? Babka? Rugelach? Honey cake?"

"Yes, honey cake," she says as she stands and stretches, covering a yawn with her hand. "A nice treat for you and Papa at work."

My father stands next and turns to her. "He's back so late and then has to work with me, so maybe skip the baking this week."

"No, no," I insist, my hands raised. "I'll get up early. Baking calms me down for some reason. Maybe because it's so reliable."

He nods. "Yes, the things we can rely on are in short supply these days, except, of course, we can always rely on The One Who Dwells on High." His head is tilted up and I wonder how helpful it is for someone to stare at the ceiling.

More and more I am taking comfort in not just eating but in actually cooking the food we eat. It makes me wonder if maybe I am supposed to be a chef. But who knows if I'll even live long enough to have any career the way things are going. Of course, it's my bad luck that just when I actually make real friends, the world turns upside down.

I head to my room at the end of the hall and retrieve the iBrain from my pants pocket. It was not one of the smartest things I've ever done to walk around town with it. I could at least have hidden it better, like Judith. I'm not exactly sure where she put hers, but I have a feeling from a glimpse I caught of her that it rests somewhere inside her blouse. And that's way more than I want to think about.

I return the device to its usual hiding place in a small metal box I took from the shop and place it behind the false bottom plate I'd constructed at the base of the wall next to my closet. Once it's tucked away, I look down at the hiding place with a feeling of satisfaction that when it comes to this tiny level of subterfuge, at least I've done something right.

CHAPTER NINE

Dani

I'm starting with the easier of the two things that Binyamin has asked me to do. Not that finding some rabbi I've never met and telling her how to get in touch with my brother is particularly easy. It's just that it's *much* easier than telling my parents that I snuck over the border months ago and spoke to my brother on my iBrain this week. Luckily, Aisha, Julia, and Trey have agreed to come with me when I tell them.

I've only been to a synagogue once. Binyamin took me after he returned from Israel and told my parents he was becoming Orthodox in order to marry Miriam and move to the GFS. Talk about a conversation that didn't go well.

He convinced me to go with him to some kind of Jewish celebration or party or whatever. I remember there were a lot of kids and adults and there was a long scroll that had been unraveled so that it ran the length of the large room where people prayed. There was a lot of singing and then there was a lot of food. I don't remember much else. The rabbi I have to go see, Rabbi Weissberg, might have been there but I don't remember her at all.

The building is kind of impressive with large, white stone blocks along the front and massive windows with smaller panes lined in lead. Some of these smaller panes have stained glass pictures and I'm hoping I can get a look at those when I'm inside.

An electronic sign outside reads Congregation Beit Tzedek in gold letters and some other information about Friday night services. I climb the front steps, a kind of light gray marble, and push hard against the heavy door. Now I'm standing in the entrance where there's an older woman with short gray hair at what I guess is a reception desk.

I stand in front of her, tongue-tied for a few seconds while she looks up at me with her head tilted, her face a question.

"May I help you?"

"Uh yes, I need to speak with the rabbi?" I finally tell her.

"Which one? We have three."

Three? I wonder why. "Uh, Weissberg."

"Okay, do you have an appointment?"

Now I know I really screwed up by just running over here and not contacting her first. I shove my hands in my jeans and look everywhere but at this woman. "No, but it's really important. Can you tell her Binyamin Fine sent me? I'm his sister."

Just then a tall woman appears. She seems to have come out of nowhere. She's broad-shouldered with dark wavy hair and eyes the same brown color. She's wearing a navy blue pantsuit with a cream-colored blouse.

"Did you say Binyamin Fine?" she asks.

"Yes," I tell her, my voice brimming with excitement. "Do you know him?"

She holds out her hand to me. "I'm Rabbi Roberta Weissberg."

I take her hand. It's soft and warm. "Dani Fine, Binyamin's sister."

We end up in her office, which she calls her study. She's seated me in a maroon armchair and is facing me in its identical twin. I realize how lucky I am that she came by the front desk when she did. I don't think the gray-haired sentry would have let me get this far.

"How is your brother and his family? Have you heard from him?"

I tell her everything. Well, not about the thing with me and Judith, but everything about my short visit to the GFS to meet my pen pal and how I gave Jeffrey my old iBrain, which he seems to have successfully reproduced allowing Julia to open up some periods of connectivity. I know from the secret messages in Judith's papercuts that iBrains are in the hands of many Jews in the GFS as well as the Gullah Geechie. At least that'll be one thing that will make my mother happy.

"So things are as bad as the rumors we're hearing?" says Rabbi Weissberg when I've finished.

"I think so. They aren't allowed to work for the government or travel anywhere anymore."

"What does your father think should be done? He works for the UPR government, right?"

Do Jews confess to their rabbis the way that I've read Catholics confess to their priests?

"Well, you see," I begin and pause, looking down at the navy-blue carpet, "I haven't exactly told him any of this. You know how parents worry."

I hear her breathe out and watch as she sits back in the chair, arms crossed over her chest. Is there some kind of punishment that a rabbi can give you? My body is tense, and I think if I move at all something terrible might happen.

"Dani, parents do worry, but they also have a right to know. Binyamin is not only your brother, he's their son."

I decide to explain my side of things. "I know but, they'll make this into a big deal, and I'll be grounded and never get to talk to Binyamin or Ju… or anyone again."

"This *is* a big deal," she says in a quiet voice.

"I know I have to tell them," I tell the carpet. "My brother actually agrees with you."

"What can the synagogue do to help Binyamin?" she asks.

I meet her gaze and shake my head. "I don't know, but he asked to talk to you. I don't know about what."

"How do we arrange that?"

I explain about the hours of connectivity and the special coordinates Julia created. "I'll let you know the next time things open up and I'll transfer the coordinates to your iBrain."

She sits there in silence, her mouth open. "This is truly a miracle," she whispers.

"Well, actually, it's just technology and a very smart young woman we call Owl, but either way it's really, really good."

* * *

Okay, one down, one to go. Before we walk over to see my parents, Aisha, Trey, Julia, and I meet up at the coffee place near my house, all of us knowing that soon everything will change.

If this wasn't difficult enough, there's the added tension of Julia and Trey's breakup. Trey's plan to spend six weeks in the ARNE was the culmination of what was building up between them for the last month.

"People change," Julia told me when she gave me the news. "We drifted apart."

"C'mon," I pressed her, "what really happened? And no more cliches."

Julia sighed and shook her head. "The initial attraction over the fact that we were each assigned the wrong gender at birth and then had to transition before puberty wasn't enough to keep us together. The longer things went on, the clearer that became."

I couldn't stop myself from asking the question that I'd been turning over in my mind the last few weeks. "Is it because Trey's going to the ARNE?"

Julia closed her eyes and again shook her head indicating I was annoying her. "It was like the last straw and finally clarified things for me. But it wasn't just that."

"It's not such a big deal, you know," I told her, my voice pleading. "Trey'll only be away for six weeks."

Julia took a few steps toward me and placed her hands on my shoulders. "Dani," she said, and I could tell by the quiet, deeper way the words came out that she really was annoyed, "it's over. You have to stop projecting your fantasy of this perfect couple onto us and concentrate on your own situation."

I stepped back to release my shoulders and turned away. I hated being lectured, even if the other person was right. Facing Julia's judgment was too much.

"Okay, okay," I whispered and walked away.

Trey and I enter the small café together. I spot Julia and Aisha already seated at a table in the back with white ceramic coffee cups in front of them. The combined smell of coffee mixed with chocolate draws me to the counter and Trey lines up behind me. A few minutes later, cups in hand, we sit in the shiny black wood chairs. I squeeze Aisha's arm, smile my hello at her and say a quick "hi" to Julia without looking directly at her. Trey just nods.

"Our date with destiny," Trey says. Julia rolls her eyes.

Aisha then takes charge, and I am relieved, since in this very awkward situation, she is the neutral party. "Okay, so what's the plan?" she asks, her eyes on me.

I stare down at the red lacquered tabletop. "I guess we tell them," I murmur.

"Riiiiight," she responds, "and then what?"

"I'm *not* handing over the code I used to get you across the border and to connect to their iBrains and getting dismissed like a good little girl." Julia says this with such vehemence that I wonder whether her anger at me and at Trey is spilling over into this thing with my parents.

"I support that," says Trey, and I turn to him thinking maybe he's trying to smooth things over with her.

"What does it matter to you, you won't even be here," Julia spits out.

Aisha places a hand on her shoulder and rubs it a few times. I know that gesture. It's Aisha's way of telling Julia that she cares but that Julia needs to calm down.

"So basically," Aisha continues, "we tell them the facts, but we don't give up our involvement no matter what they say. Do we all agree?"

There are nods and yeahs all around.

"I just want to say one thing," I tell them. "Please, nothing about me and Judith, okay?"

Aisha abandons her usual devotion to group process and answers for all of them. "Agreed."

Then she sets her cup down in a not so gentle manner, like it's a judge's gavel, and she stands. "Okay, let's do this."

The four of us file into my living room where my parents are seated waiting for us at the agreed upon time. I hadn't given them any information except to say that Aisha, Julia, Trey, and I have something important to discuss with them. As I could have predicted, my mother pushed for more, but I didn't cave.

The living room looks just as it always does, dominated by a large L-shaped light brown sofa that's the most comfortable place in the house. It's where I stretch out, working from a virtual screen when I'm alone in the house. More times than I can count, my parents have come home to find me sound asleep, the screen still blinking in thin air and my iBrain hanging off the side of my head.

Now they're sitting in the two dark brown faux leather armchairs that face the couch expecting that the four of us will assemble facing them, which we do.

After hugs of hello to my friends, my mother slaps her hands against her thighs. "So, what is all of this about?"

As usual, my father is quiet. He sits back relaxed wearing an open blue and black checked flannel shirt and one of his old Ohio State T-shirts underneath. His left knee is bent so that his white stocking foot can rest on his right leg.

"We found a way to be in touch with Binyamin and my pen pal, Jeffrey, in the GFS."

My mother is up out of her seat moving to us on the couch. "That's wonderful!" she exclaims, her arms in the air. But then her face turns into a question. "How did you…Is he okay?"

"Meredith, let her finish," my father says in his gentle, firm tone and waves her back to the chair.

I silently thank my father with a look of what I hope he can tell is gratitude.

"Silly question anyway," my mother murmurs as she sits. "How could he be all right in that... that country?"

"I wrote code that allows them to have connectivity for an hour twice a day on their iBrains," says Julia. She's folded into herself, legs crossed and arms hugging her chest. Her wavy dark hair spills forward like two curtains bordering her face.

"What iBrains?" asks my dad. "I didn't think they had..."

Here goes nothing.

"Jeffrey has my old one and he's reverse engineered it to make more."

My mother looks at me like I'm speaking a foreign language, her face all screwed up. "How did he get your iBrain?"

I hesitate. My heart thumps in my chest at the thought of telling them about the trip I took over the border.

My mother fills the silence. "Dani, you know how dangerous it is to send something like that through the mail? It could have made all kinds of trouble for Jeffrey and shut down the whole pen pal program. What were you thinking?"

"I didn't mail it," I say in a quiet voice. "I met them on the other side of the border and gave Jeffrey the iBrain."

My father's left foot is now on the floor and he's leaning forward, his arms stretched out to me. "That's impossible. There's no way you could have crossed without us knowing."

"You rebooted for fifteen minutes and I was able to stretch it to a half hour," says Julia. Her tone is a little bit too superior for my taste, but given her tech skills, I guess she has the right to gloat.

"There's no record of that."

"Yeah, I made sure of it."

"And the transport to the border and back?" my father asks, almost a whisper.

"All erased," she responds.

My father's mouth is open, his head shaking.

"Wait, hold on!" says my mother, her voice turned up a few decibels. She's standing again pointing at the four of us. "You're telling us you went down to the border, extended the reboot time, crossed and met Jeffrey to give him your iBrain?

Do you know what the GFS would have done to you if you'd been caught?"

I purposely ignore the histrionics. "Jeffrey was originally planning to come with me and seek asylum in the UPR. He's gay. I went to rescue him."

I hear my mother's sigh as she once again sits down. I have a feeling she's going to repeat this jack-in-the-box behavior a few more times.

"In the end, Jeffrey decided to stay and fight," says Aisha. "We are doing everything we can to support him and Binyamin and their whole," she pauses, "what is it Dani?"

"Minyan of Resistance," I finish.

My mother twists her body toward my father. "Steven," she says, her tone urgent, "can you do this again? Open the border so Binyamin can come home?"

As usual, she only hears what she wants to hear. To her, it's all about getting my brother back to what she considers his true home. I can't blame her, but at the same time, she's completely ignored Jeffrey and the resistance.

"I don't know. I don't know."

My father is still in shock. His job is to keep the North Ohio border safe from the GFS. I'm sure he's worried that if a seventeen-year-old could create this kind of breach, he's completely failed. He's looking past all of us on the couch, his eyes glassy. It's as if his body is still in the chair but otherwise he's left the room. My mother, on the other hand, is still very much with us.

"Meredith," says Aisha. "The minyan has made contact with the Gullah Geechee in South Carolina. Queen Olivia has an iBrain."

This gets my mother's attention. "My God," she exclaims. "They're all still alive?"

"I think I'll be able to connect them up here soon. I'm working on the coding," adds Julia.

My mother's head is now resting against her open hand. It's rare for her to be left speechless, but she's spent the last decade trying to reach the people she lived with and worked with for years before The Split. She'd begged them to relocate to the UPR, but they could not give up their islands. So they stayed, resigned to being pariahs in their new country.

My father emerges from his stupor and looks right at Julia. "I need you to explain to me exactly what you did to keep the border open. You know, Julia, you've committed a very serious violation. This is our national security you're tampering with."

She actually rolls her eyes at him. "Only if you agree not to push me and all of us aside." She gestures across the couch. "Only if we can remain involved in helping the resistance."

My mother pops up again. "You know, this is not some VR game where your avatar goes into battle to save the day. This is real life, with real guns and bullets, and an evil you've never experienced growing up here."

I sit back and stretch my arms along the back of the couch. Once my mother gets going, you just have to wait her out.

"These people are ruthless. You *know* what they did during the last Great Migration when BIPOC folks refused to leave. You all had to study this history. And now they are on the brink of electing their very first self-proclaimed white Christian nationalist. Do you know how much worse it's going to get for Jews, for the Gullah Geechee and for any of those people of color who never left? Trey, when you spend time in the ARNE you'll learn a lot from the people who for years called themselves conservatives but could not even imagine living in the GFS."

I worry that my mother has thrown a lit match on a stack of dry kindling and Julia will erupt any second. "Mom, can we maybe focus on how we can all work together to help Binyamin and everybody else?"

"Okay," my father says and sighs, his voice full of resignation. "I'll work with you, Julia, and I'll respect your expertise. Clearly, you've been able to do something I thought was impossible. How about we turn this into your Capstone project, and I'll speak with your coach."

"So you won't turn me in?" She tilts her head and glares at my dad who just shakes his head.

Back in her chair my mother breathes out audibly and stares up at the ceiling, then faces us. "Aisha, you and I can figure out how we can help Queen Olivia and her people."

Now she's pointing again, right at me. "And Dani, I want to speak with your brother as soon as possible."

I nod in agreement. "He asked me if I could connect him to this rabbi I went to see."

"What rabbi?"

"Her name's Roberta Weissberg. Binyamin once took me to her temple or whatever."

"Why?" asks my mother.

"I have no idea. Something religious, I guess."

"Well, I'm his mother and I come first."

"Okay, okay. But you'll need a code name, we all use one."

"A code name?"

"To protect their identities," explains my father. "They're trying to be careful, though I don't know how helpful these code names really are."

My mother shrugs. "I'm sure I can come up with something."

I'm relieved that this has gone about as well as it could. We're still able to stay involved and no one has gotten in too much trouble.

I smile at my mother. "If you want, I can suggest a few code names for you."

She lets a small chuckle escape. "I'm sure you can, especially since you'll have a lot of time while you're grounded at home. You think there aren't consequences for that little stunt you pulled crossing the border?"

Apparently, that's the signal for Aisha, Trey, and Julia to leave. All three stand and say their goodbyes.

CHAPTER TEN

Judith

It's the Sunday before the first day of school and the first day of my final year at Kushner Academy for Girls. My father has taken my brother Morty and his cello to the Cincinnati Youth Symphony for his audition. For weeks, the deep, mournful tones from Morty's instrument have filled the house. He's put much more time into this than he ever did for his bar mitzvah practice last year. Morty sped through his Torah reading like he couldn't wait for it to be over, which I guess was the truth. As I sat watching him from up in the women's section, I wondered what it would have been like for me if I were to stand before the congregation and read from the holy scroll, the *yad* or pointer in my hand following the ancient text. Would I have chanted everything correctly without the benefit of the cantillation trope marks that are found in books but are absent from the actual Torah? And when I finished would cheers of "*mazel tov*" have rung out around me as people threw handfuls of candy that small children would run up to grab off the floor and fill their pockets?

It's always been a silly fantasy of mine to chant one of the seven sections of the weekly Torah reading, even knowing that girls are forbidden from being called up for an *Aliyah*[15]. But now, with Reb Isaac Leventhal reinventing so many rituals, and including women in the minyan, I wonder for the first time if such a thing could be possible.

The house is quiet. My little sister is visiting a friend and my mother is sitting in her favorite sliding rocking chair reading. This is the chair in which she used to sing each of us to sleep when we were babies. Once my younger sister graduated from the crib, my mother had the chair fitted with thick tan cushions and moved it to the living room. It's commonly understood in our family that the rocker belongs to her and no one else.

Today she sits in the swaying chair with a book in one hand, her other hand lying flat on the shiny wooden armrest. I stand at the open doorway that connects the living room to the entryway right inside our front door, watching her silently, hoping to commit the scene to memory so I can draw it later.

My mother is short and rotund. Her body fills the chair and her feet hang a few inches above the floor. Sometimes she rests them on a small ottoman, a round wooden piece that's topped with the same color cushion as the chair. Today though, her feet sway with the movement of the rocker.

I guess if I was going to describe her to a stranger, I'd say my mother is down-to-earth. Unless it is *Shabbes* or a holy day, she is usually found in a housedress, one of those shapeless, long-sleeved cotton garments with patterns of small flowers or polka dots and deep pockets on each side. On her feet are simple black slip-ons, a step up from bedroom slippers.

I can't see what she's reading but I can tell from her serious, focused expression, her brow furrowed, that she is engrossed. I decide to take a chance and interrupt her.

"Mama?" I whisper.

She continues reading.

I take a few steps toward her. "Mama, what are you reading?"

---

15 A reading from the Torah.

She lowers the book to her lap and twists toward me. "Oh, Judith." Her voice has an edge of surprise to it and, I think, a bit of relief that it's me. "What do you need?"

I'm now right beside her. "Um, nothing. I was just wondering what you're reading."

"Just something Dvorah Kuriel lent me. It's a woman's view of the Torah."

I hold my hands out to her with my palms open. "Can I see?"

She hesitates, and I wait for her to lay the book in my hands. There's brown paper folded over the front and back covers. I pull it back and read the title.

"*Standing Again at Sinai*. Like Mount Sinai?"

"Of course," she says with a shrug of one shoulder. "It points out all the ways that women's stories have been left out of the Torah."

"But there are women throughout the Torah. There's Sarah, Rivka, Rachel, Leah…"

"Yes, but they are usually in a subservient position. If Jacob had twelve sons and one daughter, Dinah, then why are there only twelve tribes of Israel?" She jerks her head down with emphasis like she's stated her case.

I'm thinking this over, but before I can respond, she continues. "And do you think Sarah would have agreed that Abraham take Isaac, their only son, up Mount Moriah to sacrifice him like an animal? After she waited until she was an old woman to bear a child?"

I'm quick with an answer this time. "But Mama, *Hashem* stopped the sacrifice. It was only a test of Abraham's faith."

"Judith, no mother would have let their husband go so far as to bind their child to an altar and raise a weapon."

"Maybe that's why Sarah wasn't told?"

She nods slowly and appears to be taking in what I've said. Then she holds a hand out to me and I place the book in it.

"Well, in any case," she says as she stands, "it's an interesting book, maybe a kind of *midrash*[16], imagining a Torah where women are more, I don't know, active."

16 Expanded interpretations of Biblical text, many told as stories or parables.

She flips through the book. "Here, let me read this sentence to you. It really caught my attention." I hear a soft "ah" when she finds what she's looking for. "Okay," she says and follows the words with her finger, "'excluded from the spiritual path of legal study and argument, women might have developed other avenues to God more fully.'"

She drops the book in one of her large pockets and yawns, covering her mouth. "Food for thought, my daughter, food for thought."

I am left wondering about what was meant by "other avenues to God" when we are interrupted by the ringing of the house phone. My mother walks past me toward the kitchen. "Maybe Papa with some good news about Morty and the audition."

I follow and watch as she stands by the old ivory-colored phone fixed to the wall with the long, coiled cord hanging down almost to the floor. We have this phone in case something goes wrong with the network that runs our devices. Papa insisted we have a fallback since there might be important news he wouldn't want to miss during an outage.

After hello, all I hear my mother say is "Yes."

Then she leans toward the wall, one hand flat against it.

"Oh God! Oh God! Oh God!" Her voice gets louder with each utterance, her voice filled with anguish. She thrusts the phone's receiver at me and, when I take it, she is fully against the kitchen wall, leaning on the aging white and blue wallpaper. I can almost feel the vibration of the sob that leaves her as I hold the phone to my ear.

"Hello?"

"Mrs. Braverman?"

"This is her daughter, Judith. Who is this?" My question comes out like a command. What I want to say is, *Who's done this to my mother?*

"This is the Cincinnati Police. There's been an incident. We need your mother to come identify your father's body and pick up your brother."

I'm hearing someone say these words but they are not connecting to my brain. He probably didn't say what I thought he said. But what if he did?

"What did you say?!" I scream into the phone.

"Miss Braverman, we think your father was involved in some kind of altercation. We found him lying on the ground. He didn't survive the trip to the hospital."

There's no denying what he's telling me and yet it still makes no sense. My whole body is stiff, strung tight, with the phone clutched so firmly in my hand that my fingers are starting to ache.

"How did this happen? Who did this?" I am shouting over my mother's sobs, the phone pressed tight against my ear.

"We're investigating. Whatever happened was over by the time we arrived. Apparently, your brother found your father and someone from the symphony called us."

Oh Morty! "My brother. Is he hurt?"

"No, he's fine." His voice is flat, distant, formal. "Just a sad little boy with a big instrument we're holding for him. You'll have to pick that up as well."

My mother is quiet now, still leaning against the wall. Her silence is even more worrisome than her loud sobbing. I know she will ask me what happened, so I make one more attempt to find out.

"Why? Why did they do this to him?"

I know down deep the real answer and I also know that it's not the answer I'm going to get from the police.

The officer delivers his response with the kind of annoyance a parent would have for a tiresome child. "Like I said, Miss Braverman, we arrived after. Now, if you'll get your mother over here, we'll need to know where to send the body. You people have your own funeral homes, don't you?"

You people. The exact words the police officer used the night he stopped Solly's car when Jeffrey, Hannah, Isaac, and I drove up near the border to meet Dani. "You people stay in your own area with your own kind," he'd said. This is the way the police talk to us now.

After he gives me the address, I hang up the phone and gently pull my mother to me. She grabs onto me and I feel her tears soak through my blouse to my shoulder. Slowly I walk her over to the kitchen table, pull out one of the shiny, chrome-framed chairs with the light blue padding. She sits, lays her arms folded on the table and rests her head there.

I run to my room, grab my device, and without thinking I call Jeffrey.

"SJ?" His voice is soft and comforting and thankfully not filled with his usual teasing. I couldn't take that now.

My voice is high and urgent. My words fall on top of one another. I am close to hysterical. "Please come here! Papa's been killed downtown. We need a car. Please come!"

"Coming," is all he says before he disconnects our contact. The strength of that word allows me to exhale in relief.

When I turn to run back and comfort my mother, I'm stopped by a phrase that suddenly takes root in my brain and once again reminds me of the bond that Jeffrey and I have forged.

It's what Abraham said in response to *Hashem's* call to him. What Moses said when *Hashem* called to him through the burning bush.

Hineini.

Here I am.

CHAPTER ELEVEN

Jeffrey

Judith's face is red and puffy, her eyes watery. There's nothing I can say to her, no words that are right for this moment. I can only grab onto her and hold tight as she cries on my chest, and I just let her.

After a long moment, she raises her head and whispers, "Mama," turning toward the kitchen.

"Solly will be right here with the car. Dvorah is talking to the Hershberg Funeral Home. Hannah, Isaac, and Binyamin are on their way over."

She stares at me. Her eyes wide, mouth open. "You did all of that?"

"Um, yeah."

I take a few steps to follow her, but then turn back when there's a knock on the door. Solly, Hannah, and Isaac walk in, all of them looking like I feel. Solly's head is shaking and he mutters, "Unbelievable." Isaac's eyes are fixed on the floor. Unsurprisingly, Hannah's face is screwed up with determination as she rushes past me to Judith.

Solly rests his hand on my shoulder. "I'll drive. You sit in the back with Mrs. Braverman."

I nod, but there's a lump in my throat. What do I know about comforting a bereaved widow? I'm sure anything I say will be the wrong thing.

Before I reach the kitchen, I'm met halfway by Hannah and Judith standing on each side of Mrs. Braverman, who is bent over, smaller and older than she's ever appeared. Can a person age so much in less than an hour?

We all walk slowly and stop in the area by the front door. I watch as Judith, her face pale and drawn, ties a navy-blue silk kerchief over her mother's head and hands her her small, black purse. Mrs. Braverman grabs onto the short black strap for dear life.

Judith turns to me and holds out two papers. "Here are travel permits for you and Solly. Mama's is in her purse in case she needs it. The police said they've phoned her name into all of the checkpoints, so she shouldn't have any problem getting through."

"Are you sure you don't want to go in my place?" I ask her.

"I can't. My sisters are on their way here and I need to be with them."

I sit in the back seat of Solly's car, aware of how close Judith's mother is to me, and slowly I feel her lean into my side as if she needs me to keep her from falling over. At least I can do that much for her.

As we near one of the two-mile perimeter checkpoints, I reach for the paper in my pocket and see Solly in the front grabbing his off the empty seat next to him.

As if this horrid day could get any worse, it suddenly does when Simeon Rausch the snake, now a full-fledged member of the CPD, Jewish Unit, sticks his head in through the open window. My quick, silent prayer to *Hashem* that Simeon doesn't notice me goes unanswered. When he spots me, he spits out, "You! Schwartz!" Not bothering to hide the disgust and hatred in his voice.

I'm silent with a thousand snarky retorts bouncing around in my head, including, *Yeah, the last time we saw one another, you were lying on the bathroom floor after I finally fought back one of your sickening sexual attacks.*

I feel Mrs. Braverman shaking as she looks up at Simeon. I pat her hand to comfort her, hoping the touch is okay.

Solly reaches back and I hand him my permit. As he gives our permits to Simeon, he tells him, "You have Mrs. Ruchel Braverman's name in your records from headquarters." I take some small sense of satisfaction that Solly delivers this sentence as if he is still an army commander speaking to a subordinate.

Once we are waved through with a grudging grunt of "Go ahead" from the snake, Mrs. Braverman squirms next to me, her head turning back and forth. "Morty!" she exclaims. "We have to save him!"

I open my mouth to respond but Solly is already speaking in a calm, reassuring voice.

"He's waiting for us at the police station. We'll bring him home."

It's not hard to imagine that all three of us are thinking about the one person we will not be bringing home—the person who'll be taken on a stretcher to the back of a hearse arriving from the Hershberg Funeral Home.

How will this family survive without Reuben Braverman? What will become of his Jewish newspaper? Will it be taken over by the likes of Barak and Simeon Rausch and become a propaganda tool for the GFS government, filled with lies about how much they care about keeping us safe? I again pray silently, this time hoping that Reuben Braverman has drawn up a will that leaves his beloved *Jewish Community News* to his wife.

I expected some kind of dingy and decrepit police station, with aging furniture and peeling walls, but it's more like entering a sleek new office building with bright lights, shiny chrome fixtures and a gleaming black lacquer counter.

After we announce ourselves to the beefy red-haired uniformed cop seated behind the counter, we're pointed to a group of dark gray plastic bucket chairs and told to wait. It feels like forever, sitting there with Mrs. Braverman between me and Solly, her eyes fixed firmly on the door next to the red-haired cop. But it is really only about five minutes before a tall, thin police officer walks through followed by Morty.

The only way I can describe Judith's little brother is to say he looks crumpled. His brown pants and white shirt are creased with dark stains on his knees and dots of what can only be splattered blood on his chest and on the cuffs of his sleeves. His dark, curly hair, the same as Judith's but shorter, is messy, with portions of it sticking up on top. He's normally such a happy little guy, the kind who always has a smile for you. But now there are tear tracks on his cheeks and his brown eyes are clouded with pain.

When he sees his mother, he runs to her. Mrs. Braverman is already standing, her body in movement toward him. I hear him cry out, "Mama" through his sobs, as they cling to one another.

Solly is over by the tall cop. "His cello?" he asks, pointing to Morty.

The guy looks over the top of Solly's head. "Downstairs in Evidence across from the morgue," he says, not hiding the boredom and annoyance in his voice. He thrusts his hand toward Solly. "Here, you'll need this."

Solly takes a small yellow card from the cop, who turns away and heads back to the door. Before he disappears, he turns and looks at the four of us, his face twisted in disgust. "In the future, just stay put in your area instead of winding up in places where you're not welcome."

He's gone before any of us can respond, even if we thought it would do any good. It's not too difficult to realize that the police are placing the blame for Reuben Braverman's murder on the dead man himself.

After Solly and Mrs. Braverman head downstairs for their very depressing trip to the morgue, Morty and I sit waiting in the gray plastic chairs. Morty's hands rest on his thighs, his body bent forward, head down. I notice his bare head.

"I lost my *kippah*," he whispers in the saddest voice that makes me think he's going to break down again.

I gently place my open hand on his back. "It's okay," I tell him, thinking that should be the worst of his troubles. "*Hashem* will understand."

He raises his head and turns to me. "There was blood everywhere! I came out to meet him and he was lying on the sidewalk. His head…" He's sobbing and hiccupping, unable to finish.

I rub his back, hoping my physical contact with another male will be seen as an act of comfort and not something else. "Morty, you don't have to tell me."

He twists his body, shaking off my hand, and turns to me. "They split his head open," he yells. The anger in his voice makes me lean a bit away from him. "He wasn't doing anything!" He's still yelling. His face is twisted and tears run down his cheeks.

Then he's back in his bent-over position, crying softly. I gently place my hand on his shoulder. I wish I could tell him that the murderers will be arrested and convicted. That they'll spend the rest of their lives in jail. But what's the use? Both he and I know that won't happen. The cops will be grateful for one fewer Jew they have to contain in a small neighborhood. One fewer Jew to issue a permit for travel. One fewer Jew in their God Fearing country.

"This is all my fault," he whispers to the black and white tile floor. "I should have never auditioned."

I tighten my grasp on his shoulder. "No, Morty, don't blame yourself. We both know who's at fault here."

He turns and looks at me. "Yes, but…" He pushes out a staccato sob. "If we hadn't left the neighborhood to come downtown…"

I look into his watery brown eyes, wanting him to hear me, wanting him to put the blame where it belongs. "If parents hadn't raised their kids to be thugs. If they went after the real criminals. If they didn't hate us because they needed someone to hate." I speak these words with such speed they surprise me.

Morty's nod is barely noticeable, but I see it.

"C'mon guys, let's get out of here." Solly stands in the doorway.

Mrs. Braverman is clutching Solly's arm. His other hand is wrapped around the narrow portion of the soft black case that is likely holding Morty's cello. Mrs. Braverman is stooped over, eyes on the floor. My throat constricts with the kind of sadness that grabs hold of you just before you start to cry. I feel the tears pooling in my eyes and squeeze hard to hold them back.

I hope I never have to look at the dead body of someone I love, especially one that's been as badly beaten as Reuben Braverman. I realize that it's likely none of us will be spared this kind of tragic ordeal. Haven't I already had to stand over Isaac lying bleeding in the mud, blessedly alive but still suffering from the trauma of being beaten for who he is? Are there worse things in store for us, for me?

It's quiet in Solly's car as we drive away from the police station except for the sniffles coming from the back seat where Morty and his mother sit, his head resting on her chest, her hand smoothing his curly hair. As we pass through the checkpoint, thankfully not manned by Simeon the snake this time, I hear the distinct ripping of fabric and a gasp followed by, "Mama, what are you doing?"

I turn and see that Mrs. Braverman has ripped the seam of the collar of her pale green blouse. "This is what I must do. I'm a mourner now," she says in response, her voice a monotone lacking emotion.

A few seconds later there's another ripping sound and I turn to see Morty has ripped the seam of the pocket on his shirt, which now hangs limp. "I'm a mourner too," he says.

It's almost a relief to get back to the Braverman house and out of the confines of a car with two people wrapped up and completely overwhelmed by their grief. But it's a brief reprieve given that there's Judith and her two sisters who are at the door clinging to their mother and brother. This is their family now, a band missing its conductor, a meal with no main course.

I excuse myself and head to the small first-floor bathroom to wash my face. Already, Judith or someone has covered the mirror. There'll be no time for or interest in vanity in this house, especially during this week of a funeral and *shiva*. There'll only be mourning and remembering and the love and support of relatives and friends.

Judith's older sister Shuli holds the torn piece of the collar of Mrs. Braverman's blouse between two fingers. "Mama, you didn't have to do this. The funeral home will give us those black buttons with torn ribbons on them."

Mrs. Braverman's face is pinched with disdain. "That's not enough, Shuli. I want to rip every piece of clothing I own so they can see what they've done, so they won't be able to look away. A torn black ribbon is for a normal death, from old age or, God forbid, cancer. This was not normal. This was murder!" Her voice increases in volume as she speaks. "And I'll never let them forget it!"

CHAPTER TWELVE

Dani

Luckily, school begins online in mid-August, so I haven't had to leave the house during the past few weeks of over one-hundred-degree weather. Today, the Tuesday after Labor Day, marks the first time I'm back here in the building with my project team, minus, of course, Ibi, who graduated and is now doing his national service. That leaves us with an empty spot in the group, and with Trey's six-week trip to the ARNE, it's only me, Aisha, and Julia.

I look around our project space. Aisha's now seated at the front table that was Ibi's. We agreed that she should be head of the school news site this year, our final one at Jesse Owens High School. Her long, thin braids are tied together and coiled into an updo. The soft, glowing skin of her shoulders and neck is now visible above the neckline of her ribbed navy blue tank top. There are times like now when I look at her and I can remember why she was my first love, even though my attraction to her has morphed into an aesthetic appreciation of a close friend. She's stunning and what we all refer to as her "regal bearing"—she is, after all, the Gullah Princess—just adds to the magnetism that always draws people to her.

Normally girls flock to Aisha and she has her pick. I can say from experience that she's not a bad girlfriend. Attentive, sweet, empathetic, and affectionate. It was her insistence on remaining poly that broke us up. She stuck to what she said worked best for her and in response I got whiny and desperate. We were destined to fail. But now as close friends, I find I still get the best of what I had with Aisha before. She's the same attentive, sweet, empathetic and affectionate person, in a more platonic way. And she gives me something else that I need: the truth. Maybe she's a little blunt at times, but she always calls me on my shit and gives me her honest opinion. Fortunately, she's warmed up to the idea of Judith and even believes in all that mystical stuff about seeing souls, which has been a bit hard for me to swallow.

I watch her now at her table, immersed, her virtual screen flat on the surface and out of our sight. I somehow doubt she's working on a school project or our news site. She handed in her Capstone topic focused on the Gullah Geechee of the GFS the first week of school. No, she's likely thinking about, writing about, or fantasizing about DeAndre, the trans guy she met over the summer at Black Arts Camp where she taught creative writing to kids. In college at Morehouse in Detroit, DeAndre may be the first person who really captured Aisha's heart, and certainly the first male-identified person she's dated.

"So I guess now I'm pan-poly," she'd told me with a big grin on her face.

"Or poly-pan," I offered, which set us both rolling around giggling on the braided rug on her bedroom floor.

When she came up for air, she placed her hands on my shoulders and looked at me, her lips pursed as if she was holding back laughter. "And you, Dani Fine, are a Sapphic-monogamist." She again burst out laughing and gently pushed me backward. I lay on the floor smiling with the memory of Judith's face in my mind.

Aisha's work area faces the rest of ours. Mine is near the window side toward the back so I can make use of natural light. Julia is across from me, against the far wall, hidden behind a virtual screen she keeps up like she's projecting a permanent barrier. We're still not in a good place with one another, even with Trey out of the picture for now. We aren't openly fighting or anything, just not really talking except for a word here or there. When I complain to Aisha, she sighs, thrusts her fingers outward in a forward motion that implies "Get to it," and tells me in a clipped tone, "Fix it." I wonder, with a drop of resentment, whether she's telling Julia the same thing.

The room has an empty, eerie feeling today that's messing with my concentration, preventing me from focusing on the task in front of me, namely picking a topic for my Capstone. It's due in a week and the only thing I've come up with, encoding and decoding, isn't doing it for me. But it's a fallback if I end up with nothing else.

I just can't lose this annoying feeling that something isn't right. But I can't put my finger on what it might be. Maybe it's this unresolved business with Julia. But I'm not positive that's it. Something just feels off.

I'm doing my thing of going into my head and worrying in circles. Usually there's a specific subject attached to my low-level anxiety. Friends, my parents, my brother. But now it just feels free floating, and I can't shake it. Ugh!

I'm awakened out of my reverie by the violent slamming of the door to our room against the wall. The slam is followed by a loud and very dramatic male voice. "To quote the sainted Bette Davis, what a dump! What! A! Dump!" His loud pronouncement echoes across the room. He's looking at Aisha, his arm extended to her. Then he turns toward me and Julia.

"But fear not, student journalists, writers, and artists," he continues like he's making a political speech, "I have arrived to whip things into shape."

I stare at him, shaking my head. He's a skinny boy with short spiky hair and black-framed glasses. He's wearing a black T-shirt with red letters in an Asian language. His black jeans are the skinny kind that cling to his thin legs. There's someone behind him but he's blocking my view of them. I sincerely hope he isn't our newest project group member.

Aisha is clearly unhappy with being disturbed from what I would guess are thoughts of DeAndre. Still seated, she turns a bit toward the door, leans her chin on outstretched fingers and squints at the boy. "And you are?" is all she says.

He takes a few steps toward her in an exaggerated movement I can only explain as sauntering. "I," he responds and draws out the word, "am your savior. Kim Ji-Joon, the best thing that's ever happened to this little publication. For those of you who are Korean-impaired, the name means wise, handsome, and talented, which, as you can see, is quite fitting." He holds out his arms and takes a bow. "And this…" He pauses for effect and moves to the side, revealing a girl with long black hair tied into a thick braid. "This is my talented twin sister, Kim Ji-Kyung." He gestures to her with a flourish. "We come as a package."

She's wearing a short-sleeve, light blue button-down and a navy blue skirt that reaches a few inches above her knees. She looks up at us and then back to her brother.

Aisha's stance hasn't changed. She is broadcasting boredom and skepticism. I remember that look from our ill-fated relationship and never want it directed at me again. "Do you always feel the need to mansplain your sister? That won't work for you here," she tells him to my great delight.

"I am an artist and my brother writes." Kim Ji-Kyung's voice is soft but firm. It could be she's trying to distinguish herself from her loud, brash brother as she continues, "You can call us by our English names, Ann and Will Kim. Mx. Caro assigned us here. She said the notification was sent to your iBrain."

I can hear Aisha's sigh from my place at the back of the room as she grabs hold of her silver iBrain and attaches it to the side of her head. She closes her eyes and shakes her head, likely a reaction to the notification.

Aisha gestures to the empty workspaces in the front of the room. "Find your places and review the past few issues of the site from last spring while I finish what I'm doing. Then we'll have a project meeting."

A message from her comes through to me in the next few seconds. "Remind me to give Mx. Caro a piece of my mind next time I see her for sending us Mister Wise, Handsome, and Talented. His sister might be okay."

I smile and notice that Julia has taken down her virtual screen and is smiling too. We look at one another, both trying to hold back from laughing. It's the first positive interaction we've had in a while.

Now seated at the table closest to Aisha, Kim Ji-Joon or Will snaps his fingers to get her attention. "If you lack the cultural competency to use my real name, then I guess the English Will is okay."

His sister speaks to him in Korean and it's too quick for me to use the translator on my iBrain. But I recognize her tone. It's universal sibling code for stop being such a pain.

He's quiet for a minute or two, long enough for me to return to trying to figure out my own growing sense of internal doom. Then there's that annoying voice again.

"We've practically committed these issues to memory. Any chance we can meet now?" His tone is about one notch away from a whine.

All Aisha does is raise a hand signaling for him to stop. She doesn't even look up from whatever she's doing.

But a moment later, she finally says "Okay," and gestures to the empty middle of the room. The metal bottoms of chair legs make that grating sound as they're dragged along the tiled linoleum floor until a circle of five is assembled.

Aisha's smile at our new additions is brief. "Welcome to the Jesse Owens Brigade. I'm Aisha Wright-Bukari, the managing editor." She nods at Julia.

"Julia Sanchez, all things tech," is her quick intro. Her face is impassive, as she tucks her shoulder-length brown hair behind her ears.

They all look at me and Aisha's nod is almost unnoticeable. I open my mouth to say my name and it's at that moment the loud alarm from my iBrain goes off, the wah-wah-wah sound that tells me I have an email from Jeffrey.

Both Kim siblings turn toward the sound and stand up from their chairs. They probably think we're about to have a bad storm or a tornado.

Aisha is also standing and shouting at me: "Dani, how many times have I asked you to change that way-too-dramatic Jeffrey alarm?"

She has and I haven't.

I shut down the alarm and notice Will is walking toward me. "What's a Jeffrey alarm?" he asks, "Is that some kind of a boyfriend thing?"

I roll my eyes at his presumption. "Hardly. I don't do boys."

"I do," he says. "Is this Jeffrey cute?"

I'm surprised at the voice I hear: it's Julia's. "You'd have to go to the GFS to find out." I smile as Will responds, "What?"

"He's her pen pal." Julia again.

"I didn't think they…and we…" Ann's voice trails off, her confusion evident.

"It's a special program for Jewish teens in the two countries," explains Julia.

I tune out the rest of her explanation and walk to the back wall of the room, calling up a virtual screen. Jeffrey's email appears and it's only one paragraph followed by the jumble of Hebrew letters I will have to decode. I notice that the coded message is longer than usual, even longer than his email.

Dear Dani,

I've perfected the art of chocolate babka, not an easy task. My mother is proud. My father and friends are happy for more treats. Our last year of school begins after the High Holidays, which are early this year.

Jeffrey

The usual focus on food is what I've come to expect from Jeffrey's emails, at least the parts that the GFS government might read.

Julia and Aisha are now at my side as I execute the decoding program that Julia created. The email disappears and is replaced by the following message:

Judith's father murdered by Jew-hating thugs. Police will do nothing. We are with her but she could use your support. Shiva is this whole week.

Judith. Judith. Judith. The two syllables of her name fill my head in time to the rapid beating of my heart and what feels like the hyperventilating of my breathing. The hands that grasp my upper arms bring me back to my surroundings.

"Poor Judith," Julia whispers.

"What is *shiva*?" The question comes from Will, who for the first time speaks in a quiet voice devoid of sarcasm and bombast.

"It's a Jewish mourning ritual," answers Aisha, intuitively understanding that I can't even begin to think about words. "You visit the family and bring them food, so they don't have to worry about cooking. It's a way for community to pay its respects."

We're all quiet for a few moments. Aisha is rubbing my back in smooth circular movements, whispering in my ear, "Slow down, Dani, slow down."

My breathing calms enough for me to whisper, "I have to be with her. I have to go there."

I look to Aisha, but she's got her eyes on Julia, who tugs on my arm. "Dani, come with me," she says.

I'm all but stumbling as Julia pulls me toward the door. I swivel my head toward Aisha, who's gone back to the circle of chairs with Will and Ann.

I need to go, I need to go, I need to go. The words are a mantra I can't stop repeating as my feet tangle and untangle as I mindlessly follow Julia's lead. Are we walking to the border? Is Julia taking me to Judith, just like she did before when she short-circuited the border controls for thirty minutes? Maybe I can get there before the *shiva* ends, to sit with her, to hold her in her grief, to fold her in my arms as she cries. *I need to go, I need to go, I need to go.*

Suddenly I'm sitting on a cushion somewhere and Julia is holding a mug in front of me. "Calming tea," she says. "Sip it, Dani."

I look at the light blue ceramic mug trying to connect it to Julia's words. I squint at it.

"C'mon," says Julia. "Drink some of this so we can talk."

My fingers are wrapped around a smooth handle, and I feel the weight of the mug. The steam rises to my face, its warmth and the herbal aromas of lavender, lemon, and chamomile distract me enough that I become aware of my surroundings. We're in the small student lounge near our project room. No one else is here except the two of us. I can see the mini-kitchen area with its sink, squat refrigerator, and the three spigots for cold, hot, and boiling water. There's a gray armchair, some floor cushions, and a few of the same white plastic chairs we have in our project room. The linoleum floor is a dark purple with a variety of different rainbow arches scattered throughout.

I blow softly on the tea and take a few sips, tasting the flavors of the herbs.

"Any better?" asks Julia.

She's sitting next to me, one arm around my shoulders. I nod. I'm not really better, just more aware, less in my head. Then I remember the uneasy feeling from before Jeffrey's email arrived. My free-floating anxiety. It was about this, this tragedy, Judith's grief. I could sense it but didn't know what it was. Could it be that she and I are *that* connected?

I look down at the tea in the mug. It's the color of lilacs, a mixture of the lavender and lemon.

"I knew something wasn't right. I felt it all day," I tell the tea. "I couldn't focus on anything except this sense of dread. Now I know. It was this."

I expect the tea to respond, but instead it's Julia's voice in my ear. "It's horrible. Poor Judith."

It's not enough to say "Poor Judith" and to feel the weight of this news. It's not enough to be a Jew safely ensconced in this so-called progressive country while we shake our heads in disbelief at what's happening only a hundred miles away. It's not enough to love a girl and send her an email or a hologram or make an iBrain call for an hour a day to tell her…what? That I'm sorry this happened? That she and her family have my condolences? That I wish I could be there with her?

"It's not enough!" I tell the tea in my full voice and watch as my hand shakes the cup so hard the liquid sloshes dangerously close to the edge.

Julia gently pries the mug from my hand and sets it down on the table in front of us. She's taken my silent companion from me, which makes me sad because the tea understood. I'm sure of it. But I don't know if Julia will.

I place my hand on Julia's leg next to me and shake it. "I need to go! You have to get me there again."

"Dani," she says, drawing out my name. "You know I can't."

"Yes you can. You did it before."

"That was a fluke. I was able to take advantage of a system reboot on both sides. Who knows when they'll do that again?"

"But you work there now. You have more access. There's got to be a way."

Julia turns her body toward me, and with her fingers on my chin, positions my head so I'm facing her. I feel her hold on my chin tighten. "I could be arrested and sent to lockdown. Did you ever think of that? It's only because your father was too embarrassed about me breaking into his border system that he didn't report me before and instead decided I could help them improve security. It's my job and my Capstone, Dani, keeping the border secure. You know that."

I gently touch the hand that's still holding me by the chin and run my fingers lightly up and down the length of her arm. My heart is back to racing and I feel my throat tighten. "Julia, you saw Jeffrey's message. Judith needs me." I'm hoping my desperation comes through to her.

She pulls back her arm and stares at the floor. I know her well enough to tell that she's thinking, weighing the options, factoring in our long friendship, trying (I hope) not to put too much emphasis on our recent falling out. I sit in silence, wishing I knew how to pray, wishing I thought that prayer could help make things happen. Why do Judith and Binyamin put so much stock in pleas to God, or *Hashem* as Judith says? Can some imagined deity really come to their rescue? And if so, why let a Holocaust happen? Why let fascists gain power in a country so Jews could once again be scapegoated and attacked?

I think of that rabbi, Roberta Weissberg. How does someone living in the UPR still hold onto her faith in an all-knowing, all-seeing God even as she sees history begin to repeat itself?

Many religious people relocated to the UPR during the two years of the last Great Migration after The Split, but now most people here answer "none" when they're asked about their religion. My own mother describes herself as a "culturally Jewish Atheist," which I've always thought was how I would identify. But my brother's turn to Orthodox Judaism and now this thing with Judith, have made me start to ask questions. What do they get out of being religious? Is it the same sense of peace I get from meditating? Are all the rules about what you can and can't eat or what you can and can't do on *Shabbat* constraining or do they offer a sense of order and predictability?

I feel Julia's hand in mine before I hear her speak. "Dani, there might be a way, but it's risky."

All my senses are on maximum alert. I pivot toward her, a leg up on the couch cushion so that I'm fully facing her. She's going to help me! She's going to help me get to Judith…

"I don't care! I'll take risky as long as I can get to her."

"Please calm down."

Julia hands me the mug of tea. I sip it and silently thank the tea for helping me get through to her. Then I realize just what I've done, thanking an inanimate liquid and wonder if it's any different than praying to God.

I lower my voice so that it's quieter and slower. "Okay."

"I can definitely get you across our border and I think I can get you past theirs, so you can enter the GFS."

I'm nodding rapidly, but then stop, realizing that she's not going to say more if she thinks I'm still all manic and hyper. I fix my face into serious mode, my mouth a straight line, cheeks relaxed, eyes open but not too open.

"Here's the thing though. There's a risk they'll grab you before you get into the GFS, but I think you'll be okay even if that happens. They'll interrogate you and send you back. But it'll end up as an international incident that could hurt your father."

"And you."

She nods. "Yes, and me. But that is not the biggest risk."

When she pauses, I can see the movement of her throat as if she's swallowing her fear. Our hands are still joined, but hers is shaking. I try to steady it by clasping it with my other hand.

"Julia?" I ask her. "What is it? What's the biggest risk?"

Her voice is quiet and small and her eyes are on the purple floor. "I'm not sure I'll be able to get you back."

I know how serious this is, and I also know that she's going to try to talk me out of the whole thing. Yet even this problem doesn't deter me. Maybe I just have to go there. Be there. Maybe I have to be part of the fight.

"Just like Hannah Senesh."

When Julia turns to me, I realize I've said aloud what I was thinking.

"What? Who?"

"A well-known poet who emigrated from Hungary to Palestine before World War II. I read about her in a book about Jewish women who fought against the Nazis. She was one of three women living in Palestine, part of a group of Jews who parachuted into occupied eastern European countries during the war. They were trying to save Jews."

Julia's eyes are wide. "Wow," she breathes. "Were they successful?"

"Hannah Senesh and one of the other women were captured and killed."

"Oh no. Dani, this is not a good story to tell me right now."

"But the third woman was able to meet up with the partisans and fight alongside them. She returned to Palestine and lived a long life."

"One out of three. I'm not sure I like those odds."

"Wait till you hear what her name was, Julia."

Julia lifts her shoulders and shakes her head a little.

"It was Sara Braverman. Braverman, same last name as Judith."

"Dani…" There's doubt and a note of wariness in her voice.

"I know it sounds crazy, but I really think it's a kind of sign. I need to go. I need to be there with her and with my brother and Jeffrey. This is my fight as much as it is theirs. You have to understand that, Julia. You have to!"

She takes a deep breath in and then releases it. "Okay, I'll help you, provided I can find a way. In the meantime, you'd better start getting into shape. You might remember from your first trip to the GFS, you're gonna be doing a lot of running. Maybe even more this time."

* * *

I could have never predicted this, but the person who ends up helping me get quickly into the best possible shape is Will, Mr. Wise, Handsome, and Talented. Somehow, Aisha thought it was a good idea to let him and his sister in on, well, everything—my first trip to the GFS, the pull toward Judith, even the kissing, and now my plan to go back.

"If the twins are going to be part of this group, then we need to be open with them about what's going on," she'd told me. "Besides I told Will, especially, that if there's any breach of our trust I'll report him to the student court, and he would not be happy with the terms of their restorative justice decision."

But Will had just shrugged her off and smiled. "Lucky for Dani Fine," he told Aisha, "not only am I an unrepentant romantic, I'm also quite a fast runner. Don't be fooled by these cute, skinny legs."

Even though no one could ever replace Trey in my life, Will has partially filled that empty space, joking and teasing me, singing me love ballads in English and Korean, and pushing me to run farther and faster in the very short time I have before I must arrive during *shiva* for Judith's father.

We start out in the same place and very soon he whizzes past me. Then about a hundred yards or so in front, he stops, takes out his device and times my run to him.

"Okay, good, five seconds faster, but you really need to shave off a full minute."

I'm panting from the run, looking down at the asphalt surface of the running trail that goes through a local park. I thought I could train at our school's track, but Will vetoed that in favor of a surface that would be similar to the roads and streets where I'd be running away from the border.

I must look a bit dejected because Will puts an arm around my shoulders and says, "Don't worry Dani, I'll make sure you make your time."

I try the run again and I've shaved off two more seconds. Will is training me for both speed and whatever endurance I can muster. Today he's working on sprints, which might come in handy if I need to get away from someone or something in a hurry. He rotates sprints with distance, trying to get me to five miles, a bit of a stretch since I'm zonked at two.

"You need a running mantra," he tells me. "I usually listen to a playlist on my iBrain, but that's not going to work for you in the GFS."

Something pops into my head that seems appropriate. "I have an idea. Can I try it?"

He pats me on the back. "Great. I'll go ahead. Let's do a quarter mile. In the meantime, do some of those stretches I taught you." He takes off down the trail.

This is the longest distance I've run for speed, but it makes sense that I'll need to be able to run this long if I'm being pursued. I start with the lunges, then switch to kicking each foot back and grabbing it with my hand, and finally I stretch sideways without bending my knees.

Will's signal on my iBrain tells me he's ready. I signal back to him to start timing. Then I launch myself forward, matching my footfalls with the words in my head. I have no idea if anyone has set this poem to music because I found it in a book, so I just make up my own fast rhythm.

Eli, Eli
I pray that these things never end
The sand and the sea
The rush of the waters
The crash of the heavens
The prayer of my heart

Hannah Senesh's short poem reminds me that I need to do everything I can to make sure the world doesn't end. That's what my mother does by helping to save the earth from climate change. It's what my father does by keeping the border safe. And Binyamin, Judith and Jeffrey? They are doing everything to keep themselves and all Jews in the GFS alive. I don't know if I can ever believe that there's some God force in the world who's guiding and judging, but I do know that whoever put each of us here—whether science or God or maybe both—wants us to do something worthwhile, something that heals and doesn't destroy, something that loves and learns and spreads goodness, however small. It all adds up.

I nearly run into Will as I reach him at the quarter mile mark. He grabs hold of me as I try to catch my breath and fight back the nausea that's creeping up from my gut.

"Whatever you're doing, Dani, is working," he says. "You're only twenty seconds away from making the time I benchmarked for your quarter mile."

"It's a poem," I say between breaths, "about wanting the world to continue to exist."

He pulls me back a bit and smiles. "Deep stuff like that motivates you, I guess."

"Yeah," I say with a nod. Deep and spiritual is what I think but can't bring myself to say out loud.

* * *

True to her word and her mad tech skills, Julia gets me over the border. Just like last time, we took a vehicle to get as close as possible, and I safely ran through one side of the checkpoints after Julia disabled the video and alarms for about ten seconds. As I keep running to the beat of the Hannah Senesh poem, I listen for sirens and turn my head to look behind me for the sweep of a searchlight. But there's only the sound of the wind whooshing past me and darkness all around.

I follow the same route as before when I met Judith and Jeffrey, keeping an eye out for the spire of the church in New Hope. I slow my pace just a little and let go of the poem in my head so I can keep focused on my surroundings. A moment later, I hear something like the sound of twigs snapping. Hoping it's just a rabbit or a squirrel, I keep going until I hear the unmistakable sound of human voices. Male voices calling out to one another, the words lost in the wind.

I strain to hear whether they're behind me or ahead. I slow down and try to quiet my breathing. The voices are louder now.

"You *think* you saw someone, Thompson. You said you were sure."

Then the second voice, younger and not as deep. "I-I don't know. It could have been a bear."

A bear? There are bears here in South Ohio? I look around for a hiding place, not sure whether it would be better to meet up with these guys or with a bear. There's no upside to either.

I spot a fallen tree a few feet ahead, its light gray bark visible in the darkness. There are loose branches with their leaves still attached around it. I hide under the branches, hoping the leaves will cover me. As I lie there with my arm over my mouth, breathing quietly through my nose and trying not to move, I hear them approach as the sounds of crinkling leaves and twigs get louder.

"This is some wild goose chase you've sent us on. If we do happen to see that bear, I'm gonna let him eat you before I shoot him."

That's the first guy again. I hold my breath while they stand on the other side of the fallen tree, terrified now that I've realized they've brought guns with them. I could have been shot dead while I was running. It's likely I still could.

"Sorry, Chase." That's the younger one. "I guess we should head back. Do we still need to file a report with the border office?"

"Only if we want to be laughed out of the department. C'mon genius."

I listen intently for several minutes until I can no longer hear their footsteps. Leaves and twigs cover my hoodie, but I don't take the time to brush them off. I've got to get to New Hope quickly. It's likely that I'm already late.

It isn't until I feel Jeffrey's arms around me and hear his whispered words that I feel the tension throughout my body relax. "You're crazy to come here but it's so good to see you," he says.

"I know," I tell him as we once again stand in the empty parking lot of the church in New Hope. "I just have to be with her when she's going through so much."

We walk back toward the spot where my brother sits in his car waiting for us.

"It's going to be quite a shock when you walk into the Braverman house on the last night of *shiva*. I don't know why you thought it would be a good idea not to let Judith know ahead of time that you were coming."

Jeffrey keeps tugging at my hoodie to keep us in the shadows, behind bushes, trees, and walls of tall grass. Anywhere we can't be seen. Every time I start to speak, he responds with "Shhhh, whisper, it's still early and we don't know if anyone is close enough to hear us."

Last time I didn't see much of this town beyond the parking lot but now I catch glimpses of small houses, some with lights on since it's just after sunset.

"I knew she'd worry if I told her I was coming and she would beg me not to take the chance."

Jeffrey keeps us moving, every minute or so pulling me so I don't trip over thick tree roots. "So, it's okay for you to care about her but not the opposite?" he asks. "I know I'm no expert on romance, but that sounds a bit weird."

"I do want her to care about me, but just not to prevent me from taking care of her. How is she by the way?"

"Sad. And busy. Looking after her mother, her brother and sister and just keeping the trains running on time, if you know what I mean."

"Hmmmm, yeah, that fits."

"But she has Hannah, me, and the rest of the minyan, you know, all of us." He stops walking and pulls on my sleeve so I'll stop too. His arm is extended in front of him. "There's the car."

I see a glimpse of a chrome bumper.

"Binyamin had to camouflage the car as much as he could so we wouldn't be seen. Even if you weren't meeting us, it would still be too dangerous for any Jews to be out here without a good reason, and those are few and far between. One day I'll tell you the story of how we got pulled over by a cop on the way back from meeting you before."

As we take the last few steps to the car, I can only guess how scary that stop by the police probably was. This is another way things are different in the UPR. We don't have the same kind of police my parents had in the US before The Split. We have peace officials, community mediators and restorative justice boards. Most crimes are resolved by them. Anything more serious, like murder or rape, does involve confinement for those found guilty. But we don't have the massive prisons that I read about in *The New Jim Crow*. It's not a perfect system, and sometimes the bad guys win, but I think it's an improvement over what came before.

I get a quick hug from my brother and a peck on the top of my hoodie, then he's guiding me into the back of the car where the rear seat has been transformed into what I can only describe as a makeshift casket. The top of the seat is lifted up revealing an open box lined with foam rubber.

"Welcome to your new home," Jeffrey whispers. "Sorry, there wasn't time for a housewarming party."

I twist around to look at him and stick my tongue out, followed by a wide grin. Then I step into the casket one leg at a time and crouch down low until I can brace myself with my hands flat on the floor and twist my body so I'm lying on my side facing the back of the driver's seat. Once the cover is closed above me it's pitch dark. That's when I notice the circle of air holes, about two inches in diameter, right in front of my face.

The car is moving on a bumpy surface that I assume is the off-road area where Binyamin pulled over so the car couldn't be seen, and a few minutes later it's smooth sailing on what I imagine is a highway or paved road.

"Dani, you okay in there?" my brother asks.

I put my mouth close to the air holes and say "Yes" loud enough so I can be heard over the rush of air coming in through the open rear windows.

"Good," he continues. "Look above you and you'll see a round disk clipped to the top. It's got little spikes on one side."

I can't see much in here so I feel around the top and find the disk, pulling it from whatever has been keeping it in place.

"I have it but what is it?"

Binyamin speaks slowly, enunciating each word. "If we get pulled over, you'll hear me say 'Now!' and then you slide the spikes on the disk into the air holes so they fit securely. This way the air holes won't be discovered even if they shine a flashlight on the back seat."

"But don't worry." Jeffrey's voice. "There's enough air in there to keep you alive for a long time."

"Very reassuring," I tell him and wish he could see my eyes rolling.

No one says another word for the rest of the trip, which in my foam rubber casket feels like forever. I hear the stop at the checkpoint at the border of their neighborhood and the cover story Binyamin gives whoever is questioning them.

"Movies, huh, Professor Fine?" the deep voice asks. I can't tell whether he's buying the story or not.

"Yes, Nathan. You know from my classes that my academic focus is twentieth century world history and there was a film on campus about the famine in the former Soviet Union. I thought it might interest Jeffrey here because he's hoping to study the newest solutions to fighting hunger."

I have to cover my mouth to stop from laughing, knowing that the only way Jeffrey has any interest in ending hunger is to bake a noodle kugel.

A few minutes after we start moving again, the car finally stops altogether and the top of my casket is lifted. I'd been in such darkness that even the small overhead light in the car is blinding. I open and close my eyes a few times to adjust, and then I grab onto Binyamin's outstretched arms so I can be pulled into a standing position.

Once I can see, I notice that both Jeffrey and my brother are now wearing their yarmulkes. Their heads were bare when I saw them in New Hope. I imagine that the white fringes, knotted tassels they wear that stick out from the top of their pants—I think my brother calls them *tzitzit*—had been tucked in before but are now visible. It all makes me wonder if the GFS goons make men drop their pants to see if they are circumcised as required by Judaism like they did during the Holocaust. I make a note to ask Binyamin at some point.

"I made you a little nosh and had Isaac hide it in the Braverman's kitchen so it wouldn't be devoured by some other hungry *shiva* visitor," Jeffrey says as I stretch my legs on the sidewalk next to where the car is parked.

"Thanks," I respond with a hug. "You really are a good person, Jeffrey Schwartz."

"Yeah that's me, a regular *tsaddik*[17]. C'mon, let's take you to Judith and get the shock of the night over with."

17 righteous person

CHAPTER THIRTEEN

Judith

I've attended a few *shivas* before, but never as a mourner. Tonight is the last night and I'm both relieved and dreading it. Relieved that the house will again be quiet and not filled with enormous platters of food that take forever to clean up and put away each night, even with all the help we have. Dread because the constant flow of people, especially my closest friends and the members of our minyan, has helped me forget that my family must figure out how we're going to survive without my father.

I will admit it's a helpful ritual. People from the newspaper came and talked about how my father created one of the best Jewish weekly newspapers in the entire GFS. A childhood friend told us about my father's enthusiasm for learning and how he helped this man when he was struggling with his studies. That man went on to become a rabbi. There were cousins who remembered my father as a little boy sitting alone at family gatherings with a book in his hands. Always with a book, they said.

Others who attended my parents' wedding remembered how happy they were. I kept an eye on my mother when someone began one of those stories and was reassured that she didn't break down in sobs. Instead, she just nodded agreement, her smile sad. I think anger about my father's murder is helping her get through all of this. I've heard her say more than once, "They have to pay for this."

Like every other night during the *shiva*, Rabbi Leventhal, Isaac's father, comes with his own minyan of influential men, Bernard Blau and the horrible Barak Rausch among them, and leads a short *shiva* service with the men and women separated. Now that we all pray together in our own minyan, I've begun to resent the separation and the way women are shunted to the side with no role in the service. I'm always glad when Rabbi Leventhal recites the concluding prayer and he and his group eat a little something and then go, leaving the rest of us, the people I really care about, to hold the real *shiva* minyan.

Jeffrey usually skips the earlier service and comes later for ours. So I'm not surprised that he hasn't arrived yet. But Binyamin Fine is usually here for both. When I ask Miriam if he's coming, she nods and says, "Yes, he just has to take care of something first."

Only the few of us who need to know are made aware of the details of what Solly refers to as "our missions," so I don't press Miriam for more information.

Hannah walks toward me holding a small paper plate and lays it in my lap. Half a bagel with cream cheese and lox. "Here, you need to eat, Judith." It's her nightly ritual.

"I've been waiting to see what Jeffrey brings tonight, but I guess this can tide me over for now."

Just as I'm raising the bagel to my mouth, Jeffrey's voice calls out from the front door. "Judith, can you come here, like right now?"

I put the plate on the box where I've been sitting and walk toward the front door wondering why he is in such a hurry to see me.

"What did you bring toniiii…" My voice gives out when I see the figure standing between Jeffrey and Binyamin Fine. Black jeans, black hoodie and the shimmer of blues that only belong to the soul of one person.

"Judith." Her voice is low, almost a whisper, with a tone of wonder and disbelief.

My body takes over and I wrap my arms around her, pulling her close. For the first time since we received the call about my father, a sense of soft calm envelops me.

"I came as soon as I could," she says into my ear. "I had to be with you. I'm so sorry about your father."

All at once it's like a bucket of ice water has been thrown on my head, and the insanity of this situation hits me. I move out of her embrace, grab hold of her arm and pull her toward the bathroom next to the kitchen, which fortunately is free. I lead her into the small, blue-tiled room and lock the door behind us. As she lowers her hood and unzips the sweatshirt, I stare at her, dumbfounded at the fact that she appears so casual, like we see each other every day.

I open my mouth to speak but I can't find words. Instead, I'm rigid with the impossibility of this.

She raises an open hand. "You're not mad, are you?"

"How?" Finally, a word. I shake my head, trying to dislodge what can only be a dream or another hologram. But her beautiful soul still appears to me like tiny fireworks celebrating the many shades of blue.

"The Owl helped me again."

"But last time you…"

"I know, I ran back. Not this time. I'm here. For you, for Binyamin and Jeffrey and all of the Resistance. You know, like Hannah Senesh who parachuted into Hungary."

"And was murdered by the Nazis, Dani." Could she have found a worse role model?

"But not Sara Braverman," she says with a raised finger to emphasize her point. "She also parachuted into occupied Europe, Yugoslavia to be exact, and fought with the partisans until she escaped back to Israel where she lived to a ripe old age." She smiles at me.

"Sara Braverman?" How could I have never heard of her?

"Don't you see Judith, it's like a sign, the fact that this woman who survived had the same last name as you."

Now she's talking like Jeffrey and his obsession with Fredy Hirsch, who refused to leave Czechoslovakia so he could take care of Jewish children in the camps. Is it rational to be so caught up in the stories of these people from the past that we want to emulate their risky acts of bravery?

I breathe out a groan. "Dani, how can I keep you safe here? The way you dress and speak. How you don't know the prayers. All of it. Everyone will soon realize you're from somewhere else. Do you know how dangerous it is here? All my father did was take my brother…" My throat closes up and it's too hard to continue as the tears spill. When a sob escapes, I feel arms holding me, pulling me toward warmth. "I can't lose you too," I mumble into her neck. I cry quietly on her shoulder and feel her fingers combing through my hair and gently rubbing my back.

"Let it out. Let it out. I'm here now. I'm not leaving, and you won't lose me, I promise."

Maybe someone who hasn't seen death up close like I have can make such a promise. Someone who didn't know Rivka Blau before she was killed in a bomb blast or my father cut down on the street. How can someone who lives where she lives, who can be who she is with no fear or consequences, even understand all of this? Of course she can easily promise me she'll be okay, that I won't lose her. Of course she thinks she's another Sara Braverman and not Hannah Senesh.

But as I feel the soft fabric of her hoodie on my cheek, I'm enveloped in the kind of comfort I wasn't able to feel from Hannah or Jeffrey or even Dvorah. In that moment, I know what I have to do. I have to keep her from doing even more crazy things. I have to keep her safe and alive for her parents, for Binyamin, and most of all, for me.

"I hope you know you're out of your mind," I say into her chest and then raise my head.

She smiles again and in spite of the fact that I've been crying, I smile back at her.

Her right shoulder moves up in a shrug. "Love'll do that to you."

Now I'm back to being open-mouthed and speechless. How do I respond to that? To love? Luckily, I'm saved from responding by Binyamin Fine whose voice comes through the door. "Judith, it's just us. Isaac is about to start."

I shake my head again, roll my eyes at Dani and reach behind her to unlock the door.

"Come on. It's time for you to meet the Minyan of Resistance."

CHAPTER FOURTEEN

Jeffrey

I watch their faces as they enter the room, hoping Judith doesn't look freaked out and Dani doesn't look like she's made the biggest mistake of her life, which actually very well might be the case. But Dani is smiling, and Judith seems, I don't know, calm maybe, even though it's clear from her watery eyes that she's been crying.

Dani's dressed in all black just like she was when we met her the first time. I guess it's the required outfit for running over the border into a church parking lot in New Hope.

We're all in the Braverman living room with Isaac standing in his usual spot by the bookshelf.

"Um, everyone," Judith begins, and a dozen heads turn to her. "This is Dani Fine, uh," she pauses, "Binyamin's sister from the UPR."

Dani gives Judith a quick look, like a kind of squint, and I wonder if she's disappointed that Judith didn't elaborate on their connection. But really, how can Dani expect Judith to introduce Dani as her girlfriend? Hasn't Mrs. Braverman had enough of a shock?

Miriam Fine comes over first and throws her arms around Dani. "*Baruch Hashem, Baruch Hashem*," she says with great emphasis.

"Miriam?" Dani asks, looking a bit bewildered.

"Yes, yes, of course. How would you have known." She steps back. "I am your sister-in-law, Miriam. Our children will be so excited to finally meet their aunt."

At the mention of the children, Dani looks a bit overwhelmed and as I get up to stand next to her, Judith has placed her hand on Dani's shoulder, probably one of the bravest things she's ever done. I try to balance things out by placing my hand on her other shoulder.

Next, it's Hannah in front of Dani, asking "How did you…?" and then, "I have so many questions." Yeah, not surprising.

There are hugs from Dvorah, Solly, Isaac, and even my parents. Then Dani makes her way over to Meyer Lipsky in his wheelchair and crouches down so she's eye level with him.

"Will you teach me the holograms?" is the first thing he says to her, which makes me chuckle. Lipsky couldn't care less how she got here. He just wants to learn the tech.

"Of course, Einstein," she says, her voice soft and serious. "I'd be honored."

"It's time to begin…" Binyamin announces.

"Hold on a sec," Dani says, cutting him off in a way that none of us would ever dare speak to Binyamin Fine.

Dani whispers something in Judith's ear and Judith responds but I can't hear what she says. Then, with Judith walking behind her, Dani slowly approaches Mrs. Braverman, who is sitting in the middle of the room on a box from the funeral home. Again, Dani crouches down.

"Ms. Braverman." No, no, Dani, it's Mrs. Braverman. I hope Judith's mother doesn't catch the error. "My condolences for your loss. I am here to do what I can to stop all this and you have my word that I'll do everything I can."

I'm now standing next to Judith and can hear her let out a breath of anxiety. Her body goes rigid.

Mrs. Braverman reaches out and takes Dani's hand. "You have made a very dangerous journey to an even more dangerous place. No one of us can do everything, but every one of us can do something. When all this is over," and she gestures around the room to indicate the *shiva*, "we will have a long talk. It is good that you have family here. Family is everything."

Dani's voice is soft, just like it was with Lipsky. "Where I come from," she tells Mrs. Braverman, "we value our family of birth as well as what we call our chosen family."

Mrs. Braverman's smile is brief. "I look forward to learning more about that, and until then I hope you will extend your comfort and companionship to my daughter, Judith, who is carrying a heavy burden."

Oh, Mrs. Braverman you have no idea what permission you've just given.

Dani's smile is wide and she is nodding for emphasis as she says, "Absolutely, Judith is..."

I pray that she's pausing because she has to think before she says something we'll all regret.

"She's incredible."

Judith goes back to her box, joining her mother and her younger siblings. Just like they've done all week, Judith's older sister Shuli and her husband David attended the earlier minyan but didn't stay for this one, likely because they have a new baby at home who they've left with a sitter.

I take a seat next to Dani who has Miriam on her other side. As the prayer books are passed around, Dani whispers to me, "Why are they sitting on boxes?"

I'm reminded of how much she doesn't know. Believe me, I'm no expert on Judaism and am relieved that Dani has Binyamin to turn to for the harder questions. But you can't live in this little community and not pick up a thing or two along the way even if you aren't inclined to believe a lot of it.

"They're the mourners," I tell her, "and the tradition is they need to sit low in their grief. As if they haven't suffered enough," I add, just to throw in my own opinion.

"Seems kind of backward," she whispers to me. "We should be on boxes and they should be on the comfortable couch."

"Yeah, well, I'm sure your brother will be able to explain the Talmudic rationale that escapes me."

"Yeah, he's very good at that," she says in the kind of sarcastic tone that I guess goes with the territory of being a sibling. I'm an only child so I wouldn't know.

We move through the service and I repeatedly point out the pages and point to the prayers for Dani, all in Hebrew of course.

"You're better off not understanding everything," I tell her. "Just let it wash over you."

"But I want to understand."

This surprises me. Why would anyone from the UPR bother? "Why?"

"Well, kind of for Judith, but also for myself. I want to know more about Judaism."

I exhale my disapproval. "There's so much I wish I could unlearn."

Finally we get to my favorite part, really the only part that has any value to me—Isaac's *drash*[18]. He's been keeping them brief all week because our private minyan begins later in the evening, after all the so-called dignitaries have left. The first night he spoke about fathers and how they lift us up and hold us down. We all knew he was talking about his own father and contrasting him with Reuben Braverman, and the other fathers present, Binyamin and my papa. After that service, I watched as Hannah walked Isaac outside before any of us had a chance to talk to him. Even though it still makes me sad that I can never have anything more than a friendship with Isaac, it at least makes me glad that he has Hannah, who loves him and takes care of him.

As he begins his *drash* with a welcome to Dani and the *Shehechianu* prayer, thanking God for helping us reach the day of having her among us, safe and sound, *Baruch Hashem*, Isaac gets to the main part of his message.

"Grief, despair, hope and resilience. How do we move from one to the next, and how do we do it the next time the unending

18 A sermon, usually expounding on the week's Torah portion.

cycle of grief once again slams into us, like a powerful ocean wave we didn't see coming? We pray to God for guidance and as always we find it. Tonight, on the last night of this *shiva* week that has been filled with grief at our loss and despair over the world that has brought it about, we look to Psalm 90, the only psalm that comes from Moses, who knew grief and despair as he watched the hardships the Hebrews endured in Egypt, as he turned to see the approaching Egyptian soldiers in pursuit and the vast Red Sea that was sure to end the journey, and as he led his people into an arid, empty desert where they dwelled for forty years, a whole generation gone in favor of the next."

I wonder where he's going with all this grief and despair stuff and wish he'd get to the hope and resilience part soon.

Isaac clasps his hands behind him and looks down in contemplation of his next thought. A few seconds later he is facing us again. "So, understandably the psalm begins by acknowledging the prominence of God and His presence even before the creation of our world, in contrast of course to Man's own impermanence and short life span."

I wonder how all of this is landing on Dani and her eagerness to learn. She's probably planning her route back to New Hope and then over the border.

Isaac raises both hands, palms open and smiles. "So where is the hope and resilience I spoke of before? It comes at the beginning of the final verse.

"Teach us to number our days, that we may gain a heart of wisdom."

Isaac nods slowly as he repeats, "Number our days, number our days."

There's a short pause before he goes on. "Why is Moses telling us, cautioning us, to number our days? Well, he's already told us that our human life is a mere flash of light that quickly fades and dims. But Moses links the numbering of our days with this promise of a heart of wisdom."

He's now pacing back and forth in front of us, something I've noticed he does when he's ready to deliver his message, or as we might say in Kushner Academy for Boys, his teaching.

When Hannah or anyone else paces back and forth like Isaac is doing, it usually makes me feel dizzy and distracted. But when Isaac does it near the end of one of these sermons, I instead feel focused and attentive to his every word.

"The wisdom in our hearts comes from our devotion to *Adonai*, our God, not just in making sure that in each of these days we have numbered we follow His commandments for worship and *halacha*, but that we also devote this limited time, this blink of an eye that we have on earth, to ensuring our survival as a people through *tikkun olam*, repair of the world. I propose that those are one and the same, for the Jewish people can only survive and, yes, thrive if the wider world is just."

Dani's whisper of "Yes" awakens me from my laser focus on Isaac and makes me realize that he's been able to get through to her.

His pacing completed; Isaac is now smiling. "Well, I've spoken long enough tonight on this last evening of *shiva* for the mourners of our dear Reuben Braverman, may his memory be a blessing." There are a few murmurs of *zikhrono livrakha*, the same phrase in Hebrew.

"I'll conclude with the last verse of Psalm 90, a hopeful plea to the Almighty that is twice repeated in the verse. And we know from other places in scripture that repetition of words always has a deep meaning.

"May the favor of the Lord our God rest on us; establish the work of our hands for us—yes, establish the work of our hands."

We quickly move through the final prayers, including the Kaddish prayer for the mourners. With great relief, I stand and signal for Dani to do the same.

"Come to the kitchen, there's a little secret nosh I put away for you."

Her smile is broad. "Always the chef."

Judith catches up to us and touches Dani's arm to get her attention. "What did you think?"

Dani answers with a nod of encouragement. "I loved it, especially the parts I could understand."

Judith looks at her with this expression of total adoration. "Come let's get you something to eat."

Leaving them to their little lovefest, I tell Judith, "There's a special plate I made for Dani in the middle cabinet on the *milchig*[19] side of the kitchen."

Everyone's headed toward the platters of food set out on the dining room table, and for some reason I don't follow. Isaac's words and Dani's presence whiz around in my head, and I'm suddenly hit with the unreality of all of this—the bomb that killed Rivka Blau, the street thugs who beat Reuben Braverman to death, the lingering threat of Simeon Rausch now a member of the police department, and Dani Fine's arrival. On top of all that, there's Isaac telling us we have to number our days, a prospect that terrifies me because I have nothing to offer to this *tikkun olam* of his. If only I could repair the world with a chocolate babka.

It's either the grief-laden Braverman house or my own anxiety that makes me head to the front door for some fresh air. Just as I reach for the handle, the door opens and in walks a tall boy dressed identically to Dani—black jeans and black hoodie.

We stare at one another, heads tilted. Not only have I never seen him before, I've never met anyone who looks like him. Chinese? Japanese? Don't they all live in the UPR, or at least not in South Ohio?

"Do you know Judith or Jeffrey?" he asks.

I almost blurt out my name but I'm so filled with the enormity of every terrible thing I've been thinking about, I'm more cautious than usual.

"Who are you?" I ask in a tone that is more menacing than I mean it to be.

"I'm Will. I think my friend might be here. Um," he points to his jeans and hoodie, "she's dressed like I am, just without the glasses."

I have no idea what to do. Should I go get Dani? I've never heard her talk about anyone named Will, but we all use code names when we're on the iBrain so who knows. I just stare wide-eyed at him.

19 Dairy area of the kosher kitchen, distinct from the meat area

I see his body relax and he smiles in this cute way where he wrinkles his nose. "Oh I get it, you've never met a Korean dude before, right?"

"Uh, uh, no, I guess not." I hope I haven't offended him.

"Would you happen to be Jeffrey?"

I nod, still wary and he breaks into a grin.

"Awesome sauce. Great to meet you, man." Just as he holds out a hand to invite me to shake, I hear the distinctive sound of a *splat* behind me. A plate has hit the floor.

"Will!" Dani exclaims in a loud voice, which she then quiets a bit. "What are you doing here?"

He unzips the hoodie and there's a black T-shirt underneath. "I'm here for the revolution of course. I want to be part of the resistance."

"But why? You're not even Jewish."

He waves away her statement. "Girl, c'mon, do you think these fascists care if I'm Jewish? Don't you remember how they cut all Asians down in the street when they thought the Chinese caused that pandemic back before The Split? Or how about the Korean comfort women who were raped by the Japanese during World War Two? And I won't even get into how white people in the USA and Russia decided it would be a good idea to split my country in two."

Judith and I are frozen in place, both of us witnessing this exchange and the history Will recites that we've never heard before.

"Dani, who is this?" Binyamin Fine's deep voice interrupts this little scene and we all turn to him.

Dani's voice trembles a bit as she answers and points to our new arrival. "Binyamin, this is Kim Ji-Joon. And this is my brother."

Once again, his hand is extended, this time to Binyamin. "A pleasure, call me Will."

Binyamin offers a quick shake and then turns toward his sister, his face a storm cloud of anger. "Did you bring him here? Should I expect to see Aisha and Julia walk through this door next?"

"I…I don't think so," she says and looks meaningfully at Will, silently asking the same question.

He actually chuckles. "Fear not, dear brother, I came alone. I've been Dani's running coach and ran toward the border with her earlier tonight, then held back while she went through. Then followed. I promise she had no idea."

"How did you get all the way here from the border so quickly?" Dani asks.

"Has anyone seen you?" Binyamin is still angry.

"Not at all. I stayed in the shadows and then jumped onto a flatbed truck going south. I mapped the whole thing out ahead of time, so I knew when the truck crossed into Cincinnati."

"How did you get past the checkpoint then?" Binyamin seems a little less angry and more than a touch amazed.

Will dismisses this with a wave of his hand. "Those amateurs are like a bunch of kids playing prison guard. A little rock throwing diversion sent them scurrying so I could run right through. What a bunch of jerks."

I smile at the thought that Simeon Rausch and his turncoat companions were so easily foiled. I'm starting to like this Will guy.

Binyamin's sigh is audible. "So now there are two of you that have to be housed, fed, and hidden, to say nothing of school."

"Will is welcome to take my place at Kushner Academy," I say and grin at Binyamin.

I hear Judith's tiny giggle followed quickly by her hand over her mouth.

Binyamin's glare is intimidating, and I almost jump back. This is probably what he once did to keep his students in line. "Jeffrey, you're not helping here."

Will points to the paper plate that dropped on the floor when Dani first saw him. "By any chance is there food, preferably not laying on the floor?"

Judith immediately springs to life and scoops up the kugel and rugelach. Dani gestures toward her. "Will, this is Judith." She looks up from her place crouched on the floor and just says a simple "Hello."

Will winks at Dani. "Nice," he says. "I can see why you…"

"Not here Will," warns Binyamin. "This isn't the UPR."

"Clearly, bro. So take me to chow first and then to meet the rest of the Resistance."

CHAPTER FIFTEEN

Dani

I'm living with Binyamin and Miriam, sleeping on the daybed in Binyamin's study. The best part of this is spending time with Yuval, Yacov, and Chava, my nephews and niece. There's been lots of questions, beginning with "Are you a girl or a boy?" and then recently, "So if you're a girl, do you have a boyfriend?" Where do I begin? All of this is complicated by the fact that when I leave the apartment, I'm dressed as Miriam's male cousin, Daniel, with *yarmulke, tzitzi*, the whole nine yards. Jeffrey thinks it's hysterical but Judith frowns when she sees me, immediately removing my male religious garments and running her fingers through my tiny curls.

"I hate that they had to cut your hair," she says with a sigh.

"It's only a little shorter than I usually wear it."

"I guess," she says, her nose and eyes crinkling in disapproval. "I just want you to look like you." Then she smiles and places her hands on my cheeks. "I mean, why tamper with perfection?"

That remark earns her a lingering look and a kiss.

I have to admit, I find it interesting that Judith isn't at all attracted to the idea of me being a boy, especially since she's still not able to claim any kind of sexual identity, and she lives in a country where heterosexuality is seen as the only acceptable identity. She tells me she really doesn't care that much about figuring these things out since she's been lucky enough to meet her *bashert* and that's all that really matters. Maybe she's right?

In the UPR, it's normal for people not to label themselves, preferring to call themselves "flexi" or pansexual. Mostly, people my age just use queer and leave it at that. I'm one of the few who even says the words lesbian and Sapphic, and only when I'm asked specifically about who I find attractive. But there's more to being queer than your sexuality. Aisha and I have had long talks about this.

"You queer your life," she says, using queer as a verb. "It shows up in your chosen family, in your activism, in every decision where you push back against the norm. It's so much more than who you do or don't do under the sheets."

Tonight, Binyamin and Miriam have been invited to dinner with Bernard Blau and his sister and brother-in-law, who are visiting from somewhere in Kentucky. I'm left here as the babysitter, soon to be joined by Naomi Blau, who for some reason isn't part of this dinner. It'll be good to have help since I have to feed and bathe all three kids so they're ready for bed when their parents come home. After that comes the moment I'm dreading, when my parents log on for their hour of connectivity and my mother unleashes her legendary angry lecture over my border crossing.

"You know how she is," Binyamin said. "I'll try to help but unfortunately you're gonna get an earful."

"I know. Just don't let her convince you to ground me forever."

"I won't ground you, but I do have to protect you. So you have to stay close by and not pull any more crazy stunts."

I've heard a sweeter version of this same thing from Judith who always gets to me when she repeats what she said that first night I got here. "I can't lose you too."

I answer the knock on the apartment door and in walks Naomi Blau, who looks like she belongs at Jesse Owens High

School and not in this Orthodox GFS community. Her short blond hair is a few inches above her shoulders and she's wearing a long sleeve white T-shirt, navy slacks and a blue windbreaker. I wonder how much of a risk she's taking by dressing that way, since she stands out from all the other Orthodox girls. That's why I decided it was safer for me to pretend to be a boy when I was out in public here. But maybe Naomi gets a kind of free pass since she just lost her mother in a bombing?

"They gave me a key but I figured you were here so I'd knock."

All three Fine kids rush at their cousin and she lifts little Chava who throws her arms around Naomi's neck. The boys drag her into their room to show off the Lego castle I've been building with them.

"How did you get out of this dinner?" I ask, as we bend over the castle watching Yuval add a fourth turret.

"I wasn't invited, thank goodness. My father made a reservation at some fancy restaurant that he likes."

"Outside the checkpoint?" After what happened with Judith's father, I worry about anyone going into the city, unless they're on a mission for the Resistance.

"Oh no, there aren't any kosher restaurants outside."

Of course.

We're busy for the next two hours heating up the dinner Miriam left for all of us and then getting everyone cleaned up. Chava's bath is quick and easy and we leave her in her room to choose books and stuffed animals to take to bed. Yuval and Yacov decide to be difficult and refuse to let us give them baths.

"It's forbidden. Only our mother can do it," Yuval says with that kind of male authority that always gets me going.

"I'm your aunt! Naomi's your cousin!"

He shakes his head with great emphasis. "Doesn't matter. Still forbidden."

I look over at Naomi who rolls her eyes and gestures for us to leave the bathroom.

"You have twenty minutes," she yells through the closed door. "If you're not out of there and in pajamas, we're coming in."

I figure I can make good use of the time by reading to Chava and trying to get her to go to sleep. She hands me a book about Noah and the animals, and as I open it to begin, I hear what I think might be a telephone ringing.

"I'll get it," says Naomi from the kitchen.

A few minutes later she ducks her head into Chava's room. "That was Miriam. My father invited them back to the house, so they'll be a little while longer. You stay here and I'll deal with the boys."

Getting all three kids to go to sleep wasn't in the original plan, but we manage, even though the boys put up quite a protest.

I'm exhausted by the time Naomi and I flop onto the couch with a groan. "Why would anyone want to have children if every night is like this?" she asks.

I let out a chuckle. "That's something I'd expect me to say, not you."

"How come?"

I turn to her so my back is against the arm of the couch with my bare feet flat on the cushion. "Isn't this expected of you living here? You know, marriage, kids?"

She's not facing me, instead looking down at her legs, her hands balled up in fists. "Is it really different in the UPR?" Her voice is filled with sadness.

I have a feeling we're about to have some kind of serious talk and I hope it doesn't get interrupted by the arrival of my brother and Miriam. "It is and it isn't. There's more choices, more ways to be and to live. But there are still people like my mother who want grandchildren and hope to see their kids happily in love with someone, male, female or non-binary."

Naomi looks up, whips her body around to face me, and with wide eyes shining blurts out, "Say that again!"

"Say what?"

She gestures with her hand in a circular motion, "Male, female and, what is it?"

"Oh, non-binary. Someone who doesn't identify as exclusively male or female, but either as both or none at all."

Her voice is filled with wonder. "You know people like that?"

"One of my closest friends, Trey."

Naomi bites down on her lower lip intently focused. "How did he, she…"

"They. Trey uses they, them pronouns."

She nods slowly and is quiet. "Because he…I mean they… feel like more than one sex?"

"That's right, though we'd say gender, not sex."

Judith told me how puzzled she is about the fact that Naomi's soul is hidden from her behind a gray wall, and I wonder if I'm about to find out why. I reach over and touch her arm to get her attention. "Naomi, talk to me."

I wait, knowing from my restorative justice training that many people need time before they can say something important and meaningful and the best thing to do is to give them that space.

Naomi is staring at her lap and is silent. But I can tell by the way she shakes her head that she is working something out in her mind. Finally, she looks up but doesn't meet my eyes. "I…I feel sometimes like I'm both. I don't know. It's all so confusing." She stops and is quiet again and her anguish is clear when she begins again. "My mother was beautiful, smart, and very female."

"Feminine?"

"Yes!" Now she's able to look at me and I can see the sadness and loss in her watery eyes. "But she wasn't quiet or shy. She was forceful and unafraid." Another pause, during which she pivots her body so that we are facing one another, each a mirror image of the other with feet flat on the couch, knees bent. I take this as a sign that she's starting to trust me.

"Everyone says I look like her, and they expect me to be like her. And I want to, but only, you know, in some ways."

I nod to show I understand and decide it's now okay to prompt her. "Except for the feminine stuff?"

She reaches her arms out to me. "Well, you see, that's the confusing part. Sometimes I want all that—to wear a nice dress with my hair done all pretty. But then there's the other times…"

This must be the source of her shame because she's all of a sudden become very interested in her knees, which she hugs to her chest. My voice is gentle and I hope non-judgmental. "Tell me about the other times?"

"I want to be like the boys. I want to study and wear a *yarmulke* and be called to the Torah when I'm thirteen in a few months."

"I can understand that. Girls here are pretty confined to certain roles."

"Dani, I don't just want to be like the boys. Sometimes I just want to be a boy." She places her hand over her heart. "Like I feel it inside. I'm a boy like Yuval and Yacov. And then I'm okay being a girl, and I want to grow up and be like my mother. Until I don't and then I just don't want either one. I just want to be me." Her voice lowers to a whisper. "Whatever that is."

Next are tears and quiet sobs and when I slide over, she leans her head on my shoulder. I give her a minute and hold her a bit tighter.

"I feel like I'm going crazy," she mumbles into me.

"Only because you live here. If you were in the UPR, this would all be normal, a part of growing up and realizing who you are. You'd make friends with kids your age going through the same thing and older kids who've become comfortable with all of this. You're not crazy, Naomi. You just live in a world that hasn't made room for you."

"But the Torah says God made man and woman, Adam and Eve."

This is where I'm out of my depth. I can't refute this on her terms. "You know, there are rabbis in the UPR. I met one." Her eyes are wide. "I bet one of them would have an answer that would make sense to you. It's possible my brother would."

"Uncle Binyamin?"

"Yes, he grew up in the UPR and he's going to be connecting to this rabbi I met. Before I left, I gave her the coordinates."

"What about Reb Isaac? Do you think he would…"

"Understand?"

She nods. "I mean, he's already got us praying together."

The sound of a key in the door means the end of this conversation for now and the start of something I've been dreading. "We'll keep talking," I reassure Naomi, and make a mental note that I'll have to explain non-binary to Judith, Jeffrey, Isaac, and Hannah. The fun never stops.

"Naomi, your father's downstairs in the car waiting to drive you home," my brother says while I'm giving Miriam a rundown of what's gone on with the children.

A few minutes later, the three of us sit with our iBrains waiting to see who will connect in. There's static and a pop and the unmistakable voice of Meredith Fine.

"Is she there with you? Please tell me yes."

"Yes," is all my brother says.

"It's me." I sound like I'm even younger than little Chava.

There's an audible sigh of relief before the onslaught. "How could you? We've been worried sick, scared out of our minds. And now I have the Kims calling me multiple times a day about their son."

"I didn't know he'd follow me. That wasn't the plan."

"He wouldn't have gone if it wasn't for you. All of this is your fault, Abby." She pronounces my code name with the maximum amount of sarcasm she can muster.

"Tell them he's fine and safe."

"Do you know how dangerous it is there for him? How much he stands out?"

As usual, my brother refuses to give into my mother's drama and answers her in business-like short sentences. "Suffice it to say, he wears dark glasses when he's outside."

I know I'm digging myself in deeper, but I still have to ask them about Julia. "Is the Owl okay?"

Now it's my father's turn to sigh. "She's been ordered to headquarters in Chicago and has been assigned to make sure this can never happen again."

I worry that this will prevent Julia from signing up for a security post when we have to do national service. "Is she…"

"She'll be fine," my father responds. "They can't afford to punish someone with so much talent and expertise, which is more than I can say for you, Abby."

There's another burst of static, a pop and a familiar voice comes through my iBrain. "Princess here." I smile. Of course, Aisha would give herself that code name. "Abby, you okay?"

"Yeah, except for all the yelling and lecturing." Not a good idea to have said that because it just invites more of the same.

"Maybe if you would occasionally think before you go off believing that you alone can save the world—"

"Greta, we should be hearing from the Queen any minute."

I smile at my mother's code name. Greta, for Greta Thunberg, the girl who started a movement for climate justice.

Another pop and the clipped tones of Queen Olivia from the Gullah Geechee nation diverts my mother and Aisha to a separate group connection, freeing me from more haranguing.

Once they depart, there's Judith's soft, "Hi, are you all right?" referring to the lambasting from my mother. Her voice does more to relax me than a full body massage.

"Yeah, I expected it and was prepared for the worst."

Another pop and one more new arrival. "Heschel, are you there?"

My brother's response is enthusiastic. "Yes, it's so good to hear your voice."

I'm not sure who this is and silently ask Miriam by tilting my head and squinting. She walks over and whispers, "Rabbi Roberta Weissberg. He's been waiting to hear from her."

At least I can take credit for doing something right since I was the one who made this happen. I wish my mother could see that I'm not the world's biggest fuck-up.

"There's so much to talk about," Rabbi Weissberg tells my brother, "but I know our time is short, so at least tell me how you are doing?"

"It's not easy but we are well, BH."

Again I turn to Miriam and mouth the letters BH, and again she whispers the answer, "*Baruch Hashem*, he cannot risk saying that."

I nod at another reminder that everything we do here could result in serious consequences.

"How can I help, and please call me Regina."

I don't know why she's chosen that name but that can wait until after all of this.

"There is a young man here, Regina, about eighteen years old, an exceptionally talented person who needs the kind of training you had. Are you following me?"

"A leader of ten, correct?"

"Yes, with new ways that are very much like yours, based on his instinct and values. Could you involve him in some kind of virtual training if we are able to arrange it on our end? It would be helpful so one day he can make his role official, if you know what I mean."

"I do. Let me check here, but I think it's possible. Just a few more questions."

This conversation is about Isaac so it's a good time for me to sign off. I remove my iBrain and head to my room. A while later Miriam comes in to check on me and before she has a chance to ask if I've survived my mother, I ask, "Who's Regina?"

She smiles. "Regina Jonas, the first woman to be ordained as a rabbi back in the 1930s. If it can be arranged, I think Isaac will get the training he deserves."

CHAPTER SIXTEEN

Judith

I've been trying to prepare for the High Holidays during this month of Elul, the last month before Rosh Hashanah, taking account of the year gone by and asking for forgiveness from those I have wronged before asking the same of *Hashem*. But this year my activities for the Resistance have made all of this so much murkier than when I atoned for my transgressions before. Then it was easy to ask for forgiveness for yelling at my little sister when she got into my art desk or purposely taking too long to finish my chores. Now I'm a forger of official documents and the designer of illegal posters with messages and art that could lead to the arrest of everyone close to me. I use an iBrain to communicate with rebel organizers. And, if all that isn't enough, I love another girl. Yes, I admit it, especially now that I can be with her just about every day and we are growing closer. I love her like Hannah loves Isaac, like my mother loved my father, may his memory be a blessing.

With the holidays getting closer and with everything going on, I have no idea where my mother will want us to pray. Rabbi Leventhal will expect us in his shul, especially now that my mother has a place of distinction as a grieving widow. But Isaac is preparing a series of services for our minyan. He's about to begin his rabbinic training from the rabbi in North Ohio through her seminary. What do they call it? Oh, yes, Reconstructing Judaism. Very appropriate for our Rebel Rabbi who's been tearing down the old and reconstructing the new on his own. More people have begun to trickle into our Shabbat services at Binyamin Fine's, which have now been moved to the large room at the *Jewish Community News*, my father's paper. Isaac is becoming so popular that it's only a matter of time before his father takes notice and there's another confrontation like the one I witnessed at the dreaded Yetta's wedding.

We've been back at school for the past week. Today after the last bell rings, I'm met outside not only by Jeffrey, which I've come to expect, but also by Meyer Lipsky. While my classmates have grown used to seeing me with Jeffrey—though they haven't become any less intrusive about the nature of our relationship—Meyer in his wheelchair is an unusual presence at the girls' school.

With Yetta Freundlich now a wife running her own household, her time as a high school student has ended and her little gaggle of acolyte friends seem a bit at a loss without her. A few of them have even begun to talk to me and Hannah, though we aren't particularly interested in gaining their friendship. Our activities for the Resistance mean there are a lot of activities outside of school hours we aren't able to talk about to anyone outside of our minyan. It'll be interesting to see if any of these girls decide that their atonements for the new year include asking our forgiveness for their years of shunning us and whispering to one another while pointing at us. I'm not particularly expecting any apologies from that group. It's enough to be grateful for the fact that they no longer stare at Jeffrey and me, daring us to break the taboo of touching one another so they can report us. Though we've long since broken that taboo, we don't give them the satisfaction of acting on what they think is their religious duty.

Jeffrey beckons me over with an impatient wave of his arm. "C'mon SJ, we're going to my dad's shop. Important business."

That can only mean one thing, a project for the Resistance. When I hesitate, wondering what kind of protest art I'm going to be asked to draw, Meyer taps loudly against one of the wheels on his chair. "Can we get going already?" He raises his chin in the direction of a group of girls standing nearby. "I'm eager to get away from the pity party over there."

I see what he means. Yetta's friends have toned down their level of meanness and snark, and replaced it with long, sad faces focused on Meyer. I can just hear them, shaking their heads and saying, "Poor handicapped boy, what will become of him. What girl would marry him?"

I want to respond that they would be lucky to have one-tenth of the brain power of our Einstein and he is destined to do great things in the world. Any girl would be lucky to gain his attentions, which makes me want to tell Hannah that we have to find him somebody because I know he is looking.

But when it comes to Yetta's little, closed-minded group, it would be useless to try and change their minds. It's Meyer himself, and all he will do for the Resistance and the Jewish people, that will prove them wrong. I turn away from the pity party and the three of us head toward the town center where Mr. Schwartz has his shop.

"So, my mother went to the lawyer yesterday for the reading of the will," I tell the boys. "My father left her the newspaper. She's the new publisher." I can't help but let my pride creep into my tone of voice.

"Does she know anything about running a paper?" asks Meyer.

He's brilliant but still can be annoying. This time because he's asked the right question. "She says the idea both scares and excites her," I tell them.

"I bet," says Jeffrey.

Since my father's murder, my mother has become a different person—simmering with anger and determination, asking Dani and Will endless questions about the UPR, reading more books recommended by Dvorah, including one about new Jewish rituals for women; and now she's running a business.

We greet Mr. Schwartz at the front of his repair shop where he's working on a wall clock that's in pieces on the metal-topped counter. "There's a surprise for you in the back," he tells us.

A delightful surprise! Dani is sitting at the fancy computer that Jeffrey uses. We are all smiles when we see each other, and there's a kiss hello that I make sure is very quick since we're not alone. I have no idea what Meyer Lipsky knows about us, but it's very likely he's figured something out by now.

"Well Einstein, it's time you learn about holograms. You too Jeffrey," she says and waves them over. Meyer maneuvers his wheelchair so he's on one side of her and Jeffrey pulls a folding chair over to her other side. I take a seat on the workbench and hunt around in my schoolbag for a notebook and pen.

"I can't stay long," I tell them. "I have chores, especially now that my mother is occupied with the newspaper."

Dani swivels around to me. "I meant to tell you. Binyamin's been named editor-in-chief by your mom."

How did I not know this? "When?"

"Oh, just today. He called Miriam with the news right before I left to come here."

"This is great for the Resistance," Meyer says in a loud whisper. "Think of what we can do with a newspaper."

"Think of what we can do with holograms," says Dani.

Meyer and Jeffrey turn their attention to the screen and for the next half hour Dani speaks to them in what I can only describe as another language. It reminds me of the time Dani's friend Julia gave us all those letters and numbers and symbols the boys needed to program the iBrains they were constructing on the 3-D printer. I ignore the strange language and spend time sketching Dani's profile as she gestures to the computer's screen.

I'm getting ready to leave when Meyer rolls his chair away from the computer desk. "I have an idea for a mission, and I wanted to run it by the three of you before I go to the Governing Council. It involves the holograms, which is why I was in such a hurry to learn them."

"Awesome," says Dani. "Spill."

There's a pause as we once again try to understand what she's just said. I have a little more experience than the boys since she's been filling me in on UPR expressions in exchange for my lessons teaching her rudimentary Hebrew. I smile to myself remembering how Dani was thrilled a few days ago when I told her she'd progressed to the level of a preschooler. That's when I learned the meaning of "awesome."

"She wants to hear your idea, Meyer," I say and let out a short laugh.

"How helpful to have a UPR to GFS translator among us," says Jeffrey, with a nod of appreciation to me.

"She's helpful in all sorts of ways," says Dani, with a hint of suggestion in her voice I very much want her to keep to herself.

"Meyer, please." I urge him on before Dani has a chance to say anything more embarrassing.

"So," he begins, "you know President Fairleigh is coming to campaign in Cincinnati in a few weeks and we've been thinking about what kind of mission we can plan?"

Yesses and nods all around. At the last business meeting of the minyan, Solly explained that President Fairleigh was running against what Solly called a "self-proclaimed Christian white supremacist." Because his challenger is doing better than expected in the polls, Fairleigh has become even more radical. He's introduced a constitutional amendment to make Evangelical Christianity the official religion of the GFS and has been promising even more "protective measures" against the country's Jews.

"Well, if we can figure out the logistics, and I think we can, we'll be able to project a hologram, or maybe more than one, that can deliver a message to all the people at the rally in addition to anyone watching the live broadcast. Judith can design the hologram; Dani and I can program it."

Jeffrey clears his throat, "You mean Dani, *Jeffrey* and I can program it." He makes sure to emphasize the inclusion of his name.

"Yeah, right okay, Jeffrey. And the GC can figure out the logistics and the message."

"Did someone say message? Because no one can write a better message than yours truly."

Will Kim is standing in the doorway in his usual black T-shirt and black jeans, his dark glasses dangling from one hand and his real glasses on his face.

"Close the door!" says Jeffrey.

"Chill bro, it's just your daddy out there. He's one stand-up dude I have to say, letting me stay with you all and such."

"I believe Will is saying he thinks highly of Mr. Schwartz," I translate. Dani bends over laughing.

"So, message, message, message. I believe that's where we left off, comrades."

"Speaking of left off," I say and adjust my bookbag over my shoulder, "I have to go help make dinner."

"Judith," says Dani almost pleading.

"See you soon," I say and peck her on her forehead. And with my lips close to her ear I whisper, "My love."

CHAPTER SEVENTEEN

Jeffrey

Whatever it is that Judith whispered in Dani's ear before she left the room has Dani grinning from ear to ear.

"Ah, young love," says Will, his hands dramatically pressed against his heart, eyes raised to the ceiling.

Will is an interesting guy to say the least. One minute he's the expert on finding the right words for a message. Then he's showing my mother and me how to take the cabbage we usually stuff with a sweet mixture of chopped meat, onions, and golden raisins, and transform it into a fermented cabbage dish he calls "kimchi," which I have to admit is delicious. The next minute he's sullen and almost on the verge of tears, missing his twin sister Ann, and feeling trapped because he can't run his usual "10K," whatever that is. When that happens, I feel his sadness seep into me, knowing I'd feel the same if I were far away from my parents and Judith, who is for all intents and purposes like a sister to me.

I think of ways to keep Will's spirits up by encouraging him to teach us more about the Korean food he eats at home.

We can't always find the right ingredients, especially the spices that give his foods their heat and distinctive flavors, but we improvise, and I can tell from his smile after he takes that first bite that he's grateful.

I also ask Will a lot about what it's like to be gay in the UPR, especially for a boy.

"Boy, girl, non-binary, it's all the same except for the plumbing," he tells me.

He then has to spend the next half hour explaining non-binary in a way that I can wrap my head around.

My parents have set him up in my room on a pull-out mattress that's part of my trundle bed. They bought that for me under the mistaken impression, or maybe the false hope, that one day I'd have the kind of close friends that would want to sleep over. Suffice it to say, the trundle hasn't gotten much use. Until now.

Will's bed is lower than mine, resting on the floor, so I have to look down over the edge of my mattress to see him.

"Can you explain again about the 'they' part?" I ask as he finishes his lecture on non-binary. "I mean, doesn't 'they' refer to more than one person?"

"I guess, sometimes," he says with a shrug. He's lying on his back with his head resting on his hands. "Never thought about it that way. It's always been the case when someone says their pronoun is 'they,' we just say okay. It's really not that complicated."

I think about whether one day, after the whole Resistance thing is over, I might be living in the UPR and will need to use the pronoun 'they' for someone. Either that or the Resistance will fail, and I'll be dead so I won't have to worry about anyone's pronouns. After that not-so-pleasant thought, I decide it's time to change the subject.

"Hey Will…"

"Hmmm, yes, Jeff."

No one but no one has ever called me Jeff until now. I haven't decided whether I like it but since Will has risked his life to come resist with us, I decide to let him shorten my name. Besides, I have something else on my mind.

"Um, well, have you ever…you know…been with a boy?"

He chuckles, and then makes an effort to stop by putting his hand over his mouth and squeezing his lips together. The look he gives me is so serious that I start laughing, or maybe I'm just nervous.

"Jeff, my man, there have been many boys. So many."

This surprises me. "Did you, you know, love them all?"

"Ahhh, the famous L word. I'm sorry to tell you that the answer is no. But most of them were fun times anyway."

He's still lying on his back with his head resting on his hands. His eyes are closed and there's a big smile on his face, his eyes crinkled at the edges. I can only guess what he's remembering.

Then the image of the horrible Simeon Rausch slithers into my brain like the snake he is, and I hold my breath while my body trembles at the memory.

"Will?"

He opens his eyes. "Yeah?"

"All those boys you mentioned. I mean, like, did you want to, you know, with them?"

"You mean because I didn't love them?"

How can I explain this to him without falling apart? "Not that so much. More like, you weren't, you know, forced to or anything?" I choke out a sob and cover my face with my hands.

He sits up on his mattress and grabs hold of the edge of my bed. His voice is quiet and there's no longer a trace of laughter in it as he says, "It was all consensual, Jeff, on both sides, I promise."

All I can do is nod to show I've heard him.

"Were you…?" he asks.

I nod and pivot my body away from him so that I'm facing the wall. I admire his courage and his boldness so much I can't stand letting him see me like this.

Then I feel his warm arms around me and his breath on the back of my neck. "I've got you, bro. It's supremely fucked up what happened to you. You didn't deserve it. You're such a good guy."

We're both quiet for the next few minutes while he holds me and I'm able to pull myself together. His closeness is kind of like what happened when I told Judith about what Simeon had done to me and she hugged me to her, but it's also different in ways I can't put into words.

"Go to sleep," he whispers in a soft voice that's worlds apart from his usual brazen pronouncements. "I'll stay till you do."

But that's not possible while I'm still thinking about what happened to me. So I decide to start a new conversation. "Will? What's it like being a twin?"

"Huh? Where did that come from?"

"I need a change of subject before I can fall asleep. Is your sister just a female version of you?"

I feel his body shake as he laughs. "Not really. Ann is more like the anti-Will but in a good way."

How could the anti-Will be good? "What's she like?"

"Quiet, thoughtful, kind. She always lets me take the lead and shoot off my mouth. Then she softly steps forward and cleans up my mess."

He's quiet for a moment as I try to picture this calmer and caring version of Will. Then his soft sobs shake me out of my reverie.

"I miss her," he says as he hiccups for air between sobs. "So much."

I turn my body so we're facing each other and pull him toward me, amazed that in the space of a few minutes we've switched places. Now it's me comforting him. As I rub calming circles on his back, I feel him settling down.

"Thanks," he finally says.

What a pair we are. Two guys falling apart. I doubt this is the kind of thing Will usually does when he's lying in bed with one of his boys. Of course, I would be the one who gets to hold him while he cries instead of, well, the other stuff.

Will's voice returns to its usual, easygoing manner. "Let's call it a night, dude. I'm wiped."

But instead of moving back to the trundle, he stays with me, and before I can turn around again, he does it instead.

"You be the big spoon, Jeff."

It takes me a few seconds to understand what he's said. First, I think he's using some UPR lingo I don't know. Then it dawns on me that he wants me to hold him from behind. I move close and place my arm around his waist and feel him back up against me.

I close my eyes and a smile slowly slides onto my face. *Peace* is the last word I'm conscious of before sleep takes hold. When I wake up the next morning, Will is back on his trundle mattress fast asleep.

* * *

I dress quickly for school and rush into the kitchen for a fast breakfast. I'm running late and the sadistic prison guards at Kushner Academy for Boys would only be too happy to punish me with detention for a tardy.

My mother stares at me with her hands on her hips. "Oy, Jeffrey." She shakes her head, comes over to me, and starts to tuck my white button-down shirt into my pants, gently pulling out the strings of my *tzitzit*.

Always gentle with me, she doesn't lecture, but instead leaves the room and comes back with a hairbrush and a hand mirror, holding both out to me. "Your hair," is all she says.

There's a plate on the table with leftover potato kugel and three cinnamon rugelach and a cup of the Earl Grey tea I like. I hand her back the brush and the mirror, receiving a nod for my grooming efforts and sit to scarf down my breakfast.

My mouth is filled with kugel when my father calls out from the living room, "Both of you, come quick!"

This is not very unusual. He's always watching, reading, or listening to the news and feels the need to invite us in to hear whatever it is that's shocked or outraged him. It's never good news but a lot of the time it's not such a big deal. Something in my gut tells me today might be different.

When we enter the living room, I see that he's got the local morning news show up on the screen. A correspondent is talking to the anchor. I open my mouth to ask what's going on, but before I can utter a word, he shushes me.

I look up and there's Will, likely awakened by my father. He's leaning against the doorway, black hair pointing in multiple directions, his T-shirt creased from sleep. With eyes wide and his head shaking a bit, he gives me that look that says, "What's up?" I shrug back at him and point to the screen as the newscast starts.

"Our sources in the nation's capital in Dallas tell us that President Fairleigh is coming to Cincinnati tomorrow to announce new protection measures for Jewish populations in the GFS," the correspondent tells the anchor.

My stomach lurches with the realization that my father isn't crying wolf this time.

"And these new measures would include a change to guest status, similar to other non-white, non-Christian populations in the country?" the anchor asks.

"That's what we're hearing. Guest status and consolidation into a few regional communities with protective entrance and exit measures similar to what Cincinnati has already put in place. That may be why he's making the announcement here where we've seen a decrease in the kinds of disruptions that occurred when there were no limits on mixed interactions that drained police resources."

I roll my eyes at the thought that they now have a new term—"mixed interactions"— they're using to mean antisemitic violence. And as for police resources, that's the biggest joke of all.

The anchor smiles, signaling that this is somehow good news. "I know how much the people of Cincinnati will be looking forward to the President's visit in the midst of what's proving to be a very competitive election campaign."

The correspondent signs off and the anchor goes to a commercial, promising a look at the day's weather upon his return. My father clicks off the screen.

Will's migrated to the couch; his elbows resting on his thighs, head buried in his hands. The perfect response to what we just heard.

I'm frozen in place, barely able to stand but not yet able to sit either. My father is shaking his head and my mother lets out an audible sigh.

Will bolts up from the couch. "We'll fight this, right?" he bellows.

My father looks to me like I have an answer. I blurt out the first thing that comes to mind and I pray that it's actually true. "The minyan is planning something."

"Oh yeah," says Will. "Lipsky's thing." He pauses and looks at my parents. "To which I've already contributed greatly."

"Um Will," I say with a shake of my head, "the less said about that the better, okay?"

The Governing Council just approved the mission and will be giving us the details and our assignments tonight. My chest burns at the thought they'll be telling me to do something that's completely out of my depth.

The doorbell rings, the four of us jumping a bit at the jarring, unexpected intrusion. It's Judith, her eyes cast downward, head shaking. She's somehow been able to combine sadness, anger and disbelief into one silent expression.

"You heard," I greet her.

"Yeah," she breathes. "I couldn't bring myself to walk to school yet."

Will's voice is a bit too loud right behind my back. "We're gonna fight them! We won't stand by and let them do this."

I turn and lower my hands so he'll quiet down, especially since the front door is still open.

Kushner Academy for Boys might as well be an ostrich farm today with so many heads in the sand. There's a lot of talk about leaving for Israel with no one stating the obvious that we've been forbidden to leave the country. I overhear a couple of boys in my senior class having an insane conversation during lunch.

"Who needs to be a citizen anyway?"

"Yeah, if they want a *goyisha*[20] government, they can have it. Our parents came here to live on our own without their laws breathing down our necks. This just makes it official."

"No one in my family ever votes anyway."

These are the kinds of guys who'll celebrate when the day comes that we are walled off in a ghetto, the modern equivalent

20 Derogatory term for non-Jews

of a city in Nazi-occupied Poland. Until they are crowded in with six other families in a small apartment and wonder where their next meal is coming from. I don't even bother to argue with them. I have Lipsky and Isaac here for sane conversation and the rest of the Resistance that sees the true reality of what's going on.

Sitting in Talmud class, Lipsky and I are supposed to be discussing Rabban Gamliel's interpretation of two verses in Deuteronomy, but neither one of us can concentrate.

"Will's writing the script for the hologram of the President's Daughter," I tell him.

"Does he even know who she was?" asks Lipsky as he looks down at a page of Talmud, his finger pretending to follow the Hebrew from right to left.

"I told him what I know—former USA president's daughter, Jewish convert, protector of the Chosen People in the GFS, blah, blah, blah."

"Keep your voice down, Schwartz," Lipsky says as he nods in the direction of the teacher walking up the aisle toward us.

"So, we can discuss Torah everywhere except the bathroom or the bathhouse? Isn't that what Rabbi Yohanan says?" I announce in a voice that I hope reaches the teacher's ears and makes him go away. I have to admit, if I heard some students discussing anything about a bathroom, I'd get as far away from them as possible. It works.

"Okay, we're good," says Lipsky, his finger still moving across a line of Hebrew. "Back to the President's Daughter."

"It's interesting. Will says that in the UPR Marianna Fredricks, who we've always called the President's Daughter, is seen as a traitor to the Jews, a sellout."

"Does it surprise you that they have a different take on her?"

"I guess not. All it makes me realize is how much I don't know or understand about the UPR and what Will and Dani grew up believing."

Lipsky then launches into a whole monologue about how people like him, who Dani calls "differently abled," are treated in the UPR. I half-listen since Will's mentioned this to me as well. It's this whole thing he calls accessibility with curb cuts, ramps and kitchen sinks built at wheelchair height instead of higher.

The other half of my mind is focused on Will and how strange and fascinating he is. My first gay male friend. I wonder what it would be like to kiss him and to feel his chest pressing into mine. I wonder if his chin would feel scratchy against my cheek and if I would like that. I'm not ready to think about anything else beyond that, especially in the middle of Talmud class. I'm sure the rabbis have commented on something in Deuteronomy that these thoughts are violating. I already know what it says in Genesis and Leviticus about men being with men, and that's been enough for me to turn my back on Torah and the whole enterprise of obsessively parsing every word for its true meaning.

It's this kind of stuff that's made me give up on some aspects of Judaism, the study and worship parts, not the food, of course. Though there might be some hope for me and Judaism yet now that our Rebel Rabbi is finding new meanings and creating new rituals. Maybe I can ask Will to find out what Isaac thinks about the whole Sodom and Gomorrah mess and that "man shall not lie with man" stuff. I'm too scared and worried to ask him myself. I don't want to lose his friendship if he says something hurtful. But what if he doesn't? What if, like everything else he's been doing, Isaac comes up with some new interpretation that gets us away from the "abomination" thing?

I can see it now. A new Talmudic tractate. *"Rebel Rabbi Isaac Leventhal says that Lot's neighbors were not sinful for engaging in homosexuality, they were instead sinful for…"* and then Isaac would have some masterful insight that I could never think of. But what if he could?

CHAPTER EIGHTEEN

Dani

I knew coming here was the right idea. Not only am I getting to know my sister-in-law, niece, and nephews, and spending a lot of time with Judith, but I'm actually making myself useful to the cause. Plus, and this is the bonus, Judith and I get to work together on this mission.

We'll be interrupting the GFS President's speech with the projection of two volumetric images, similar to holograms but easier to create without all the equipment that isn't available here. Judith has been sketching the figures and I'm programming the computer so it can work with the scanned drawings.

We sit next to each other at her little table in the basement, our shoulders touching. She's drawing and I'm coding on an old laptop of hers. The computer is fine for my purposes today, but we'll need Jeffrey's father's Xio4000 desktop to run the program that will enable us to generate the three-D appearing images. Then they'll be loaded onto a projector Binyamin took from the university after they eliminated the Jewish Studies Department and fired him. But the projector by itself won't work with these kinds of images so Meyer and I retrofit it to become a volumetric projecting device.

I pause what I'm doing to watch Judith, her head bent in concentration, dark curls hiding a part of her face; the scritch-scratch of her pencil the only sound in the room. Her hand pauses and she turns to me, head tilted.

"It's hard to concentrate with you staring at me."

"It's hard not to stare at you."

Her cheeks are pink as she shakes her head and reaches for my shoulder, gently massaging it. Her lips pucker and I hear the soft pluck of a kiss followed by a whoosh of air as she blows it to me.

"Now, back to work and no more staring," she says and smiles at me.

But I'm not done with her yet. "Is there a reward if I do a good job? And don't tell me the reward is the mission will be a success. I'm talking about a more…" I pause, "um, personal reward."

Again, she shakes her head, "Let's just say that when we're done, the kisses won't have to be blown from a distance."

I grin at her. "Okay then, c'mon, let's get back to work. The sooner we finish, the sooner the reward."

She chuckles, picks up her pencil and lowers her head.

Judith and I haven't gone beyond kissing. I mean, that's great and all, but I have no idea if she'll even agree to go further. This is one of those things that's so different here from what I'm used to in the UPR. By now, any girl I'd been with, especially one I feel so strongly about, would have been on the same page as me, meaning, we would have done it already, likely more than once. Aisha and I didn't waste any time, that's for sure. But with Judith, I know it's different. I have to be patient. I have to understand that this is just another of those things where we come from separate worlds.

I focus on the laptop screen, still not back on task. Instead, I wonder if Judith is so religious that she would only have sex after she was married. Is that still a thing here in the GFS? I take a deep breath in and let it out, closing my eyes and tightening my face muscles so I can relax them and push these thoughts aside, at least for now.

I feel Judith's hand wrap around my wrist. "How's this?" she asks and slides her drawing on top of the laptop's keyboard.

I look down and am in awe of her talent. I take in the figure that will become a projected image, astounded by its likeness to the real person.

"It's okay if it's not good enough," she says with this self-deprecating tone I've heard her use before about her art. "I can start over."

She reaches for the paper and I grab it before she can.

"It's amazing," I tell her. "It's like she's alive again."

Binyamin argued and argued with me about going out on the mission, but in the end even he knew that only Meyer Lipsky and I have the tech know how to load and launch the figures and troubleshoot if we run into problems. Meyer worked so hard on creating the projecting device, so Will and I tried to find a way to include Einstein in the group of us heading out to the park where the president's speech was being held.

"I'm too conspicuous and you know that," Meyer told us, putting an end to our brainstorming session. "Besides, I have an important role to play so you guys can get back in. In the meantime, I'll be here with Schwartz for any tech support."

Tonight, Will and I are again in the black jeans and hoodies we wore to cross the border. We've put Hannah in a similar outfit though she's wearing a long skirt and blouse over it so she won't arouse any suspicion when we go through the neighborhood checkpoint. Solly Hershel leads our small group and has made us promise repeatedly to follow all his directions.

Will's hands are on his hips in a defiant pose. "This isn't the army," he says.

"Mr. Kim." Solly practically barks his name. "If you want to come out of this alive or not in a prison cell, you will do everything I say. No arguments. Let me hear you tell me you agree."

Will rolls his eyes and gives Solly a limp salute. "Yes, Captain Herschel, I agree." His mocking voice makes me wonder if he really does.

Once again, I am shut up in that casket of a back seat in Binyamin's car, but this time with Will crammed in next to me. We'd rehearsed every step of the mission this past week, making sure both Will and I could fit in this small hiding space. Instead of lying on my back like I did before, Will and I are pressed against each other on our sides.

"Cozy digs," he says as we squeeze into the back seat coffin. "Good thing we're not into the opposite sex, huh?"

I don't answer him because I'm just not in the mood to kid around in the way I usually can with him. This is serious stuff we're about to do. I make sure the thumb drive with the images loaded onto it is still in my pocket. Binyamin has hidden the small projector under his seat along with a tiny but powerful amplifier that will blast our messages into the park, another specialty from Meyer assisted by Jeffrey's father. Binyamin, Hannah, and Solly hold forged permits courtesy of Judith, but Will and I are strangers here and would attract suspicion even if we could show the guards a permit.

I feel the car stop and the guard's voice asking for the permits. Binyamin explains that he is taking Solly to visit a friend from his former chess club and Hannah is headed to the GFS museum's nighttime exhibit for a school project. The cover stories work, and Binyamin deliberately mentions he will come back alone after dropping them off.

"Fine, fine," the guard responds, and for a minute I'm confused about his use of my last name, worried I'd somehow been discovered. But then I realize what the guard meant and I know we're okay.

Once I feel the car moving forward, I exhale and relax, surprised by how tense I was. I feel Will's similar exhale on my face and I nod to him.

The top of the seat casket finally opens and Binyamin lifts me up so I can stand. Will gets up on his own and both of us shake out our arms and legs to help us get moving.

"Thanks for the ride, bro," Will says. "Your sister and I had some great bonding time."

The car is parked according to plan, in the darkness under an elevated highway. Hannah and Solly remove the clothing covering their all-black outfits and Solly gives each of us a black ski mask and black latex gloves. Binyamin hands Hannah the mini projector and gives Will the amplifier.

Solly looks at me. "Thumb drive?"

I nod. "In my pocket."

Binyamin hugs each of us and whispers in my ear, "Don't take any chances or Mom'll kill me."

I shiver a bit at the thought of my mother back home, worried and angry, blaming everyone in creation for what I've done, especially herself. It's the first time I've even felt a tiny bit of sympathy for what she might be going through, with both her children far away and in danger.

We wait and watch the car disappear into the night and then take the route mapped out by Solly that keeps us amid foliage and away from street and highway lights and the crowds streaming into the riverside park where the President will speak.

Solly has mapped out three waystation hiding spots for us as we wait for the event to begin and for the countless opening speeches to end. Each spot brings us closer to the park. He's ordered us not to speak and to keep our eyes on him at all times.

Of course, Will disobeys at the first opportunity. "Some power trip, that guy," he whispers to me. Again, I don't answer.

From where we wait behind a row of dumpsters, we can hear the speakers praising President Fairleigh, "a good Evangelical Christian" they call him, mentioning his wife and three children, one of whom is apparently a popular minister in Dallas, the GFS capital. The Cincinnati mayor is the first to mention what he refers to as "our model solution to curtailing violence involving the Jews." I notice that he doesn't say *against* the Jews.

We move to the final hiding spot when the vice presidential candidate is introduced. He's the last of the speakers before the president. His speech ends with a chilling endorsement of Fairleigh as "the only man who can ensure that this country becomes and stays a purely white Christian nation as God intended."

Hearing this, Will grabs my hand and all but crushes it. I look over at Hannah whose terrified eyes-wide, mouth-open expression changes in an instant to livid, eyes scrunched and her mouth a tight straight line. The change brings to mind Judith's many stories about Hannah's bravery and steely resolve.

I wonder what Judith's doing while she waits for us to return. But before I can feel badly over the certainty that she's sick with worry, Solly gestures for us to move to our staging area. It's showtime.

The crowd is yelling and chanting Fairleigh's name, the deafening noise covering any sounds we make as we get into place and set up the amp and the projector with the thumb drive tucked into it. Will and I are focused on the task, while the other three are lookouts. Solly has the authority to abort the mission if at any moment he feels we could be caught; but we are counting on the element of surprise to buy us time until our projected images are finished delivering their messages.

I look to Solly for the signal. The plan is to let Fairleigh begin and then wait until he announces his proposal to restrict Jews to their neighborhoods before we launch the projector.

My eyes are fixed on Solly at the president's first mention of GFS's Jews.

"I commend the forward-looking citizens and elected officials of this great city for the innovative order of protection you have issued to put a stop to Jewish-related violence." He's interrupted by applause and cheers. He continues, "In fact, I'm so impressed with what you've done that if I'm re-elected I will take your program nationwide with orders of protection in every area of the country where Jews live." More cheers and chants of "Four more Fairleigh," his awful slogan.

My hand moves to the switch but there's still not a signal from Solly. What could he be waiting for?

Fairleigh begins speaking again. "But," he goes on, "I'm not stopping there. Not at all. In my second term, I will make sure the GFS Congress passes legislation that revokes the citizenship of Jews in the GFS, downgrading them to the status of Guest Resident, just like we have done with any of the small numbers of non-white settlements that insisted on remaining here after The Split."

I'm so paralyzed with fear and disgust at what I've just heard that I've blocked out the crowd's cheers, and it takes me perhaps a full minute to realize and react to Solly giving me the signal to begin. I flip the switch and in a few seconds the images are loaded onto the projector.

"Did he just say what I think he said?" Will whispers, his voice shaking.

I can only dip of my head once as the light from the projector reaches up into the night sky and the first 3-D image comes to life.

She is a few years younger than me, with dark hair a bit shorter than Judith's and tied back with barrettes. Judith drew her in a white dress with a decorative pattern of a band of tiny flowers around her collar extending down in two lines over the bodice and repeated on the sleeves.

"*Hello, my name is Anne Frank,*" she begins, the voice of Naomi Blau coming through loud and clear. "*For many years, my family hid with others in the attic of a house in Amsterdam before we were betrayed to the Nazis and sent to a concentration camp, where we were murdered or left to die from disease like I did. Perhaps you read the diary I kept during that time in the attic, though it may not be available in your country. If you did, you'll know that the only reason we had to hide and were murdered was because we were Jews. In fact, Amsterdam wasn't even my home. I grew up in Germany until the Nazis declared that Jews were no longer citizens and we were beaten on the streets with the police looking on and doing nothing.*

"*All of this happened because Hitler wanted Germany and the countries he invaded to be pure white and Christian, what they called Aryan.*

"*So I ask you people of the GFS, are you going to try again to exterminate us, first by confining us to ghettos and then revoking our citizenship? Is purity worth the price of genocide, a crime against humanity? Maybe you need to ask yourselves, what kind of country do you want to be?*"

With this last question, she fades away. There's silence for a few beats and then the murmur of voices.

President Fairleigh looks a bit shellshocked but then grasps the microphone.

"Ladies and gentlemen, don't be swayed by this…"

But before he can go on, there's a second image above him in the sky, someone this crowd knows quite well. She's a beautiful blond older woman, perfectly made up with no wrinkles or other signs of age, just as she was up until the day she died in a plane crash.

"It is so good to be with you once again," she says in Dvorah Kuriel's voice. *"I've missed my country so much since my untimely passing last year. I'm Marianna Fredrichs, the daughter of the former president of the USA and the man who laid the groundwork for The Split and the GFS. I was so delighted when this country was founded and proudly settled here with my family, working in the government as a member of the country's first cabinet.*

"As you know, I converted to Judaism before The Split and lived in the GFS in an Orthodox Jewish community. We lived side by side with our Christian neighbors, all proud citizens of our new, conservative country, a beacon of freedom to the world.

"But since my death, things here are changing. And now I shudder to think that had I still been alive, my own citizenship would be revoked even though I've worked so hard to help establish this incredible nation.

"I ask that in my memory you reconsider these actions against our Jewish neighbors and continue to live peacefully together as the God-fearing nation we so love."

Once she fades and the voices of the crowd begin again, Solly waves us to get going, and we race off, reversing our route with stops at the hiding places, until we are far enough away from anyone who could be looking for us.

When we get to the row of dumpsters, Will climbs up and retrieves an ax we hid in the middle one. As quietly as possible, Solly smashes the projector, amp and thumb drive into pieces, and we distribute the remains among the dumpsters.

Sirens in the distance grow louder. Solly urges us forward. It's about a three-hour walk back to our neighborhood and we have to get there on time so that Meyer can play his part.

The plan is for the four of us to stick together to get back through the checkpoint without anyone left behind. When Solly first explained this to us, Will told him he was crazy.

"We have a much better chance of evading capture if we each go our separate ways," he insisted. "We can map out four different paths back to the checkpoint and meet there."

"No!" Solly said in that awful military voice of his. "This is the best way. All together. I know what I'm doing."

But now the sirens are getting even louder, closer, and there's not just one. It's more like a wall of high-pitched wails closing in on us.

Hannah and I run alongside Solly, both of us looking to him for guidance. To my horror, I see what I'm pretty certain is doubt and fear on his usually relaxed face. His mouth is open, eyes wide, staring straight ahead.

Then Will appears in front of the three of us, jogging backward like he did at times when he was training me. "I can create a diversion and make them go after me," he says, his voice loud above the sirens.

"T-t-too dangerous," Solly calls out, his normally deep voice higher than I've ever heard it.

"I'll be okay, I'm the fastest," Will calls back to us. "I can outrun them."

Solly looks down at the ground and is quiet for a few seconds. The sound of car brakes squealing to a stop is so close I'm afraid to turn my head in their direction. Hannah and I are still looking to Solly, who raises his head and nods at Will, motioning to him with his hand. "Go!" he shouts. "Do it!"

Will turns toward the sound of slamming police car doors at the same time that Solly grabs Hannah and me by our arms pulling us in the opposite direction. I'm winded from running, and my throat is closing, making it almost impossible to breathe. Luckily, Solly steers us behind a row of stores and we hide inside a loading dock, which is dark enough to conceal us. "You two okay?" he whispers.

We both nod, and though I want to ask him if he has a plan for getting us back, my throat still feels closed and the pain of fear has settled in my gut. I can't imagine how Will is going to escape all those police and the weapons they carry. I don't want to think about how he might have to sacrifice himself so the three of us can get away. I remember my mother telling us how his parents were worried, calling her constantly. And his sister, Ann, his twin. What if they lose him? I'd never be able to live with myself.

We wait in the loading dock for what feels like forever but is probably ten minutes.

"I mapped out an alternate route back in case something like this happened," Solly tells us. "Let's get going."

We walk for what feels like much more than three hours, but by this point I've lost all sense of time. When we cross a two-lane highway, Hannah pulls on my arm.

"We're close to home and we haven't seen Will. Do you think he's all right?"

I think back on all the times Will ran ahead of me during my training for crossing the border. "He's fast so maybe he's at the checkpoint already."

She nods. "I hope so."

The checkpoint has a small, white guard house and the same kind of barrier usually found at railroad crossings. There's a chain-link fence on either side with cameras set up all along it. How they can call this anything but a ghetto is beyond me.

There are four cops in uniform standing outside the guard house, talking in a group.

Solly signals to wait behind some trees until we see Meyer approach the checkpoint from the other side, the metal frame of his wheelchair visible in the dark. Luckily, we had him add a half hour to our expected arrival time before he initiated his part of the plan. This way, if we were delayed, he wouldn't miss us.

He finally rolls up to the guards and we hear them say his name.

"Why are you out here in the middle of the night?"

It's a question we anticipated.

"I couldn't sleep, came outside and got disoriented. It's part of my condition."

All of this, of course, is a big lie. Meyer is the last person who'd ever become disoriented, and his "condition," his broken spine, has no effect on his mental abilities. But these guys, who think living with a disability means you have no chance at a meaningful life, will believe anything.

It's then that Meyer begins to spin around in his chair, faster and faster. The cops tell him to stop and try to grab onto his chair, but he doesn't let them slow him down. And then, as they're yelling and grasping onto him, he tips the chair over and falls to the ground, just as he told us he would. When he thought up this idea, Meyer promised us he'd be fine. He explained that he'd long ago learned how to fall off his chair without hurting himself.

As all four cops bend down to check on him, that's our cue to run under the barrier and as far away from the checkpoint as we can get before they realize what's happened.

Hannah and Solly split off from me and go back to Solly's place where Isaac is waiting. I head off to Binyamin's so that he and Miriam can see I'm okay. But throughout all of this, there's been no sign of Will. Could he have sneaked past the checkpoint just like he did when he first arrived? That's hopefully what's happened.

To my surprise, I find Judith standing in Binyamin's living room. We run to each other and she holds on tight. Binyamin and Miriam envelop us in a hug and even after they pull away, Judith holds on. She's whispering something in Hebrew. I hear a few familiar words that the minyan repeats during its services. *Baruch ata Adonai.*

"What were you saying?" I ask when she finally releases me.

She looks down, a little embarrassed. "Prayer of thanks and the *Shehechyanu*, giving gratitude to *Hashem* for allowing us to reach this time."

When Binyamin's device beeps, we all freeze in place, our eyes on my brother who lifts the little black piece and answers. He mouths "Jeffrey" to us. "It is? Really?" Binyamin asks.

There's a pause. "Well, yes they would explain it that way." Another pause. "No, not here. Not with you?"

His face falls and his eyes close a bit. It's his worried look. "I'm going out to the paper to see what I can learn. I'll keep an eye out...yes, sure...bye."

He slides the device into his pocket. "Will isn't with Jeffrey. When was the last time you saw him, Dani?"

There's a queasy feeling in my stomach that moves up into my chest. "A while back. He's the fastest among us, so he left us to run toward the police and create a diversion so we could get away. I thought he'd meet us at the checkpoint or even sneak through ahead of us."

Binyamin rubs the top of his head, messing up his hair. "This isn't good. Why don't you turn on the news and I'll go see what I can find out."

We tune into a national news station and wait for them to talk about President Fairleigh's speech. A reporter standing in the same park where we launched the volumetric images summarizes the main points of the speech, focusing most of his report on what Fairleigh intends to do to the Jews.

I realize it's the first time Judith and Miriam are hearing this. Miriam is hugging herself, her legs up on the couch bent at the knees and tucked into her chest. Tears silently slide down Judith's cheeks and I reach my arm around her shoulders, not knowing what to say.

All three of us are staring at the screen when the news anchor says something about a "late-breaking report."

"Police have informed us that they've arrested a teenage illegal, likely from the UPR. Non-white, possibly Chinese or Japanese, heading away from the park and carrying an illegal communication device. It is believed that he is responsible for a brief disruption during the president's speech that you may have heard if you tuned in live. The illegal was injured during the arrest and has been taken to the city hospital. We'll update with further details as they become available."

We sit there, silent, clutching one another, all three of us crying. They got Will and hurt him so bad he had to be taken to the hospital. It also seems likely that they got his iBrain. Could he have taken it with him even though Solly said not to?

Judith is pressed up against me and I feel the vibration of her device. When she doesn't reach for it, I take it out of her sweater pocket and hand it to her.

She sniffs "Hello" through her tears. "We know…okay." She hands me the device and I put it back.

She can hardly get the words out. "Jeffrey. Sobbing. He's coming over."

It's quiet again. Then I feel Judith turn toward Miriam. "I'm sorry," she says. "I didn't ask. Is that okay?"

Miriam nods. She hasn't said a word since we turned on the news. The program drones on and we let it in case there's more they can tell us about Will.

I sigh. "This fucking country. Calling him an illegal and not being able to figure out that he's Korean." I look down at the carpet and watch a tear drop onto it. "Poor Will." I don't say what I'm thinking which is that I hope whatever they did to him doesn't kill him.

Sounds drift toward me and I only catch snippets. Weather. Sports. Useless information. Then knocking, three times, then three more. Miriam is up and opens the door. Jeffrey runs to us and he's sobbing, voicing the thoughts I didn't say aloud. "They'll kill him! Then they'll come after all of us." He's on his knees, his head in Judith's lap. Judith shushes him, rubbing his back.

"I don't think they'll kill him but we don't know how badly he's been hurt," says Miriam. I can hardly hear her as she shakes her head and speaks softly. "And it's possible they could force him to give up information that would implicate us all."

Miriam's device buzzes and again we freeze. With the device still in her hand, she straightens her legs and stands.

"Binyamin wants us to come to the paper. Hannah, Isaac and Solly are already there. Jeffrey, your mother is on her way to watch the children. You three go and I'll wait until she gets here."

CHAPTER NINETEEN

Judith

Dani runs on ahead of us, hiding in the darkest places along the streets to the town center where the *Jewish Community News* has its office. Jeffrey and I walk at a more normal pace as if we're out for an evening stroll. As if nothing terrible has happened.

Phrases from a kind of reverse *Dayenu*, the song we sing at Passover, cycle through my mind. Instead of saying '*dayenu*, It would have been enough,' about each good thing in a list of many good things, I'm thinking that each horrible event by itself '…would have been too much."

It would have been too much if we were just going to have our citizenship revoked.

It would have been too much if they got a hold of one of our iBrains.

It would have been too much if one of us was arrested, injured and sent to the hospital.

And it certainly would have been too much if the person arrested was a non-white kid from the UPR.

Before we left Miriam, Jeffrey and I washed the tears from our faces. But now as we walk, I hear occasional sniffles coming from him and know how difficult it is to keep myself from dissolving back into sobs. I want to take his hand or slip my arm through his, but we're out in public and the last thing we need is some busybody deciding that the community has to know we are violating standards of purity.

There have only been a few times that I've seen Jeffrey scared silent. He normally covers his nervousness with chatter; either joking around, putting himself down or going off on one of his speeches about the many varieties of brisket. But now he's quiet and all I hear is the sound of an occasional car passing us or a baby crying for a night feeding from the houses we walk by.

Worrying about Will and what he must be going through feels too terrifying, so I think instead about what it means to have my citizenship revoked. Would it be any worse than being confined to the neighborhood the way we are? Would this give the GFS the right to treat us worse? Probably. But how much worse?

The paper's office is on the second floor above the kosher supermarket. Dani steps out from behind a parked car and meets us. Jeffrey enters a code on a number pad at the entrance and I hear the door click open. We walk upstairs and through a heavy metal door that brings us into a large room with messy desks set out in three rows, each with a computer screen on top.

There isn't anyone in the room, but I spot a few closed doors along the opposite wall. Then one opens and Hannah comes toward us. I'm a bit taken aback that instead of hugging me, she takes hold of Jeffrey. This could be the first time they've ever touched.

"Don't worry, we'll get him out," she says in that voice that leaves no room for doubt. But still I wonder. How?

Once we're in the meeting room, there's more hugging and reassurances until we are all seated around an oval table. The four members of the Governing Council—Binyamin, Dvorah, Solly and Hannah—are together at the head. Next to Hannah is Isaac, then Jeffrey, me, and Dani whose hand rests on mine. Normally I'd be a little worried for everyone to see this show of affection, but under the circumstances the only way for me to feel any sense of calm is to be comforted by the warmth of her touch.

Jeffrey's father is seated on the other side of Binyamin, with a chair next to him left vacant for Miriam; and Meyer rounds out the group between Miriam's spot and Dani. I'm not sure how Meyer was able to get up to the second floor since the building doesn't have an elevator.

The only one missing is Naomi Blau, likely because of the late hour. I find myself wishing she were here. I have a vague sense that we haven't yet realized how valuable she is to what we're doing but I don't know why I feel that way.

Binyamin looks at me. "Judith, your mother knows you're here so don't worry about how late it is."

My nod is accompanied by an exhale of relief. After what happened with my father, I try never to make my mother worry.

Binyamin begins the meeting. "We've been discussing how we might get word to the UPR about Will. We think their government might be able to get him released."

"Would they?" asks Jeffrey. "He's not like a spy or anything or some important prisoner."

"There's an extradition treaty between the two countries," Solly explains. "We're pretty sure there are GFS citizens in custody who could be returned in exchange for Will. We just have to let the UPR know."

"So if they do that, he'll have to go back?" asks Jeffrey. The sadness in his voice comes through, making me realize just how close the two of them have become.

I feel Dani's body shift from side to side next to me followed by a knock on the table as the hand not holding mine hits the wood surface. "Can't we just break him out of the hospital so he can continue working with us? Isn't there a way?"

Binyamin sighs and looks at his sister, shaking his head. "It's too dangerous, Dani. I'm sure they're watching him every second. Plus, we don't know what shape he's in."

"And even if we were successful," continues Solly, "he's too exposed at this point and could only work behind the scenes."

"And they have his iBrain," adds Meyer.

True to form, he's focused on the technology and steers the conversation away from Will. Jeffrey gives Meyer a hard look, his mouth a straight line. "Really, that's what you're concerned about?"

"Schwartz, it's been the only way to communicate with the outside world."

"We can't use them anymore," Binyamin says with a note of finality in his voice. "There's too great a chance that the GFS can listen in on anything we say. That's another message we have to get to the UPR as soon as possible as well as to our allies throughout the GFS."

There are nods around the table except for Meyer who has his head in his hands.

"Dani, are any of your friends able to open your email?" asks Hannah. "We can send a papercut code tonight with the message."

"Yes, I gave Julia the password before I left just in case."

"Tonight?" My voice squeaks with alarm when I ask this. It's already late and Hannah knows how long it takes me to make a papercut, let alone to code the message.

"It's doable," says Meyer in that arrogant tone of his. "Once we have the message, there's a program we can run so you'll know which Hebrew letters to use for the papercut."

"Just a simple design, Judith," says Hannah. "Spend most of your time on the Hebrew."

I nod. I guess it is doable.

Binyamin's device buzzes. "That will be Miriam. I'll fill her in." He stands and gestures to Jeffrey's father. "Mr. Schwartz…"

"Please, call me Zalman. We're way beyond niceties here."

Binyamin's smile is brief. "Okay, Zalman. Please take Jeffrey, Judith, Dani, and Meyer back to your shop so they can get the message out to the UPR. And if there's time, could the four of you run this message through the coding program?" He hands Jeffrey's father a folded-up paper. "We'll have to use the newspaper to get the word out to our friends in the Resistance."

"What about the Gullah-Geechee?" Dani asks. "They have an iBrain."

"I'll make sure our Federation chapter in South Carolina gets word to them," he responds and then claps his hands together. "So let's act fast, people. We have to do our best to keep everyone safe."

I see Mr. Schwartz glance over at Meyer and look back at Binyamin with his mouth open in an unspoken question.

Binyamin responds, "Solly and I will get Meyer down the stairs."

Dani's anger comes through in her voice. "You might look into an elevator or a ramp, bro. You take away someone's dignity when you deny them accessibility."

Binyamin sighs at his sister and raises his hands in surrender. "I know, I know. It's not like we didn't both grow up in the same country."

"And yet, only one of us learned anything," she says and turns her back on him.

"What did I walk in on?" asks Miriam as she comes through the door.

CHAPTER TWENTY

Jeffrey

Judith is drawing and cutting. Meyer and Dani are staring at the computer monitor, their heads almost touching. What am *I* doing? Not a friggin' thing.

The truth is I'm useless. That's a fact. Will is in a hospital bed fighting for his life. They're probably torturing him so he'll give them information. I'm certain he's being called all kinds of horrible names and insulted constantly. They're probably starving him. And all our mighty Minyan of Resistance can do is hope (hope!) that the UPR government will free him because some random group of Jews sends a secret message in an email to a teenager. Great plan.

I tap Dani on the shoulder to get her attention and she swivels her body to look at me. "Can I talk to you for a minute?"

Judith looks up and scrunches her eyes at me, asking wordlessly what this is about. Meyer, of course, stays fixated on the screen, his fingers tapping away at lightning speed.

The room is small, but I head to a corner and motion for her to follow. She has that same questioning look on her face as Judith. "What's up?" she asks.

I keep my voice as low as possible. "Do you really think there's a way to break him out of the hospital? I'm just not really feeling optimistic about this whole government prisoner exchange. I think Solly's been reading too many spy novels."

She looks down for a few seconds and then back at me. "It's a longshot. I just don't know if we can do it without Solly or my brother," she says with a shrug.

"Hannah and Isaac could help," I offer.

"We'd need to know what kind of shape he's in and the level of security around him. Also, we'd need an ironclad plan."

I feel a tap on my arm. Judith. "What are you two talking about?"

The heat of fear rises in my chest. She'll never agree to let us do this. "Aren't you supposed to be cutting?"

Judith tilts her head and stares at me in annoyance. "I *would* be if your little conversation didn't distract me."

Dani's arm goes around Judith's shoulders. "We're talking about…"

"No don't tell her! She'll never agree."

"To what?"

I know Judith hates it when I underestimate her, which is why I think we might be on the verge of an argument.

"It's about Will," is all I say.

Dani holds up her pointer finger. "If we can come up with a good plan…"

"No! It's too dangerous," Judith blurts out.

"They'll torture and probably kill him." I'm whining.

"The UPR government…"

"Would take forever, if they even decide to do anything." I've stopped whispering and am on the verge of shouting and sobbing.

Meyer remains facing the computer. "Maybe you should ask if I have any ideas," he says with a hint of impatience.

The three of us surround him.

"Do you?" I ask.

"Maybe."

"Meyer," says Dani, drawing out his name. "Just tell us."

"Well," he begins. "The police seem very capable of being fooled and distracted. We've proven that."

When the door to the workroom opens, we all jump. My father stands there and breathes out audibly before he speaks. "I just heard on the news that they'll be moving Will to a GFS prison hospital in Dallas on Monday. Let's get that message out to the UPR as soon as possible."

When he closes the door, I crumple to the floor and tuck my knees into my chest, making myself as small as I feel. Dani and Judith squat down to check on me.

"Seems time is of the essence, my friends," says Meyer. "Let's get to work."

The three of us look at one another and rise to our feet, once again standing around our very own Einstein.

CHAPTER TWENTY-ONE

Dani

Meyer angles his chair to face us. "One of the physical therapists I see works in that hospital. She's Jewish."

"I thought they all worked in the Jewish hospital?" asks Judith.

"She's part-time in both places. I have an appointment with her tomorrow at our hospital. I'll ask to see if she can find out what we need to know about Will."

I'm reluctant to add another person to the mix. "Is she trustworthy?"

"We have less than a week," adds Jeffrey.

Meyer sighs in response. He's a great guy, but still a guy. And he continues in a calm but arrogant voice. "Sophie and I have had many conversations about what's going on and we're on the same side. Once she can let us know the situation, we can put my plan into action. *If* we find the right person to help us."

"What? Who? What person?" Jeffrey asks, shaking Meyer by the shoulder.

"Schwartz stop it. Sophie has enough work to do with me tomorrow without you adding a dislocated shoulder."

"So what do you mean by the right person?" I ask.

"The guy who'll pretend to be a doctor."

"That won't work," says Judith in her quiet voice. "They know who all the doctors are. We can't just make one up."

"We can if he's being sent from the Dallas prison hospital to evaluate the patient," Meyer answers in a triumphant voice someone would use if they figured out how to solve the world's most difficult puzzle. It's almost like an announcement.

For the first time all night, Jeffrey breaks into a smile. "Brilliant," he says. But then his expression deflates. "But who can we get?"

"Well, that's the biggest question," says Meyer. "Who?"

"My brother and Solly won't do it."

Meyer shakes his head. "They're too recognizable anyway."

"My father's too old and Jewish looking," Jeffrey adds. "No one would believe he's some government doctor from Dallas."

We're all quiet for a while. This plan is too good to be scuttled over this. There has to be somebody, but I can't offer any suggestions. I'm the least helpful here.

"Anyone from school?" asks Jeffrey, who then answers his own question as he shakes his head. "Dumb idea."

"There is someone," whispers Judith, "but I don't know if he'll do it. But he'd be good at it if he agreed."

Three voices come together at once, all with a lot of urgency behind them. "Who?"

"My brother-in-law, David. He's tall, with light hair and blue eyes, so he doesn't look typically Jewish. Not a lot of people outside the neighborhood know him because he works as an accountant for Bernard Blau's company."

"Doesn't Blau's company own buildings all over the city?" asks Meyer.

"Yes, but David isn't very high up since he just started there."

"Is he on our side?" I ask. This is the second new person we're thinking of involving. Widening the circle increases the danger.

"Yes, I've seen his soul. I made sure it was a good one before he married Shuli. Plus, David and my sister have been to Isaac's services, and my mother has talked to them." Her voice is a bit wobbly as she continues. "After my father was, uh," she breathes out a sob, "murdered, they…" And she can't finish the sentence.

"They're angry like your mother?" asks Jeffrey.

Judith nods, unable to speak. I take her hand. "Can you ask him?"

"I can go with you," offers Meyer. "I've seen enough doctors in my lifetime to give David excellent acting lessons."

"Take Isaac too," adds Jeffrey. "David might agree if the Rebel Rabbi thinks he should do this."

It's a great plan but there are too many details we still have to figure out. "He'll need a doctor's coat."

"Sophie can get one."

"Identification," I continue, "and one of those badges with his name on it. Plus a visitor's pass."

Meyer's back with that arrogant voice that drives me nuts. "Easy. Judith makes the ID and we three-D print the badge. What else?"

I look right at him with my eyes wide and my head tilted to the side. "How do we actually get Will out?"

* * *

Judith's brother-in-law David does make a pretty convincing doctor and Hannah, wearing a blond wig, is his nurse from Dallas. The technician aide they bring to wheel in the diagnostic instruments and machines is yours truly, complete with a long light brown braid running down my back.

Meyer was able to hack into the Dallas prison hospital's network and create an email address from the newly minted Doctor Gregory Taylor, who sent word to the city hospital here that he'd be arriving early Friday morning to examine the prisoner.

Sophie, the physical therapist, turned out to be a gold mine of information. There are two guards assigned to Will's room; one for daytime and one for night duty. Hospital security fills in during their breaks. The shift changes at eight in the morning and eight at night.

Will, we learned, is recovering from multiple broken ribs and breaks to his left arm and wrist from when he was arrested. I'm sure once they saw that Will is Asian, they were especially rough on him, though I also suspect he did his best to resist arrest, which may have also contributed to his injuries.

In any case, we'd have to be gentle with him, but it appears we won't be endangering his health by taking him out of the hospital.

Isaac has borrowed Solly's car, using an excuse about preparing for Shabbat or something, and David and Hannah get through the checkpoint with me hiding under a tarp in the trunk. Since arriving in the GFS, I've come to appreciate so many things about my life in the UPR, including the ability to sit upright in a vehicle. I will not miss riding around confined to cramped spaces with only warm, stagnant air to breathe.

Once in costume, Hannah uses a fake account on a ride hailing app to have us picked up by a taxi van where we can store the metal cart we've assembled along with the phony equipment, all of which is covered by a black cloth secured with bungee cords.

A police captain and Will's doctor meet us at the hospital entrance. Following our plan, David does all the talking.

"Dr. Taylor, I was in med school with Dr. Patrick Drummond, who I believe is a colleague of yours in Dallas?" asks Will's doctor.

David pauses to pretend he's thinking. "Hmmm, the name rings a bell but I'm kind of isolated at the prison hospital, so I don't come across many other staff very frequently." That's the response we rehearsed should this kind of question be asked. I'm hoping David's answer satisfies Will's doc.

"In any case," David goes on, deftly switching the subject, "what we're more interested in hearing about is the condition of the prisoner. What's his name again?"

As we move through the lobby crowded with people walking in every direction, the captain, who introduces himself as Bill Sargent, complete with what is likely his usual joke about being promoted over his family's name, speaks in an angry voice.

"We've only been able to get some kind of foreign words from him." He reaches in his pants pocket and pulls out a small black book. "Ji-Joon," he says slowly and with some effort. "I have no idea what that means. We've got our language guys working on it."

Could this country be any more racist? They think Ji-Joon is some kind of Chinese spy code instead of a common Korean name.

"And his condition?" David asks, turning his head to Will's doctor.

"Stable," he answers. "Multiple fractures healing well. Alert and mildly sedated. I see no reason you shouldn't be able to move him to Dallas on Monday."

"That's the plan," answers David as we step into a spacious elevator, "assuming all goes well."

"Doctors, I will take my leave here so I can get back to headquarters downtown," Captain Sargent says with a slight wave of his hand.

Will's doctor, whose name badge reads Nicholas Trask, MD, points to the cart I'm holding. "What do you have there?"

"Just some diagnostic instrumentation," David answers. "Custom mechanisms created specifically for the prison hospital."

"Really? I can't think of anything medically unique that's different than what we're doing here. Can I take a look?" He reaches over to the cover just as the elevator stops at our floor.

"Maybe later," David tells him, "or better yet, I'll follow up by email with full descriptions and photos. I think you'll find it really fascinating."

This guy deserves an Oscar. Even though we fed him most of these answers, his delivery is totally perfect. I'm even starting to believe he's a doctor.

Dr. Trask introduces us at the nurses station and a nurse comes up to shake Hannah's hand. "So happy to have you here. How are things in the nation's capital? You're awfully young. Are you right out of nursing school?"

David interrupts before Hannah has to answer. "Nurse, I'm terribly sorry but we have limited time here and we need to spend most of it with the prisoner."

We're already quite a bit past her when she responds, "Of course. My apologies, Doctor." It's clear she has no problem accepting her subordinate role and defers to the men. My guess would be there are few if any women doctors here and likely no male nurses.

As expected, a big, hefty, uniformed cop with a blond crew cut and very little neck stands by the door of Will's room. Since we're about ten minutes away from the shift change, the cop looks like he's about to fall asleep on his feet.

Dr. Trask introduces David "and his staff" to the officer who nods in response. "What's all that?" he asks, pointing to the cart.

When David answers "Medical instrumentation," the cop nods again and lowers his head, looking like he's on the verge of conking out.

"Shall we?" asks Dr. Trask, who reaches for the doorknob.

"Actually, Nicholas, our protocol requires that only Dallas prison hospital staff can be in with the prisoner during the examination. If I neglected to mention that in my email, I sincerely apologize. But it's standard procedure for us."

"Oh? But I'm the attending physician here. This is highly unusual."

David places a hand on Trask's arm. "I understand your confusion, of course. But for us this is standard operating procedure and we need to proceed immediately. I'm scheduled to be back in Dallas by lunchtime." He then moves that same hand to the door. "May we?"

Trask mutters his okay and takes a step back. We know from Sophie that the door is solid without a glass panel for viewing.

Will is the only patient in the drab, windowless room with walls painted a color I can only describe as vomit green. Hannah and David stand back as I approach the bed. His face is pretty banged up with black and blue marks on his cheek and the bridge of his nose. It looks like he's had stitches to close a cut on his forehead.

"Will," I whisper, "it's Dani." I place my hand on the shoulder of the arm that isn't broken. "Will, wake up."

He groans and I see his eyes open and then close again.

"Hurry!" Hannah whispers in an urgent voice behind me.

I turn back and see that they have unloaded the cart to do what is needed to accommodate Will. There's white padding and a small pillow on the bottom level. We'll have to have him lie on his side with his broken arm on top. Extra blankets will protect his ribs. At least I hope they will.

Hannah moves to the foot of the bed so she can lift Will's legs. David slips both hands under Will's torso. I'm at his head.

I try one last time. "Will, we're getting you out of here. But you have to be really quiet."

"Hmmm? Huh?" His voice is low and raspy. "D-D-Dani?"

"Yes, it's me." I give the signal and we lift him just like we did with a makeshift dummy we pieced together last night, weighted to approximate Will's heft. But the cast on his arm is heavier than we planned for and I feel his body sink a bit as we lift it off the bed.

Hannah, David, and I look at one another open-mouthed. The thought of dropping him and then us being found out pushes us to make an extra effort.

"Will, think light thoughts. Visualize yourself as a cloud or a feather." I have no idea if he can understand me much less put into practice UPR meditative visualizations. But it's worth a try.

Whether it was Will's visions of weightlessness or our own fear-induced adrenaline, we manage to get him into the cart and cover him up. I shush him when he groans. "Go to sleep Will."

As I cover him, Hannah and David fill the bed with the cushions and pillows we brought, including something Judith fashioned to look like an arm cast. They'll soon discover him missing, but this ruse might give us enough time to get away.

There's a new guard at the door and we meet Dr. Trask at the nurses station assuring him that Will is indeed able to travel to Dallas on Monday but that he needs peace and quiet for the next hour to rest after the examination.

"Keep the room dark with no interruptions by staff to check on him." David looks at his watch. "Give him at least sixty minutes before you go to him."

Trask still has that skeptical, questioning grimace on his face that tells me he's not sure he understands why and he might not listen to David's instructions.

David again looks at his watch. "Oh wow, we're running late." He turns to Hannah who has already called for the taxi van. "Nurse, is the van outside?" She nods to him.

David says a quick goodbye and thank you while we wait for the elevator. He assures Dr. Trask that we can find our way out on our own.

We are silent on the elevator. I'm too terrified I'll say something to give us away and panicky that we could still be found out.

Once in the lobby we move a bit faster but not fast enough to hurt Will. The taxi driver helps us lift the cart into the back of the van.

"I need to sit with my equipment at all times," I tell him and squeeze myself next to the cart. When the driver closes the back door and heads to his seat, I quickly uncover Will's face and see that he's asleep and still breathing. I keep his face uncovered throughout the trip so I can watch him.

David instructs the driver to pull over onto a side street next to the train terminal.

"I can let you off right in front," he says, confusion clear in his voice.

"We need a quiet place for a few minutes to file our reports," David tells him. This was not a rehearsed answer and I want to hug David for being so quick and believable. Then I want to kiss Judith for suggesting him to begin with. And then I want to kiss her some more, assuming we get back alive.

Isaac is parked on the street and we quickly remove our costumes and carefully lift Will into the well cushioned back seat. Hannah sits with him and David is in front.

By the time we get to the checkpoint, it is swarming with police.

There's an opening in the hidden rear section of the trunk next to where I'm lying to let in air. It also allows me to listen in on the conversation. I hear Isaac open the window.

"What's going on here?" he asks.

"Prisoner escape," says the guard. "That Chinese illegal." I roll my eyes. "We've been ordered to search every vehicle."

I hear doors open and about a minute later, the guard says, "Front's clean."

Isaac's voice is next. "Can we get back in?" Two doors close so I assume that he and David are in the car again. Then more doors are opened and I imagine Hannah is out. Now comes the real test.

"What's this?" asks the guard. And then, "Oh, wow, oh, okay. Sorry. Um, good *Shabbes* Isaac. You're good to go. We won't need to check the trunk."

As the car moves forward, I breathe out the longest breath I have ever held. I hear three voices speaking Hebrew and know they are praying their thanks to God. This would be a good time for me to pray my own thanks. I decide then and there to learn the prayers, not just the one to give thanks, but all of them. Getting through this mission has, of course, taken detailed planning and perfect execution. But still, there are so many things that could have gone wrong. We could have been discovered at any point. So it's entirely possible that maybe something greater than us was at work here. Something that has made me feel like I'm finally ready to take a leap of faith.

When we pull into Jeffrey's driveway, the trunk is opened and I am helped out by Hannah. We're both beaming at one another. She reaches for me and draws me into a hug. "I'm so glad you're here," she says.

I smile back at her. "Me too."

I wait to thank Isaac and David, especially David. It's time now to gently get Will into a real bed.

Isaac reaches into the back seat, removes a blue velvet cloth cover, and slowly lifts out a Torah scroll that was placed next to Will to distract the Jewish checkpoint police. It's clothed in burgundy velvet with Hebrew letters embroidered in gold. The thick, polished wooden dowels are visible at the top and bottom. Isaac kisses the velvet and looks up, still holding the Torah, and chants something in Hebrew.

Hannah takes my arm and points to Isaac. "We had help from the Highest of the High," she says. "We call the Torah the Tree of Life and today we've seen just how it lives up to that name."

CHAPTER TWENTY-TWO

Judith

I've never been so grateful for Friday early dismissal as I am today. I only wish it were the same for the boys' school. But the boys aren't expected to help their mothers prepare for the Sabbath the way we are, so when I step out of the school building, Jeffrey isn't walking up the street to meet me.

It would have been too suspicious for all of us to call in sick today, so only Hannah and Isaac did, while the rest of us went about our day like everything was normal.

As I walk down the front steps of the school, I notice a large crowd of girls standing together talking. Normally that wouldn't interest me since they usually talk about boys. But something makes me think today it might be a good idea to listen in.

"So scary," one of them says.

"He could be anywhere, even here."

"I heard the teachers say they're searching every car coming through the checkpoint."

"Are the Chinese dangerous? I've never met one," asks a younger girl, holding her older sister's hand.

"All illegals are dangerous," her sister tells her.

I want to shout, *He's not Chinese, he's Korean and not the least bit dangerous*, but of course I can't.

Instead, I rush over to Jeffrey's house knowing at least that Will is no longer in the hospital but also that the police are looking for him. What I still don't know for sure is whether Dani, Hannah, and David are all right.

Poor Jeffrey and Meyer; stuck in school for a few more hours. They must be going crazy, especially Jeffrey. Since the night Will was captured, Jeffrey's been crying on and off and refusing to eat, something I never thought he'd be capable of. My eyes sting with tears at the memory of Jeffrey at *kiddish*[21] after *Shabbes* morning services, a plate of food piled high and a big smile on his face. I just pray I get to see him like that again.

Mrs. Schwartz greets me at the door. "They're all inside, honey. *Shabbes* tonight is here. Your family is coming."

"Dani?" I ask. She can probably hear the fear in my voice.

"In the basement with Will." She points to the door leading downstairs. "Go," she says and smooths down my hair.

Dani is standing at the bottom of the steps looking up with a big smile on her face. I rush down the stairs and nearly tackle her as I grab hold of her.

"Shh, Will's sleeping," she says into my ear and then plants a soft kiss on my neck.

"How is he?"

"Still recovering. Come see."

She leads me to a daybed against the rear wall of the basement. This room looks like a larger version of the workroom at Mr. Schwartz's shop. Wooden tables crowded with metal and plastic parts. Blenders, food processors, sewing machines, clocks of all types disemboweled with wires sticking out at all angles. At least the floor is clear, likely Mrs. Schwartz's handiwork.

Will is lying on his back, dressed in loose navy sweatpants and a navy sweatshirt with one sleeve cut off because of his cast. The sweatshirt's zipper is open, and I can see the white bandages that are keeping his broken ribs stable. His good arm is at his side with his hand resting on his stomach.

---

21 A buffet lunch served to a congregation after Saturday morning Sabbath services

I'm relieved to see the slight movement of his chest that tells me he's breathing. There's another bandage on his forehead but his face is relaxed, his mouth slightly open.

I feel a strange desire to get a sketchpad and pencil and draw him in this position. Embarrassed at the thought, I look away and instead softly recite the *r'fuah sh'leimah*, the prayer for healing. I hope he's sleeping peacefully. Resting will help him recover.

Dani and I turn at the sound of somebody coming down the stairs. I haven't seen Hannah and Isaac yet, so maybe that's who it is. But instead Naomi Blau, who's also been dismissed from school early, walks over to us and stands next to Dani looking down at Will. She's kept her hair short and has already changed out of her school clothes into dark blue jeans and a light pink button-down shirt. I wonder if her father, Bernard Blau, one of the most prominent citizens of our community, knows how she's dressing.

Naomi leans in front of Dani and looks over at me. "Judith, Reb Isaac is upstairs and wants to talk to you."

It's sweet that she's addressing him this way. I always try, but Isaac and I are just about the same age since I'll be eighteen in a few months, and he was my friend before he was my rabbi, so I don't always remember.

As much as I'd like to see Isaac and Hannah, it's hard for me to break away from Dani. There's always this pull toward her.

"Right now?" I ask Naomi. "Can't it wait?"

I feel Dani's arm encircle my shoulders. "Go ahead," she tells me. "I'll be right here. I'm sure Isaac has a good reason."

* * *

At *Shabbes* dinner, Dani and Binyamin resume the argument they started the night Will was arrested.

"They were going to send him to Dallas in a few days," she says forcefully, her fork raised for emphasis. "We had to act quickly."

"This little scheme of yours has placed us all in danger," her brother responds, anger clear in his voice. "Now everyone is being searched at the checkpoint and I've heard they may go house to house looking for him."

"And what if he needs more medical attention?" adds Solly. "That will mean finding a doctor we can trust who won't turn us all in."

"Sophie knows people," says Meyer with a wave of his hand that brushes off Solly's concerns.

At Binyamin's questioning look, Meyer explains about Sophie and how she helped us by gathering information about Will.

"There was no telling what they would have done to him in Dallas to get him to talk," says Isaac in his calm, rabbi voice. "It's likely we saved his life, and you know the Talmud in Sanhedrin 37a says that if you save one life, you save the entire world."

Binyamin sighs aloud with exasperation but stays quiet so as not to challenge Isaac on Talmudic interpretation.

"Let's just hope everyone at this table can be counted among those in the *entire world* who get saved," says Solly with more than a note of sarcasm.

"Well now he's stuck here, thanks to all of you," says Binyamin with resignation in his voice. "I doubt there's going to be very much the UPR can do for him if he's a fugitive."

The only good thing about this conversation is that Jeffrey isn't hearing any of it. He's downstairs watching Will and hasn't left his side since returning from school. At least he finally agreed to eat something.

After Mrs. Schwartz lit the *Shabbes* candles I went into the kitchen and piled a plate high with food and brought it down to him along with a bowl of soup. He looked at me for maybe five seconds, pointed to an open spot on a nearby table and went right back to focusing on Will.

"You'll eat, right?" I asked.

"Yeah, yeah," he said in a way that made me feel dismissed.

CHAPTER TWENTY-THREE

Jeffrey

I shovel brisket into my mouth while staring at Will as his eyes slowly open. Lowering the plate to the floor, I lean over toward him.

"Hi there, pal. You're safe now, back with the Chosen People." I'm not sure he gets the joke.

"Jeffrey?" His voice is groggy and hoarse. "You're here? In the hospital?"

I smile at him. "Nope. *You're* here in my basement. It isn't much to look at, but it beats a prison hospital."

"But how? Did they...?"

"Discharge you to me? No way. The Minyan of Resistance—well mostly the younger members–orchestrated an ingenious prison break and brought you here."

His face is a question, so I explain what happened, who did what, and all of the various costumes that had to be created, including the fake arm cast.

His eyes are wide with amazement. "So they don't know I'm gone?"

"They know now, but as you can see, they haven't found you yet, and we'll make sure they don't. But you're confined to the house or any other hiding place we think of because they're out there looking, and as always the Jews are their number one suspects."

"Where is everybody else? I want to thank them."

"Upstairs having *Shabbes* dinner. Oh, that reminds me, you need to eat."

I help him sit up a bit, which puts a little pressure on his ribs, causing him to wince and moan. Once he's in position, I have him hold the bowl with his good hand and spoon chicken soup into his mouth.

"Mmmm, this is helping my throat." His voice is less hoarse.

"They don't call chicken soup Jewish penicillin for nothing, bro." I realize I've started to use some of his UPR lingo. "It's a universal cure for just about anything, and my mother's is the best."

"Jeff, listen," Will says after he's eaten about half the soup. "I messed up, big time."

I shake my head at him. "No, no, you saved Dani, Hannah, and Solly. They got away because of you."

He hands me back the bowl and spoon and looks down at his lap. "They got my iBrain," he whispers. "I forgot to leave it back here. I'm just so used to having it with me all the time."

"I know." I lower the bowl down onto the floor next to me and put my hand on his good arm, squeezing it gently. "It was a mistake. We all make them, especially me."

He looks at me and now he's shaking his head. "It's major, man. We're screwed because of me."

"It's already taken care of. Everyone in the GFS with an iBrain has been told to stop using it and we're going back to emails and papercuts. A bit slower, but it worked before and Judith can, you know, snip, snip quite fast." I smile at him. "She's a real speed demon with those scissors of hers."

"Jeffrey, come up and have dessert," my father calls out in a loud whisper from the top of the stairs.

I tell him Will is awake so he leaves the basement door open, and while Will and I continue eating, we listen to our family and friends singing and telling stories about ancient rabbis encountering hidden prophets.

Will doesn't eat anything other than the soup, but that's enough for now. Maybe solid food would hurt his ribs. I don't know. I'm no doctor.

I set him back down to relax as we listen to the singing. I'm usually not a big fan of any of the *Shabbes* stuff other than the food, but the thought of my parents and friends up there bringing in the Sabbath together fills me with an emotion that constricts my throat and brings tears to my eyes.

I look over at Will and he's smiling, but also trying to fight the urge to drop off to sleep. I smooth his forehead. "Go ahead and close your eyes. You can sleep easy now."

I watch him give in to it. His face is calm with a small smile lingering. Looking at him like that just heightens my emotional reaction and I feel the tears escape and roll down my cheeks. At least now I'm silently crying from happiness and gratitude. I hear the words and melody of *Tov l'hodot* from upstairs and I whisper along.

It is a good thing to give thanks to God, and to sing praises unto God's name, O Most High

When the song ends, I can just about make out Isaac's voice beginning a story about the Baal Shem Tov[22], probably something about a poor shepherd or farmer becoming a revered rabbi and scholar. They all seem to go that way.

I stare again at Will and let the feelings I've held back come into my consciousness. I love him. He's strong and smart and cocky and impetuous, but also warm and caring. He didn't have to leave the comfort of the UPR to fight alongside people he had no connection to. But he did because he knows it's the right thing and he wants to be part of what's right.

I lean over and plant a soft kiss on his forehead. "I love you Will," I whisper so I don't wake him.

I've always been drawn to Isaac and I guess you could say he was my first, real crush. But this is different. Will Kim is my first, real love. A boy who's also gay. A boy who would never

---

22 The revered founder of Hasidism.

hurt me. Who's patiently taught me so many things. A boy. I love him.

* * *

Dani, Judith, Hannah, and Isaac all take turns sitting with Will over the next week. I try to figure out a way to get Meyer down to our basement, but even the bulkhead has steps. At least he's able to come into the house through the ramp my father and I built after Meyer and I became friends. Given how few friends I had before, I think my father would have done anything to make it possible for the one friend I had back then to visit.

I lost the battle with my parents about staying home from school to look after Will. My mother said she was perfectly capable of feeding him and getting him up when he needed to use the bathroom. I'm not sure how helpful it's been for me to spend any time at Kushner Academy for Boys since all I do is sit in class wondering how Will is doing and counting the minutes until I'm back home with him. But, as I said, I lost that fight.

Tonight, Dani comes by and she and I take dinner down to Will, the three of us eating together. Then she shoos me away after my father asks me to come up and watch the news with him.

I've never been all that interested in the news. It's usually just more propaganda about the perfect lives we've been given in the GFS. There's only so much one can roll their eyes before they start to ache with the effort. But now that things have gotten worse for the Jews and seem to get even more horrible every day; and now that the hunt is on for the so-called "illegal," the news at least gives me some sense of what these antisemitic goons are up to.

I bring up our dinner plates to save my mother another trip up and down the stairs and take my seat on the old living room couch that's seen better days. My mother keeps covering it with a series of different fabrics draped over the back and the seat cushions. Inevitably, something spills, and the cover is soon replaced with a new one. Tonight, it's a silky olive-green fabric that she's tucked in all around to keep it from slipping off.

The news opens with coverage of the presidential campaign and a new poll showing the race very close. After a second story that I half listen to about a Christian mission to the Middle East, the anchor announces a "special report" on the status of the search for the "UPR illegal" and his likely connection to the Jews.

A young reporter with more hair on the top of his head than he apparently knows what to do with, speaks into his handheld mic. "We've learned that the illegal is not Chinese or Japanese as originally thought, but a Korean from the UPR named Ji-Joon Kim. Just eighteen years old, it is not yet known how he entered the GFS or who he's working with."

I'm a little amused they finally figured out Will is Korean but worried that they now know his name and age.

"Growing evidence," the reporter continues, "points to an alliance with Jewish radicals in the Cincinnati area who helped the illegal interrupt President Fairleigh's campaign event with distortions of history meant to drum up sympathy for GFS's Jews."

So now I'm a radical. I have a feeling that'll please Dani very much from all she's told me about the UPR.

The screen splits and a second man, older, gray-haired with wire-frame glasses appears.

"Our guest this evening is Dr. Charles Kingsley, head of the Institute for Historical Accuracy. Dr. Kingsley, thank you for being here. Can you shed some light on the meaning of the messages that the illegal and his accomplices unleashed on an unsuspecting public?"

I roll my eyes, knowing that whatever this guy is about to say will be the very definition of a distortion and the exact opposite of accuracy.

Kingsley nods. "Yes, of course. These half-truths are very typical of what we often see from Jews bent on playing the victim, raising their suffering above everyone else's. It would be like you or me constantly going on and on about how the Romans fed Christians to the lions."

I wonder if Binyamin Fine is listening to this garbage comparing the murder of Jews in the Holocaust to Christians in ancient Rome. I bet that six million of them weren't murdered in the span of a decade, and that doesn't even begin to account for the persecution of Jews over hundreds of years before.

If my father weren't sitting next to me, I'd switch off the screen right now, unwilling to listen to another word from this charlatan. But I sit tight as he continues.

"Just the fact that they would exploit the story of the teenage Anne Frank to their own ends shows the lengths they will go to distract us from the facts."

The reporter breaks in at this point. "Can you set the record straight for our audience?"

"I'd be happy to. When this country was founded, we generously extended residency to Jews from the former United States and granted them the religious freedom they'd been wanting for years. We left them alone to pursue their faith and customs, even though many were antithetical to our new Christian nation. We gave them permission to send their young men to the Israeli army and to visit the Holy Land whenever they chose. And yes, Marianna Fredricks, daughter of a beloved US president, herself a Jewish convert, was helpful in setting up our government, even serving in the first cabinet. But very quickly her influence diminished, and after her father's death, she was effectively sidelined. To now lift her up as some kind of icon is just ridiculous."

So much for the revered President's Daughter, our great protector. I want to interrupt and ask my father if this is true, if the President's Daughter lost her power to protect us. But I know better than to bother him while he's watching the news. It's like a second religion to him. Instead, I sit there and continue to listen to this jerk.

"Look, this country gave the Jews everything and all we got in return was a public safety headache that's left us with no choice but to restrict their access to areas where the public could not be harmed."

"So illuminating," says the reporter nodding. "Dr. Kingsley, thank you for coming on the show and helping us separate fact from fiction. Now back to you, Bob."

I shake my head and utter "Unbelievable" under my breath. My father responds by shushing me.

The anchor appears. "Before we break for a commercial, we've just learned from Janice Chandler, our correspondent in Dallas, that the House will vote tomorrow on the bill to revoke the citizenship of Jews living in the GFS, reducing them to guest status. The legislation is expected to pass and could reach the president's desk as early as next week."

A commercial begins, advertising the newest release of the home helpers that my father refuses to buy. He clicks off the screen.

I look at my papa. "So much for historical accuracy."

He sighs. "Jeffrey, these are people who will lie to your face even if you are watching the truth right in front of your eyes on a video screen. They have no shame."

We're interrupted by a knock on the door. Binyamin stands before me with a look of dread on his face that I've been seeing a lot lately, not just on him, but on almost everyone.

My mother runs in from the kitchen and offers him many things to eat and drink. He knows better than to refuse her, so he agrees to a cup of tea.

"I'll bring it with a slice of the honey cake Jeffrey made. It's delicious."

Binyamin smiles at me. "Nice to see you back in the kitchen, Chef."

I shrug. "Yeah, well, gotta keep the masses fed."

At my father's gesture toward the armchair, Binyamin sits, his legs spread apart and his hands pressed together pointing forward. "Listen, I have some concerning news. Someone from Baruch Rausch's office dropped off a press release at the paper that will be in tomorrow's edition."

"What does that traitor want now?" I ask.

Binyamin takes a deep breath. "There'll be a house-to-house search in the community starting tomorrow to look for Will. Rausch has put his son Simeon in charge."

Just the mention of the snake is enough to make me feel like I'm going to lose my dinner.

"So…" Binyamin continues.

"There's no time to waste," my father picks up the thought. "We have to figure out where we can hide Will."

* * *

Let's hope this idea that Dani and Meyer cooked up, to create a smaller version of the underground room that Dani has at home to keep her family safe during a superstorm, works to hide Will when the snake and his goons come knocking.

Dani stands by the wall we've drilled into in my basement with a diagram in her hand, acting like she's the foreman at a construction site. *A little to the left there, to the right here.* I'm waiting to see if she's actually gonna grab a shovel and do a little manual labor like the rest of us.

"I hope this works," I say as I wipe the sweat off my forehead before it drips into my eyes. "All this hiding didn't turn out so great for Anne Frank, you know."

Dani looks back at me, shaking her head. "It'll be fine Jeffrey, if none of us betray Will. That's how Anne Frank was captured. Did you know she was on the last train of Jews deported out of Amsterdam? That's how close she came to surviving the war."

"More work, less talk," Solly barks at us. "They could be here any day, and Dani, you'll have to get in there with Will. No one knows there are two so-called illegals here and I'd like to keep it that way."

Luckily, my papa has all the tools we need to drill into the basement wall, create a short passageway and then a room just large enough for two chairs for Will and Dani, plus water and snacks, of course. Meyer assured me multiple times that he's done the calculations and there will be enough oxygen to keep the two of them alive for the time it takes Simeon and his goons to conduct their search. We just have to make sure when we see them coming down the street, we get Dani and Will into the little room and close things up so the hidden door is actually hidden.

My papa has always had a suspicious streak. Some might even call him paranoid. He thinks the little round helpers that

Judith's mother uses to recite recipes or time an egg boiling in a pot are really secret listening devices that the government uses to spy on us. He watches the news every night so, as he says, he can always stay one step ahead of "them."

But perhaps the pinnacle of my papa's paranoia can be found in the faux brick paneling that covers our basement walls. It's the best wall covering for creating a hidden door, which he's already drilled out along the lines of mortar surrounding each brick.

When I asked him why we couldn't just use a moveable bookcase like they do in the movies, he said that was too obvious. I think he's giving Simeon and his buffoons way too much credit.

We were smart to start right away because they begin their search of the neighborhood on our street. We have just enough time to get Will and Dani into their little room. Luckily, Will's ribs are healing well so he no longer needs to be bedridden. He's even been up in the kitchen with me a few times. One night I surprised him and made his spicy *kimchee* with a modified version of what he calls *bibimbap*, though it looked more like a plate of vegetables, rice, and cubed chicken with a fried egg on top. As they say, it's the thought that counts.

The knock on the door is persistent and loud. As we discussed ahead of time, my father answers and politely ushers them in.

Simeon stares daggers at me and I look right back at him unafraid, even though my heart is racing thinking of Will and Dani behind the basement wall.

"I want a top-to-bottom search of this house. Leave no stone unturned." He sneers at me as he walks by. "I don't trust these people at all."

"Mr. Rausch," my father says.

"It's Officer Rausch," he growls.

"Of course, Officer Rausch. We have nothing to hide and will stay out of the way of you and your men while you do your business."

I smile to myself, trying not to laugh out loud, knowing that "do your business" is my father's phrase for going to the toilet.

They run upstairs and I'm sure they are ransacking everything they can get their hands on. Even though I hate the thought of Simeon touching anything of mine, the only thing I didn't want him to find was my iBrain, which I sent into hiding with Will and Dani. In fact, they have just about everyone's iBrains in there while these searches are going on.

I hear the thuds of our possessions being dumped on the floors of our bedrooms and heavy feet walking from room to room. Finally they emerge, and now we get to witness just what they will do to our living room and kitchen. More destructive dumping.

After this second act of barbarism, they head downstairs to the basement. As we agreed, only my father goes with them. With the door open, I can hear everything.

"Did we tell you to come down here with us?" Simeon shouts at my father.

The longer he's here the more I want to once again use my Krav Maga and leave him on the floor in agonizing pain. But I know that assaulting a police officer would only land me in jail and I have no interest in living through another separation from Will or becoming the reason for Dani and Meyer to plan another prison break.

"Officer Rausch," my father says in a voice filled with politeness that makes me cringe to hear him belittling himself to this barbarian, "as you know I own a shop that uses many of the same tools that I store here in my basement. I am happy to have you look around down here, but I ask that you not destroy anything that could hurt my livelihood."

"We'll do what we need to do," he responds in that same mean tone he's been using.

I hear things being moved, the sounds of metal clanging as it hits the concrete floor.

"Look for a secret door down here," Simeon instructs his minions, causing my throat to close in fear. My mother comes over and puts her arm around me and I pull close seeking the same comfort I had from her as a child.

Finally there's the deafening sound of their boots on the stairs. I move away from my mother and watch as they come back up followed by my father.

"Schwartz," Simeon says, standing over me, "I don't know what you think you're playing at but you'll never get away with it."

I still say nothing and keep my face as neutral as I can, showing neither fear nor anger.

Simeon turns to the others and gestures to our back door. "Men," he says. "Let's take a look at the backyard, and then over to the next house."

He waits while they all leave and then turns back to the three of us. "We'll be watching you," he says in what passes for him as an ominous tone. Then he's gone and my father peers through the kitchen window for a good five minutes until at last he looks over at us and says, "They're gone."

CHAPTER TWENTY-FOUR

Dani

When Jeffrey opens the door, and Will and I emerge from the little room, I get a quick hug and notice a much longer embrace between the boys. Could something be going on with them? I just hope Will understands how new this all is for Jeffrey and how tender his heart may be if Will is his first love. I know how that was the case for me with Aisha.

But I have no idea if I'm even reading this right. I have so little experience with boys that it's possible I'm misjudging what I'm seeing. I guess time will tell.

For the next few hours, Jeffrey and I, along with his parents, put the house back in order. Closets emptied with their contents thrown everywhere. Blankets and sheets littering the bedroom floors. Everything on a shelf in every room was pulled off. Anything delicate was broken, including a set of glass candlesticks that Jeffrey's parents received as a wedding gift. When I look over at Mrs. Schwartz, her cheeks are wet with tears.

I notice Jeffrey and his father kissing the bindings of religious books before placing them back on their bookcases. At my questioning look, Mr. Schwartz explains that this is respect and love for holy writings that include the name of God. For some reason, this gesture makes me choke up with emotion and I turn away before Jeffrey sees the look of awe on my face and makes some kind of sarcastic joke. I can't believe that Simeon Rausch and his men would be so intent on searching for Will that they would throw holy books off the shelves.

They invite me to stay for dinner but after all of this, I need some time alone to process everything.

"I don't want you out by yourself, Dani, no matter how careful you promise to be," Mr. Schwartz tells me.

I was hoping the walk back to Binyamin's would help clear my head but maybe riding in a car, once again covered up by a blanket or a tarp, is the safer plan. If I'd become too preoccupied by my thoughts on a walk, I could very well make some stupid mistake, especially with Simeon roaming the neighborhood .

Miriam is helping the children with homework so I volunteer to start dinner.

"Oh Dani, that would be great. There's defrosted flounder filets in the *milchig* refrigerator. If you could bread them and get them frying, and prepare baked potatoes and a salad, I would be eternally grateful. I'll be in to help as soon as I can."

I'm happy for the time alone. By this point, I know my way around a kosher kitchen, so I easily find the flounder on a shelf in the dairy refrigerator. The meal prep is pretty simple so I have time to think about the issues that have been pressing on my mind since the day we freed Will.

It's true that I miss home and my parents and friends. And it's also true that I'm living in a community under siege where I have even less legal status than the GFS Jews. Yet, these problems aren't preoccupying me. Instead, I keep picturing Mr. Schwartz kissing the bindings of those books. I keep remembering the sound of the prayer of gratitude chanted by Hannah, Isaac, and David as we drove past the checkpoint after rescuing Will. These memories have triggered a longing in me for something that until now, I've never known I needed.

Is this how it started for my brother way back when? Did he witness something that summer he was in Israel that ignited a yearning for a deeper connection with, with…what? God? Judaism? Prayer? I'm not sure. I just know something has changed in me while living here and it's about more than my feelings for Judith.

I've been learning a little Hebrew with her but aside from enjoying the time we spend together, the lessons haven't brought up these newer feelings. Instead, it's been like learning a new language, something I'd do at home, in school or online. I've thought of it as a challenge—figuring out how to read unfamiliar letters grouped into words running from right to left.

But what I'm feeling now is more spiritual instead of intellectual. It's lodged in my body. Judith would probably say it's seeped into my soul and she could be right. But actually, I feel it in my solar plexus, right in the center of my being. It's the longing for a magic key that will unlock something in me. That will enable me to develop reflexes I want but don't have, like automatically reciting a prayer of gratitude without thinking. Like recognizing the holiness of an object and kissing it to express my love. I want these things to be part of me, unconscious actions that are as natural as breathing.

While I'm watching the fish filets in the frying pan, getting ready to turn them over, Miriam joins me in the kitchen. "The boys are able to finish their homework without me and Chava is busy coloring, so what still needs to be done?"

"Can I ask you something?" I begin.

When she hums yes, I take the plunge. "Why did Binyamin become Orthodox? Was it just so he could marry you?"

She smiles and a short chuckle escapes. "No, he told me that's how your mother explains it, but I think he always had a desire for a deeper connection with *Hashem*."

"Like a yearning?"

She hesitates and all I hear is the scritch of the peeler against the cucumber she's holding. "I guess you could call it that. He said at the time he felt he'd suddenly woken up to himself. To be honest, Dani, I don't think your brother could have made the transition from a secular life in the UPR to our life here as Orthodox Jews without a spiritual need that wasn't focused on wanting to be with me. This is the kind of change that has to come from deep inside you. Otherwise it will feel forced, like an imposition. But you might want to ask him to explain it."

I check the potatoes wrapped in foil in the oven. The tines of a fork slide in without too much trouble. They're nearly ready.

"I'm going through something, Miriam, that I can't fully explain yet, even to myself. And it's not because of Judith. It's like a longing for something, something more." I tell her about the prayer uttered in the car and the books. "It's like they did these things automatically, without thinking. I think I want to learn to be like that. I think I need to."

We hear them before they come running into the kitchen. Three pairs of little feet coming toward us, and Yacov's high pitched voice, "Mama, we're hungry."

Miriam comes over to me and puts an arm around my shoulders. "This is a big realization, Dani. Why don't we pick it up again after the children are in bed? Binyamin has a governing council meeting after dinner, so it'll just be you and me."

It's quiet in the living room when Miriam and I finally get to sit down with mugs of hot tea set on coasters placed on the low table in front of us. We're both seated at an angle toward one another.

"It feels almost like a luxury to be able to sit and have an adult conversation after the children are asleep," Miriam says and smiles. "So tell me more about what's going on for you."

Hesitating, I lift my mug and blow on the tea before taking a first sip. The action takes me back to that day in the UPR with Julia after we found out that Judith's father had been murdered. I'd gone deep into myself, grief and resolve winding themselves around one another. I hold back a smile remembering how I'd turned the tea into a sympathetic friend, worried that Julia wouldn't understand my need to be with Judith.

"Part of it is wanting to learn more about Judaism. I mean, Judith is already teaching me some Hebrew, but what I want to learn are the deeper, more spiritual things."

Miriam sets her mug down. "There are many ways to learn, Dani. Our way here is one way certainly, a bit easier if it's what you've grown up with, but not impossible to absorb and practice much like Binyamin has. But as your brother has told me, there are Jews in the UPR who observe in a variety of different ways."

I nod. "Yes, I met that rabbi, Roberta Weissberg. She leads a synagogue in the UPR."

"Right. She's the one who was hoping to get Isaac into a rabbinical program. Well, that is, before we had to stop using iBrains."

The thought of why we can't use our iBrains stops us both. Poor Will is so down on himself about that even though Jeffrey and I have tried to reassure him. And though I don't blame him for the mistake he made, I have to admit what we've sacrificed by not using our iBrains. It was the only way my parents and my friends could reach us. It was the only way the Resistance throughout the GFS could stay in touch.

Miriam interrupts these thoughts when she turns toward me and holds up a finger as if she's figured something out. "Our young Rebel Rabbi Isaac has introduced so many new rituals and ideas into our services. I never thought I'd be able to pray seated next to my husband, and now that I do, it feels so natural and more and more obvious that *Hashem* would approve of this if it's what we choose to do. So some of those reflexes, as you call them, are just what we've been told are what's required. But as we create this new minyan, we're able to study and figure out what is truly *halacha*, meaning what is commanded of us by *Hashem*, and what is merely custom and tradition that can be molded to our purposes and re-created."

My mouth is open as I take in the full meaning of what Miriam is saying. "You know," I begin, my hands open in front of me like I'm holding onto something, "I think because I've never been to the synagogue that you all grew up in, the one where Isaac's father is the rabbi, where the women sit separate from the men, the only way I've experienced and observed Judaism is through the minyan that Isaac leads. So because he's being more creative and treating women and men as equals, I can develop these reflexes I want from him, and also from Judith and all of you."

Miriam nods. "Yes, while Isaac's observances are very rooted in Torah, he's opening us up to new interpretations and rituals that seem more infused with meaning than those from his father's shul and more connected to the challenges we are facing. Like teaching us an old Yiddish partisans' song from the time of the Shoah. It's a song that speaks of hope and purpose even when facing tremendous danger."

I take in Miriam's words about these new rituals and interpretations that balance change with the Orthodox Judaism that the members of the minyan have always practiced. Maybe this is the path for me. I wouldn't have to sacrifice my own values about justice and equity in order to have the spiritual life I seem to be craving. It's starting to feel like this is all coming together.

Excited about what lies ahead, and grateful to Miriam for the insights she's given me, I spring forward and throw my arms around her. "Thank you!" I exclaim.

She's laughing at this sudden show of affection. "For what?"

I pull back but am all but bouncing up and down on the couch. "For this." I move my hand back and forth between us. "For giving me a way to find a path. You know?"

I stand and pick up my mug to bring it back to the kitchen. Miriam looks at me with confusion, her head tilted to the side. "Where are you going?"

I realize that I've suddenly ended our conversation. "Oh, sorry. I just have so much to think about, I'm excited to get started and I can't wait to share it all with Judith."

CHAPTER TWENTY-FIVE

Judith

I've made more papercuts in these last few weeks than I can count. Before I was asked to hide secret messages in my art, I'd spend a week, maybe two, creating something intricate that wasn't just a repeat of what I'd made before. Now that the codes are the main reason for the papercuts, the designs are simple—a small tree, the Star of David, a Torah scroll. These are papercuts that take about an hour to complete. Much more time is devoted to cutting out the Hebrew letters that contain hidden messages for the Independent Jewish Network throughout the GFS.

After we learned that the police had Will's iBrain and we could no longer communicate that way, Binyamin wrote an article in the newspaper praising how art is used to celebrate Jewish culture. He then announced that each issue of the *Jewish Community News* would include photos of papercuts created by various artists, all fake names to protect my identity. These are the papercuts with the hidden messages for the members of the Independent Jewish Network.

Between this time-consuming task, schoolwork, and preparing for my big day tomorrow at Shabbat services, I've had very little free time to spend with Dani. That's been the worst part of all of this. I have no idea how long she's going to be able to stay in the GFS, and there's still so much we need to share and discuss. Can there be any future for us beyond this visit? Why would she even want to stay here permanently, given the way things are going for Jews in this country? Would I even want that for her?

These last few days, with Chanukah approaching, I've been given a short break from both schoolwork and creating papercuts for the newspaper. Tonight, the first night of the holiday, is also Shabbat, so I've been working with my mother to clean the house like I would normally do on a Friday. Dani should be here any minute to help make the potato *latkes*. She told me that making *latkes* for Chanukah is one of the few Jewish activities she learned from her mother.

I want to know more about her parents. Sometimes when she talks about her mother, she tells me how much she admires her work as a scientist traveling all over the UPR to help people deal with the superstorms and the floods. Other times, Dani will complain about how rigid and controlling she is. How she's angry at Binyamin for moving here, refusing to understand why "becoming religious," as Dani calls it, was something he felt he needed to do. Dani says her mother actually blames Miriam for all of Binyamin's decisions, as if his wife had forced him.

I wonder what Dani's mother would make of me, similar in some ways to her daughter-in-law, and probably in her mind, a bad influence on Dani. Dani says her parents have no problem with the fact that she likes girls or, I suppose, that Jeffrey likes boys. That amazes me, especially when I think about what my own mother would say if she knew the real nature of my relationship with Dani, at least as much of it as I've been able to figure out so far. I can't imagine she'd react in the same way that Dani's parents have, and at this point I don't want to find out.

Three short buzzes on the doorbell, the signal we agreed to, and I know it's her. When I open the door, I see a boy with a yarmulka, white *tzitzit* fringes sticking out from under his shirt, and one of Jeffrey's navy school blazers. The adorable face, complete with a wide grin and sparkling eyes, belongs to Dani. I take her by the arm, pull her inside and she envelops me in a hug. Immediately I'm filled with that warmth I always feel when she is this close. She smells like the fresh air from outside and faintly like coconut shampoo.

"Judith, was that Dani?"

I pull away quickly at the sound of my mother's voice but not before Dani plants a tiny kiss on my lips. Even that small kiss causes a vibration radiating through my chest. "Yes, she's here," I call out, and the two of us chuckle quietly.

My mother sets us up with a ten-pound bag of white potatoes, a five-pound bag of onions, peelers, knives and cutting boards. The peeled potatoes will be dropped into large bowls of water to prevent them from turning brown before they are cut and fed into the food processor along with the onions. Once the mixture is ready, we'll squeeze out the moisture and add eggs, matzoh meal and salt and pepper.

We've been left to this task while my mother goes upstairs to finish cleaning with my sister, Leah. We don't expect Morty home from school for at least another hour.

Dani is peeling the dried brown layers off the onions, wiping her eyes every minute. "If the onions are annoying you, we can switch," I tell her. "They don't seem to bother me much, and it makes me sad to see you cry."

"Maybe in a little while. I'm okay for now." She pulls another onion out of the bag. "Naomi Blau came by my brother's last night."

"Oh?"

"Yeah, it was kind of strange. He and Miriam took her into his study and stayed there for like an hour."

I smile, knowing just what they were doing. Dani looks over at me. "You know something, Judith Braverman. C'mon, spill."

I can't keep the smile off my face as I shake my head. "It's a surprise, but I promise, you only have to wait till tomorrow."

"You won't even tell me, your one and only *bashert*?"

"Shh, not so loud." I take a few steps toward her and the scent of the onions fills my nose. "It's because you *are* my *bashert* that I want to surprise you," I whisper in her ear. She turns her head and I'm rewarded with another peck on the lips.

Once I'm back peeling potatoes, I pick up our conversation. "You know how I told you I had trouble seeing Naomi's soul?"

"Mmmhmm."

"Well, last time I saw her, it finally came through, nice and sparkly. I wonder why?"

"I think I know," says Dani, looking very satisfied with herself. "And unlike you, I will reveal all and not keep you in suspense."

I stop peeling and turn to her. "All right. As you would say, spill."

She smiles. "You're so cute."

I blush in response and then motion with my head for her to continue.

"Okay, so this is gonna take a bit of explanation. The bottom line is that Naomi is enby. Non-binary."

This must be another one of Dani's UPR terms because I have no idea what she's talking about. "I need a translation."

"Yeah, well, you see, um..." She's kind of motioning with her arms, which I've learned is her way of trying to figure out how to explain something. "You know how Naomi cut her hair and sometimes wears pants and sometimes dresses?"

I nod.

"Well, that's because she doesn't feel like she's completely female all the time. Sometimes inside her she feels like she's a boy and other times she's comfortable being the gender she was assigned at birth. That's non-binary, at least it is for her."

Even though I know every word she's said is English, I have no idea what Dani's just told me. "How can she feel like a boy when she's a girl?"

Dani places the onion she's holding down on the cutting board and walks over to me. "Judith, try to keep an open mind, okay?"

I also stop what I'm doing and give my entire attention to our conversation. "I want to understand but you have to help me. Just like with everything you're having to learn here, there are things you grew up with that are completely foreign to me."

She nods and reaches over to touch my arm. "Okay. So." She takes a deep breath. "There's male and female, right?" She gestures with her right-hand palm down. "Male." Then does the same with her left. "Female." She keeps both hands in place. "That's the gender binary. Either or. Okay?"

"Right."

"But for some people the binary doesn't fit because they don't feel wholly like one or the other, or maybe they feel like neither."

I look back and forth at her hands marking the sides of this binary she's described. "How can someone be neither?"

"Well, first you have to separate the concept of sex, meaning the parts of our bodies, from gender, how we feel inside about ourselves. So, for Naomi, even though her sex is female, at times she feels and wants to express herself as a boy, while other times she's comfortable expressing her gender to conform to her sex—female."

The picture of Dani at my front door dressed as a boy enters my mind. With her short hair and male clothes, she's been able to convince people she's Daniel, Miriam's cousin from Louisville. That leads me to ask a question that feels a bit urgent.

"Is this how you feel too? That you're also a boy?"

Dani shakes her head slowly. "I've thought about that from time to time, but I don't think so. Did you ask because I make such a convincing Orthodox boy?" Her smile is wide and I know she's teasing me.

"Uh, I can't say the thought didn't occur to me."

She nods. "Yeah, it's true that I don't express my gender like you or Hannah, wearing dresses and skirts and keeping my hair long. But that's because I've always felt more comfortable in jeans and a hoodie. In the UPR there's more leeway for that. The gender binary is less rigid. So as someone whose sex and gender are both female, I can still do what feels right for me and be a little gender non-conforming in the traditional sense. Do you understand?"

I turn back to the potatoes, knowing my mother will be annoyed if we aren't making progress.

"Judith?" Dani's voice is close to pleading.

"I'm thinking about it."

I hear the crunch of the dried outer layer of an onion that tells me Dani is back at work. "Just one other thing," she says. "Because I was able to explain all this to Naomi, she now has the words to describe what she's been feeling. Instead of thinking she's crazy or abnormal. That's why I think you've been able to see her soul. Before, her soul was kind of blocked, not just from you but from her too."

For some reason, this last explanation completely makes sense to me and opens a door to everything Dani has said. Maybe it's because she's finally explained things using an image that is part of my world, this gift I have for seeing souls. It's provided the key I needed to unlock my mind.

I finish peeling a potato, drop it into a bowl of water on the counter, take a few steps toward Dani peeling onions at the kitchen table, and stand close behind her. "I'm starting to understand. Thank you." I place a soft kiss under her ear and walk back to the counter where most of the ten-pound bag of potatoes awaits me.

Except for the sounds of crunching onion layers, scraping peelers, and knives cutting against wooden boards we're silent until Dani says, her voice a bit hesitant, "While we're on the subject of big revelations there's something else I wanted to talk to you about. That is if your brain isn't already close to exploding."

I chuckle and do my best to respond in kind. "Will it require more translation?"

"I don't think so. It's about me."

I want to keep up this light conversation, but I'm filled with dread, convinced she's decided to sneak back across the border. After Will's arrest, I have little confidence Dani could get back home safely. Plus, how would it feel to not have her here with me? When would we see each other again? "Okay," I say slowly, trying to keep the fear out of my voice, but knowing I haven't succeeded.

"Stop worrying. I'm pretty sure this will make you happy."

Now I have no idea what she's about to tell me.

"You know how you've been teaching me a little Hebrew? Well, while that's been fun and interesting, I've realized it's not enough. I want to learn how to become a more observant Jew, not just by learning a language or the rules for keeping kosher, but also, you know, inside me. Do you get what I mean?"

The first question that comes into my head is whether I'm hearing this right. Does Dani want to become Orthodox like her brother? Once again, I stop what I'm doing and turn to her. She's already abandoned the onions and is facing me wiping tears from her eyes with her sleeve. I'm not sure if they're from the onions or because of what she's telling me.

"Can you explain more about that?" I ask. But before she has a chance to answer, the full meaning of what she's said takes hold of me and I run over and hug her. I feel her body shake with laughter.

"This was unexpected since you seemed not to understand what I'm saying."

I pull back but still stand close. "I want to know all of it. I just want you to know how much this means to me."

"I get that. But I want you to understand this is something I figured out I need for myself. It's not just because I want to be with you." She takes my hand. "You know what I mean?"

I bite down on my lower lip and nod. "That makes it even more meaningful to me. This isn't something you do for someone else."

She places her hands on my shoulders. "How about we attack the rest of those potatoes. I've pretty much finished the onions."

We stand side by side quietly peeling and cutting for a minute or two until Dani picks up the conversation. "This all started the day we rescued Will, though maybe it was building up even before, I don't know. I realized that when something incredible happens, like finally getting away with sneaking Will out of the hospital, I felt this need to express my gratitude. As we drove through the checkpoint, I heard Hannah, David, and Isaac recite a prayer out loud, automatically, like, without even thinking. That's what I wanted, the ability to feel something so deeply that it just bubbles up like a reflex."

"It's called *kavanah*," I say.

"It's like a real thing with a name?"

"*Kavanah* is the intention behind prayer or any religious act. It's what drives the thing you call a reflex. Without it, you or anyone are just going through the motions of observing or praying. That's not what *Hashem* wants from us because it's basically empty."

"Yes, that makes a lot of sense. So it's not just the reflex by itself, it's like the feeling that gives it meaning. What did you call it? The intention?"

"Right."

I finish peeling a potato when I suddenly remember something I'd once read about *kavanah*. "There's a saying about this I should probably include in a papercut one day. 'Prayer without *kavanah* is like a body without a soul.'"

Dani puts her arm around me. "That's a very Judith Braverman saying, don't you think?"

I gently push against Dani's side. "I guess it is."

We go back to our work quietly for a few minutes. I hear the plop of a potato Dani has tossed into a bowl of water.

"I want to learn to observe with *kavanah* the way you do."

I turn to her and take her hand in both of mine. "I think in your case, the *kavanah* is already there. You just need to learn how to put it into practice."

CHAPTER TWENTY-SIX

Jeffrey

I wish Will's first Chanukah hadn't fallen on such a lousy day. I wanted us to load up on *latkes* and find out if he prefers his with applesauce or sour cream. I wanted to watch his face when he takes his first bite of one of my perfect *sufganiyot*, or jelly donuts. Instead, the new law that's taken away my citizenship and knocked me down to the status of guest hangs over our heads like a storm cloud that threatens to burst.

My mother does her best to keep things festive, asking my father to tell Will the story of Chanukah.

I try to give him the short version. "Only enough oil for one night magically lasted eight days. That's why we eat greasy food for a week."

My father gives me a serious look that causes me to sit back in my chair. "There's more to it than that. You know better," he says, wagging his finger at me.

So, Will is then regaled with the tale of the Maccabees, who were able to defeat the Greeks and rededicate the Second Temple in Jerusalem, which involved the lighting of the lamp with the miraculous oil that lasted eight days.

It's a simple story that Jewish families are telling all over the GFS tonight, imagining ourselves as modern-day victors against the foreign invaders. But all I can take from it is the irony that on this day of our great historical triumph, we are once again facing insurmountable odds. I wouldn't belong to the Minyan of Resistance if I didn't think it was important to do my part, which these days is pretty much confined to making sure Will isn't found by Simeon and his goons. But the truth is, Cincinnati, South Ohio in the God Fearing States is not worth defending as if it were some reincarnation of ancient Jerusalem. I'd much rather they just let us all leave so Will and Dani can return home and the rest of us can live in peace in the UPR.

Will apparently leans toward the savory, leaving the applesauce alone in a bowl and placing small mountains of sour cream on his *latkes*. "You know, I bet these would also taste good with some kimchi," he says as he spears a few more from the platter onto his plate.

In the next few seconds, a container appears on the table courtesy of my mother. Will places two pieces of the spicy, pickled cabbage onto a *latke*, cuts a piece and closes his eyes as he savors the combination. He cuts a second piece and offers his fork to me. "Korean and Jewish, just like us," he says and smiles.

I lean forward and slide the food off his fork with my mouth, closing my eyes the way he did. The fried potato mellows the spiciness, and the *kimchi* adds a zing to the *latkes*. He's right. It's a great combination. And as I give him a thumbs-up in response, I say a silent prayer to *Hashem* that this food pairing is some kind of culinary prophesy of what could happen between me and Will.

We've buzzed off most of Will's hair and dyed the remaining short hairs blond. He's dressed in a yarmulke and *tzitzit* with dark glasses hiding his eyes. Even with all this disguise, it's a huge risk to take him out of the house to Shabbat morning services at the newspaper's office. But this is a special day, and I can't miss it, which means Will has to come too since I won't leave him alone in the house.

He sits in the back of the congregation between my parents. Binyamin has already figured out a hiding place for him in case we have any uninvited visitors. But we've heard rumors Simeon the snake has reported that "the illegal" is not hiding in our neighborhood and the house-to-house search has been called off. Still, I wouldn't put it past the GFS and their lackeys to burst in on a religious service and start asking for identification.

Isaac, our Rebel Rabbi, is up front getting ready to begin. I spot Dani, dressed similar to Will but without the glasses, sitting between Binyamin and Miriam. Judith is up front with Hannah and Naomi Blau. Naomi's big shot father is nowhere to be seen. He's probably *davening* with Isaac's big shot father.

"*Gut Shabbes*," begins Isaac, greeting us with the same Yiddish welcome my father uses. "I'm sure some of you must be wondering just how good a *Shabbes* this is given yesterday's news." He looks from one side of the room to the other, nodding slowly. "How can I blame you if you are? But let's remember that when a Jew sadly passes away on a Friday afternoon, we are forbidden from holding his or her funeral on the Sabbath. Why is that? Because *Adonai* our God gave us *Shabbat* as a kind of gift or refuge from our everyday lives. Even in the wake of a devastating storm or an evil decree as we've just experienced, we are commanded to keep *Shabbat* and to delight in its sweetness."

He pauses, likely to let all of this sink in. Since I know what he's leading up to, even I find it hard to disagree with his insistence that we separate ourselves from the horrors of the outside world, if only for these few hours of reprieve.

"Today is indeed a sweet *Shabbat*, because today we will celebrate three *b'nai mitzvot*, three of our community reading Torah for the first time. This minyan of ours is like the blue and white braided Havdalah candle that we will light tonight after sundown to mark the end of *Shabbat*. For us, one color of the braid is *mitzvot*—the commandments that God has set out for us in the Torah. The other color of the braid represents the new ways of worship we are creating so that we can hold fast to Torah in a manner that brings its full meaning to all of us. These strands of color are wound around one another, strengthening the braided candle and ourselves."

The service proceeds as it normally does with the usual order of songs and prayers we all know by heart, except of course for

Will and Dani. Isaac has enlisted Morty Braverman as his young cantor to lead the singing and chant portions reserved for the *hazan*. Luckily Morty is past bar mitzvah age so his voice has settled into a smooth tenor. Listening to him, I choke up a bit thinking how proud his father would be to see him up there.

The Torah scroll is laid out on a table in front of the lectern where Isaac usually stands. Morty calls each person up to the front for their *Aliyah*[23], one to recite the blessings before and after the Torah portion and the other to read from the Torah. The first four of the seven readings proceed as they normally do. Since I chanted last week, I'm relieved from this responsibility (what others refer to as a privilege) and am called up only to recite the blessings before and after Meyer chants. As expected, Lipsky pulls it off perfectly, hitting all the right tropes and not pausing for even a second.

After Isaac himself finishes the blessing after the fourth *Aliyah*, he looks out over the small congregation and smiles. "Now, for the final three *aliyot*, we will look to that second color of the braid, the one that helps give the other its full meaning." He looks over to Morty who calls up to the front Sharon Goldwyn and Hannah Goldwyn, chanting their Hebrew names. I hold my breath as Hannah and her mother come forward. Mrs. Goldwyn recites the first blessing and the congregation responds as it knows to do after she chants the first line. All is quiet as she finishes and Hannah picks up the thin, silver *yad* used to help the reader follow the text in the Torah scroll.

It is strange seeing Hannah swallow visibly and breathe out to calm her nerves. I've never seen her be anything but fearless. But a lot is riding on this reading, the first by a woman, and it's clear she knows it.

Her reading is a relatively short one, recounting the early years of Joseph's time in Egypt working for the Pharoah's chief butcher. Naturally, Joseph the mensch is soon put in charge of managing everything the butcher owns.

Relief shows all over Hannah's face when she finishes without making any mistakes, just two short pauses in the

---

23 The honor of being called upon to read from the Torah. Typically, each week's portion is divided into seven readings.

middle. When Mrs. Goldwyn completes the closing blessing, mother and daughter hug and Isaac makes a point of shaking hands with each of them, saving a special open-mouthed smile for Hannah. "*Yasher koach*," he says out loud, and all around the room members of the congregation repeat this expression of congratulations for a *mitzvah* well done.

My stomach tightens as Morty calls up the two people for the sixth *Aliyah*. Dvorah Kuriel and Judith Braverman. Judith has been a wreck over this ever since Isaac first asked her to do it. She insisted we not tell Dani, wanting it to be a surprise. Whatever. I don't pretend to understand how things work between those two.

As she stands next to Dvorah while the blessing is recited, Judith appears calm, more relaxed than Hannah. As she lifts the *yad*, she looks over at Dani with a big smile on her face. Surprise!

Judith's reading is not a fun one. When Joseph rebuffs the butcher's wife's advances, she tells her husband that Joseph propositioned her and he finds himself in prison. It's too bad that Judith's first *Aliyah* has to be about a woman who tells a terrible lie. But soon after he's beyond bars, Joseph, that loveable mensch, is running the place.

Judith's voice is high and sweet and she glides through the reading in true Meyer Lipsky fashion. Once Dvorah finishes the blessing, there are many handshakes and hugs, including a pretty long one from Dani. Have these girls forgotten that we're living in the GFS? I decide that I will wait and congratulate Judith later. There's still one more *Aliyah* left in this tale of Joseph, son of Jacob.

But again, instead of having Morty launch into calling someone up, Isaac addresses the congregation.

CHAPTER TWENTY-SEVEN

Dani

I'm sitting here overflowing with pride, glad that Judith saved her big secret so it could be a surprise. She was amazing, with her beautiful voice, so calm and strong. Binyamin whispered to me that reading directly from the Torah scroll is challenging. Apparently, there are no vowels and no little marks that guide the melody to tell you when to chant a high note, a low note, or let the word linger for longer than a beat.

Miriam mentioned that the Torah reading today would be the beginning of the story of Joseph, the guy with the Technicolor dream coat, though she didn't use those words. But I have some memory of the play so at least I wasn't completely lost.

"Before we have our esteemed young cantor call forward two of our congregation for the final *Aliyah* of this week's portion, I ask that you indulge me first with some brief words of *midrash* from the sages."

Binyamin leans over to me. "*Midrash* is an interpretation or exposition of Torah." I nod, grateful that my brother is helping me follow along.

Isaac looks down at a piece of paper on the lectern and then back up at us. "Our understanding from Torah of how the world is ordered has always been that there are two genders, male and female. We've been taught that each gender has its defined role in life, the male realm and the female realm. Yet today, we've delighted in watching and listening to women in our congregation come forward for their first *Aliyah*. Each one has shown us how they cannot only chant so beautifully and accurately, but with the soul intention of *kavanah*."

Isaac steps to one side of the lectern and holds his hands up. "Now at my young age, I do not profess to have studied the ways of the Hasidic mystics whose writings are recorded in the book of the Zohar. But after speaking with the young person who we'll be calling up for this seventh *Aliyah*, when I did a little exploration, I learned that our sages have written about the existence of gender beyond male and female. For example, Rabbi Yirmiyah, son of Elazar said, 'When God created the first earthling, it was created an *androgninus*; thus is it written, male and female did God create *them*.' And in *Devarim*, or the book of Deuteronomy as it is referred to in English, while reviewing the obligations of men and women when offering the first fruits of Sukkot, the rabbis pondered those who fall outside the identities of male or female. The Mishnah says 'An androgynous, who presents both male and female physical traits, is in some ways like men and in some ways like women. In some ways, they are like both men and women, and in other ways, like neither men nor women.'"

My mouth hangs open in amazement. I would have never imagined that rabbis in ancient times would have written about the existence of what we now call non-binary or gender non-conforming identity. I can't help but wonder how everyone here is reacting to this.

Isaac steps over to the table where the Torah scroll is open and stands next to Morty Braverman. "Again, I turn your attention to our braided candle, the symbol of our congregation, with three strands of *halacha* and three strands of new ways wound around one another. This joining not only makes us stronger, as I've said, but also creates room for each of us to be the person we know our self to be." Isaac places his hand on Morty's shoulder and Judith's brother calls out in a loud, clear voice the Hebrew names of Miriam Fine and Naomi Blau.

I smile at Miriam as she stands and passes in front of me to walk up to the table with the Torah scroll. She joins Naomi who's dressed in flowing blue pants, a cream-colored blouse and a thin tie knotted over her chest. Just like everyone, male and female, who've been called up, Miriam and Naomi each have a blue and white tallis draped around their shoulders. Miriam, like most of the married women here, is wearing a simple gray hat with a thin brim. But just like Isaac and Morty and all the men and boys, Naomi is wearing a blue *yarmulke*, the same color as her pants.

Seeing my sister-in-law proudly standing beside thirteen-year-old Naomi Blau who is wearing clothes that feel right for her, I am more and more convinced that this minyan of Isaac's is the place where I can satisfy the yearning within me.

* * *

The original members of the Minyan of Resistance, along with a few others, including me and Will, have been invited to Dvorah Kuriel's house to mark the end of *Shabbat* with a Havdalah service, where the braided candle that Isaac described this morning is lit and extinguished in a cup of wine. After that, there'll be the candle lighting for the second night of Chanukah and the surprise I have for Judith and everyone else, I guess.

I arrive with my brother and his family, carrying their contributions to tonight's dinner prepared yesterday before sundown. Judith has spent the afternoon with Hannah on their weekly Shabbat walk. I imagine they have been celebrating their great accomplishments from this morning.

I pace around Dvorah's living room, impatient for Judith's arrival. I'm nervous and excited about two things tonight—one I'll tell her right away and the other that's the surprise.

"What's with all the pacing, Dani, or should I say Daniel?" asks Jeffrey as he walks alongside me matching my steps.

I stop and look down at my clothes, realizing I'm still dressed like a boy. "Oh, I guess I need to change," I tell him and walk toward the bathroom.

"Don't change too much," he calls after me, and I can hear him laughing at his own joke.

I realize how comfortable I've gotten being around Jeffrey and everyone else here in this little minyan. I never thought I'd adjust so easily to life in the GFS. Not that there isn't horrible oppression of just about everyone who isn't white, straight, cisgender, and Christian, but it's almost like I've known Jeffrey, Meyer, Hannah, and Isaac my entire life. Judith, of course, is in a whole different category, one focused more on a future than the past.

When I emerge without the *tzitzit* and blazer but still wearing the *yarmulka*, I smile at the memory of Naomi Blau standing in front of everyone dressed as her authentic self. That kid has inspired me to find my own way of being observant starting with this *yarmulka*, which just feels right.

Judith and I spot each other at the same time, and we walk toward one another grinning.

"Did you guys have a nice afternoon basking in your great accomplishments?" I ask after we hug hello.

"We walked for hours and I felt like my feet didn't even touch the ground. I was so happy."

Her face is radiant and for a few seconds I am overwhelmed by how beautiful she is. Luckily, she continues talking.

"Hannah, of course, spent the entire time going on and on about how amazing Isaac is, and I guess I can't disagree. Can you imagine what he'll be like after he goes through the actual training and becomes an official rabbi?"

"I feel like I already learn so much every time I listen to him. And what he did for Naomi Blau was beyond impressive. I can't believe the stuff that those old rabbis said about gender."

She smiles and I know she's amused by how I've described what Isaac said. "Yes, the *midrash*." I don't mind her correcting me because I want to be able to have the right words for everything.

"I'm glad you explained…" She pauses. "What is it? Um, oh yeah, non-binary. I'm glad you explained that to me before so I could understand what Isaac was doing and then describe it to Hannah."

"Was she okay with it?"

Judith shrugs and rolls her eyes. "Of course. She never questions anything Isaac says, at least when he's speaking from the *bimah*."

I look down at the floor, embarrassed. "The *bimah*?"

I feel Judith's finger on my chin lifting my head. "It's fine not to know everything, that's what I'm here for."

I grin at her. "Among other things."

Now she's the one with pink cheeks. "Anyway." She draws out the word. "In a regular synagogue, the *bimah* is a raised platform where the rabbi and cantor conduct the service. I hope one day Isaac will be the rabbi in a real synagogue that's worthy of him."

She looks over to where everyone is congregating in Dvorah's living room. "It looks like they're starting."

I realize I haven't said what I meant to tell her. "Can I tell you something real quick?"

"Oh? Sure."

"You know how I told you we have to do a Capstone project in order to graduate in the UPR and I hadn't decided what I wanted to do?" I don't wait for her response and forge ahead. "Well, I have." I'm bouncing on the balls of my feet I'm so excited, which makes her laugh and grab my arms to hold me still. "My Capstone is going to be about how I'm studying to be an observant Jew and everything I've learned here. What do you think?" I'm practically holding my breath waiting for her to tell me.

"I think that's perfect," she says and I exhale in relief. "I mean, if your school is okay with that topic."

"They'll be fine. It's a pretty open assignment. I just have to show that I've put a lot of work into it, which I will."

Isaac has us all stand in a circle for Havdalah. Judith is on one side of me and Jeffrey is on the other, whispering in my ear every few seconds. It's not the first time he's given me his own version of commentary during a service, part explanation and part cynical critique. But tonight, he begins by letting me know that I'm in for a real treat.

"I know Isaac has a thing about the braided candle, but really Havdalah is all about the spice box. Just wait."

I'm drawn in by the easy melody and find myself singing along using the wordless syllables yai-yai-yai between the actual Hebrew blessings. "It's kind of like a formula that the blessings all begin the same way with *baruch at-ah*, right?" I whisper to Jeffrey.

"Yes, yes," he says, "gotta give God His due since, you know, since He's the Creator and all."

"You think of God as male?" I ask him.

Jeffrey sighs. "Dani, after Isaac's little lecture this morning about not male, not female, but sometimes male, sometimes female, I have no idea. Plus there's all the stuff you and Will have told me."

Immediately I worry that he'll make some joke in front of Naomi that could hurt her feelings. "You and I need to talk," I tell him. "It's really important that you not say the wrong thing to Naomi since she's just figuring all of this out for herself."

"Okay. Until we talk, I will only smile and nod at Naomi."

I feel Judith lean over. "Are you two really going to spend the whole time talking to each other?"

"Jealous?" asks Jeffrey.

I elbow him. "We'll be good."

"Besides," he says, "it's just about time for my favorite part."

I now get Jeffrey's obsession with the spice box. That little silver cube on a stand filled with spices smells amazing. When I pass it to Judith, she says, "We never got to do this at Isaac's father's shul." She sniffs and a little moan of pleasure escapes. I guess Jeffrey's not the only one who's grateful to be included in this ritual.

Once the Havdalah prayers have finished, Isaac looks around the circle. "With the end of *Shabbat*, we can now turn to the second night of Chanukah."

Dvorah leaves the circle and returns with a menorah and two small boxes, one containing candles and the other kitchen matches. She inserts two blue candles next to one another and a white one in the center raised above the others. I already know that the white candle is called the *shamash*, which means helper, and the candles are inserted from right to left but lit from left to right. It's a lot to remember but as I become more observant, I'm determined to figure out what I need to hold onto and what I can leave behind. Tonight, though, I know what I need to remember.

"The story of Chanukah," Isaac begins, "is widely known in our community and, given our current challenges, brings to mind many old clichés, such as 'what's old is new again' and 'the past is never dead, it isn't even past.' And, yes, I had to look all of that up." He smiles and there are a few chuckles from the group.

"A small army of pious Jews fight and defeat a mighty oppressor in order to keep our faith and its traditions alive. I don't think it's too much of a stretch to say that we here in the GFS are modern-day Maccabees. And just to extend the comparison even further, both our forebears and our own minyan have a heroine by the name of Judith."

He extends an arm toward our Judith and I see her shaking her head as she stares down at her feet, unable to look at anyone directly.

Isaac smiles at her. "It is true that our Judith is not planning to woo an enemy general and cut off his head while he sleeps."

"Too bad," Jeffrey interjects to more laughter.

Isaac smiles at him. "But both the Judith of ancient times and our own Judith do what the Talmud demands of us— partner with God to make the impossible possible. In other words, we are not permitted to just pray for *Adonai* to make a miracle out of thin air. But instead, we must ask for the strength and the help to bring the so-called miracle about. It can be a code embedded in a piece of art or a complicated ruse that frees a captive. Regardless of our current challenge, it is upon us, in partnership with The One, to prevail against the evil that would destroy us."

He lets this thought sit with us for a moment. Judith turns to me and shakes her head a little, signaling that she is still not thrilled to be compared to a Biblical heroine. I, on the other hand, know that Isaac got it right, so I nod yes to let her know I agree with him and take her hand then quickly let it go. I know she's nervous her mother might see.

"Tonight," Isaac begins, "we continue our new ritual of inviting someone up here for their first honor. Dani, please come forward to light the Chanukah candles."

I can't decide if I'm more nervous or excited for this. As I step forward, I turn and look back at Judith whose mouth and eyes are wide open. "Surprise," I whisper back.

As I reach into the box to take out a match, I silently pray for the strength to strike it successfully on the first try. Maybe what Isaac said about partnering with God is true, since the match lights right up.

I light the *shamash* and lift it to first light the candle added for the second night and then the one next to it. With an intake of breath, I begin the blessings as I replace the *shamash* into its holder.

I had Miriam rehearse this with me about a thousand times, so I begin the prayer in Hebrew using the melody she taught me. I even know what I'm saying because I made her translate it.

Blessed are you, Our God, Ruler of the Universe, who makes us holy through Your commandments, and commands us to light the Chanukah lights.

Blessed are you, Our God, Ruler of the Universe, who performed miracles for our ancestors in their days at this season.

Once I start, the rest of the group sings with me, which makes me feel like I can get through this without totally embarrassing myself. When the prayers are finished, even though they all carried me through by singing along, I'm still congratulated with hugs and many compliments of "*Yasher koach.*"

It's only when I'm getting my hug from Dvorah that I overhear Mrs. Braverman say to Judith, "She is a generous and brave young woman, just like you. I don't understand everything about the two of you, but I want you to know I approve."

When Judith and I finally face one another, she once again has her mouth open in what I can only describe as extreme surprise or maybe even shock.

"Did she just say what I think she said?" I ask.

Judith can only nod, her head moving up and down repeatedly.

I can't help myself, even with everyone crowded around, I throw my arms around her and pull her in for a hug.

"I'm...I'm..." is all that manages to come out of Judith's mouth.

I don't want to let go of her. Happiness and relief course through my body along with the excitement and warmth of having Judith close. Finally, I pull back so I can look directly at her and gaze into her beautiful, dark brown eyes. I bite down on my bottom lip and then break into a smile. Leaning in again, I whisper words meant only for Judith. "*Baruch Hashem.* I guess it's true what they say about Chanukah and miracles."

Other Books by Cindy Rizzo

Getting Back (Ylva Publishing 2015)
Love Is Enough (independently published 2014)
Exception to the Rule (independently published 2013)
All the Ways Home: A Collection of Short Fiction (New Victoria Publ. 1995)

Bella Books, Inc.

Women. Books. Even Better Together.

P.O. Box 10543
Tallahassee, FL 32302

Phone: 800-729-4992
www.bellabooks.com

CPSIA information can be obtained
at www.ICGtesting.com
Printed in the USA
JSHW030259250822
29684JS00002B/2

9 781642 474107